THE OTHER SIDE

By JT Todd

©2019 by JT Todd

All Rights Reserved

THE AUTHOR AND PUBLISHER HAVE PROVIDED THIS E-BOOK TO YOU WITHOUT DIGITAL RIGHTS MANAGEMENT SOFTWARE (DRM) APPLIED SO THAT YOU CAN ENJOY READING IT ON YOUR PERSONAL DEVICES. THIS E-BOOK IS FOR YOUR PERSONAL USE ONLY. YOU MAY NOT PRINT OR POST THIS E-BOOK, OR MAKE THIS E-BOOK PUBLICALLY AVAILABLE IN ANY WAY. YOU MAY NOT REPRODUCE, COPY, OR UPLOAD THIS E-BOOK, OTHER THAN TO READ IT ON YOUR PERSONAL DEVICES.

Copyright infringement is against the law.

This is a work of fiction. Names, characters, businesses, places, events and incidents are either the products of the author's imagination or used in a fictitious manner. Any resemblance to actual persons, living or dead, or actual events is purely coincidental.

CHAPTER 1

Noah Walker gazed blankly into the black pool of liquid swirling in the large mug. Darkness. It was the only thing he could count on. He knew it was futile to deny what was going to happen. This was the worst dream yet. So many people were going to die and he was helpless to do anything about it. He let out a long breath and took a swig of his coffee, nervously eyeing the other patrons sprawled in deep couches and cushy armchairs that populated the trendy bistro.

The dreams had plagued him since childhood, molding and shaping him into who he was today. His failure to change the outcomes of his dreams fueled an angst that was unbearable. Even when he tried to warn people, the result was always the same. People got hurt when he dreamed. Some people even died.

He ignored the elderly woman peering at him dismissively as she shuffled by his table. Though it bothered him, he was used to people staring at him, to being an outcast. If only he didn't have to suffer through the dreams and their inevitable consequences, he might seem normal like everyone else.

He picked up his phone and once again re-read the text he composed to his parents, grimacing in frustration at the cold words on the screen. He truly wasn't certain what to tell them. Even though they always tried to comfort him, his parents were equally baffled about what to do. As Noah receded deeper into himself through the years, they pushed harder to reach him, but it didn't help. He set the phone down. He would send the message when the time came. They would miss him dearly, but it was better this way. Better that he was dead.

Noah glanced at the large mahogany clock hung prominently above the stone fireplace. There was no doubt that the man in the overcoat would be arriving any minute. Below the clock, the fire flickered ominously, dancing before him. He knew it was a trick of his mind, but for a moment, only briefly, it appeared the flames coalesced into the image of the horrific destruction from his previous night's dream. He slunk back into his chair and tried to still the trembling in his hands as he waited for what was to occur. Even though Noah dreamt about this very moment two weeks earlier, something about the man he was about to meet made him anxious.

THE OTHER SIDE

The door to the coffee shop opened, bringing with it a burst of cold winter air that sent a shiver through Noah. A man entered wearing a dark grey overcoat, his hands tucked into his pockets. After scanning the room, the stranger walked directly to Noah's table and sat down across from him. The man's eyes locked on his for a long moment and Noah couldn't help but stare back. The man's eyes hinted at secrets and a deeper understanding of this life.

"My name is Riley O'Connor," the stranger said. "I have been sent to find you." His voice was warm and friendly, as if he had known Noah for years. "What a relief I wasn't too late." The man extended his right hand from his pocket in greeting, just as Noah knew he would.

Noah hesitated for a moment before shaking the man's hand, the uncertainty of the situation causing his legs to tremble slightly. This was the point where his dream ended. Now anything could happen.

"So what do I call you?" Riley asked with a slight smile on his face. He was a handsome man with chiseled features and small dimples on each side of his face when he smiled. His light brown hair was speckled with grey but still thick. Noah guessed he was in his fifties based on the deep etched wrinkles across his forehead.

Noah slowly pushed his long bangs from his face. "Noah," he mumbled.

"Hi Noah," Riley said warmly, attempting to

put him at ease. "It is a real pleasure to make your acquaintance."

Noah frowned. Riley's voice was not threatening, but he still didn't trust the man. "Did my parents send you?"

"No one sent me," Riley responded, the flash of a frown quickly replaced by another smile. "Let's just say I was led to find you."

"Then why are you here?" Noah challenged, his mind racing through his options for escape. His legs fidgeted uncontrollably under the table despite his effort to remain still. His instinct told him to flee at all cost, yet for some reason, he ignored it.

Riley took a deep breath, obviously sensing his distrust. "Noah, I am here because of you. I do not know what is going on in your life, but taking your own life is not the answer. It is never the answer, no matter how bad life gets. Your life is precious to your parents, to me, and to God."

"Whaaattt?" Noah stammered, shaking his head wildly. "How could you know?"

"What if I told you I dreamt about you the other night?"

Noah's breath caught for a moment, but he didn't say anything. It was an odd question for anyone to ask. *Could this man know about his struggle against the dreams?*

Noah was five years old when he suffered his first dream. Even today, he remembered every detail. The coolness of the autumn air.

The leaves falling in a cascading array of bright orange and maroon as a cold wind blew through the line of maple trees along his street. His neighbor, a girl just two years older than him, riding her bicycle along the sidewalk headed towards the intersection, oblivious to the pain she was about to experience.

In the dream, he watched a large pit bull strike her at full gallop, knocking her from her bicycle and sending her several feet into the busy intersection. The dog began to attack her savagely. Her screams still echoed like daggers piercing his eardrums. Within seconds, his father had come to the girl's rescue, confronting the dog with a baseball bat. It was a week later, while having dinner with his parents, when he learned his dream had become a reality. That was the beginning of his torment. The beginning of his desire to end his miserable existence.

"I dreamt I was at your funeral," Riley stated, pointing his finger at Noah's chest. "You were lying in a white coffin, dressed as you are now." Riley paused for a moment. "Around your neck was a noose made of bright yellow cord."

Noah's eyes went wide in shock and began to dart around the room erratically. *Could they both suffer from the same curse?* He had to find out.

"Do your dreams ever come true?" Noah asked in a voice so soft Riley had to lean over the table to hear him.

Riley slowly settled back in his chair, analyzing the implications of Noah's question. After a long moment, he responded casually, "No, I can't say they do, but the dreams do give me information. In your case, the dream gave me your face and an indication of your personal struggle."

Noah lowered his head, disappointed by Riley's response. He placed his hand in the front pocket of his jacket, gripping the object held inside. It gave him comfort to know that at least something in his life was certain. He didn't know what compelled him to do it, but a moment later, he placed the spool of bright yellow nylon cord on the table. Noah felt the tears forming in his eyes as he looked at Riley defiantly. "I am going to do it tonight," Noah said, cramming the spool back into his pocket.

Riley reached out his hand and grabbed Noah's arm. There was a look of fierce determination in the man's eyes that demanded Noah's full attention.

"Son, listen to me. I don't want you to do that! I came here to find you because I need you."

"Me?" Noah responded in surprise. No one ever needed him for anything.

"Yes," Riley stated, slowly releasing his grip on Noah's arm. "It is true." His eyes brightened with intensity as he stared at Noah. "I need you for a very special purpose. I need you to help me save humanity."

CHAPTER 2

Riley O'Connor was an intuitive man by nature. He possessed the innate ability to read people and see beyond the obvious. His unique skill was an asset in his line of work as a senior operative for the Central Intelligence Agency. Profiling terrorist suspects and finding common denominators between seemingly unrelated events was his passion. That is why he was the best in the agency. His work took on an even greater significance three years ago, when a drowning accident gave him the opportunity to direct his passion towards an even greater cause, protecting the future of mankind.

The thought of being dead for that long still sent chills up his spine. The doctors believed the freezing temperature of the water was the only thing that saved his life. Riley knew otherwise. There was a bigger plan in action and he was now a key part of it. He met face-to-face with God that day. It was an encounter that forever changed him from the inside out.

"Save humanity???" Noah gasped. "Are you crazy?"

The young man stared at Riley suspiciously, like a dog trying to determine if a stranger is a friend or a threat. Riley studied Noah as well, analyzing his appearance and mannerisms to draw opinions, form conclusions, and direct his next move.

In a glance, Riley noted the complete blackness of Noah's outfit, accentuated by pale skin that covered his small, bony frame. He guessed Noah was seventeen, maybe eighteen, yet his eyes reflected a knowing skepticism of someone many years older. Light from the overhead lamp reflected off a series of tiny silver globes pierced in a small arc from his temple to a spot beside his hairline. Noah's hair was jet black and cut in a very peculiar manner—shaved in the back and on the sides, with long bangs drooping across his forehead that obscured grey eyes encircled with black liner and mascara. Even his fingernails were painted black. Noah radiated rebellion and perhaps something deeper like depression.

In an effort to foster trust, Riley slowly removed his other hand from his pocket, placing it on the table, palm side down. "You see, in addition to the dreams, we have something else in common."

Awestruck, Noah stared at the prosthetic hand. Science had made great strides in creating lifelike prosthetics and Riley owned one of the latest models, complete with fingers and a soft rubber membrane that mimicked human skin. He could control his hand to open or close with slight flexes of his bicep. But Riley knew Noah was not much interested in his hand itself. Noah's eyes were locked on the glossy black fingernails. On a powerful internal prompting, Riley painted the nails of his fake hand just an hour ago.

Immediately, Riley felt another prompting. It was like an idea forming, but it carried emotion. Since his accident, Riley learned to act on the overwhelming sensations. This prompting was so strong that he knew it was right. Even so, he hesitated, reluctant to deviate from his plan. To do so would mean he would expose his deepest secret to a complete stranger. After a moment more of consideration, he trusted his instinct.

"Noah, I have a secret to share with you." Riley inched closer to Noah. Only one other person in the world knew what he was about to share and that was the man Riley worked for. "I have special gifts."

"What kind of gifts?" Noah asked hesitantly. Riley sensed Noah was genuinely interested, but still very much on edge.

"The Bible refers to them as gifts of the Holy Spirit."

Noah frowned, the confusion evident in his expression.

"It is difficult to fully explain, but let me share an example. I am led to do things by strong thoughts, feelings, and impulses about people or events. Almost like an inner voice is telling me information I would not normally know."

"You mean you read minds?!?" Noah exclaimed.

"No, I don't read minds," Riley responded shaking his head. "In some cases, I see patterns in people's actions and behaviors that are not detected by others. Most of the time, I just know, deep down inside what to do. Call it an inner wisdom, if you like."

"I still don't understand," Noah said folding his arms. He leered at Riley, "Why are you here?" The same question Noah posed earlier, only this time curiosity replaced Noah's distrust. But Riley also detected a new, barely perceptible emotion—hope.

"My employer is in need of someone like you to work on a special mission."

"Your employer?" Noah asked, beginning to fidget again, causing his coffee to spill as his knee bumped the table. "Who do you work for?"

Riley easily recognized Noah was becoming uncomfortable with this new direction of conversation. His reply was purposely calm and measured. "I work for the CIA."

Noah pushed back his chair and glanced at the entry door. The redness that entered Noah's face told Riley that Noah's heart was racing and

THE OTHER SIDE

he was getting ready to run. Riley decided now was the time to gamble. "Noah, please listen to me! I know what you can do. I know you dream about the future."

Noah stared at Riley, his expression a swirl of disbelief, pain, and fear. Slowly, a look of relief emerged across Noah's face. Riley's smiled again. As always, the prompting had proven correct.

Noah scooted his chair back to the table. "I don't understand. How do you know?"

"As I said, I have a gift. Like you, I keep my gift hidden from others."

"Are there others like me, I mean... us?"

"Yes, I believe so. But your gift is truly special. It is very unique among the gifts. Very few people in history have been able to predict the future."

"There were others?" Noah asked. "Like who?"

"Did you know there were many people in the Bible who experienced dreams of the future? In one case, a young Hebrew named Joseph interpreted the dream of an Egyptian king that came true."

Noah perked up, his curiosity overcoming his fear. He glanced suspiciously from side to side to make sure no one was listening. "Did they dream about people dying?"

"Yes, in a manner of speaking," Riley nodded. "Joseph interpreted a dream about a seven-year famine that would have killed thousands of people."

"What do you mean would have?" Noah asked urgently, "I thought you said the dream came true?"

"Yes, the dream did come true. The famine the Egyptian King dreamt about did happen, but Joseph used the knowledge from this dream to prepare for the famine, saving many people who would have perished otherwise. In short, one man changed the future that could have been."

"He changed the future?!?" Noah exclaimed, leaning in intently. "Is that possible?"

"Noah, I have learned that anything is possible, if we have faith. You must believe that a different outcome is possible." Riley's eyes glimmered for a moment, catching the reflection of the fire. "Please trust me."

Noah leaped out of his chair, his bangs swishing wildly across his face as both his hands grasped Riley's right hand in a vice-like grip. "Can you help me? Please?" Noah pleaded. "Can you help me to change the future?" The tears were beginning to stream down Noah's face, leaving long streaks of black.

Breakthrough. Riley went for the close, knowing he now possessed the key to recruiting his target. "If you come with me, I will do more than that," Riley promised. "I will help you learn to control your dreams as well."

Noah nodded eagerly in response, the tears still streaming down his face. Riley settled back

THE OTHER SIDE

into his chair and offered a silent prayer of praise. The first stage of his quest was complete. One down. Four more to go.

CHAPTER 3

New York City, New York

Cooper Williams bypassed the long line of tourists waiting anxiously to be screened by security. Every morning, it was the same scene, and after all these years, he completely ignored the disturbance. It was an expected nuisance that accompanied working in the most iconic building in America. The Empire State Building was a majestic display of architecture and everyone wanted to see it.

He rode the private elevator reserved for tenants to the eightieth floor in a daze. He just didn't feel right. As he exited the elevator, dizziness overwhelmed him and he stooped to one knee. He checked his pulse. Everything seemed normal, except his head was now ablaze in pain. Maybe it was stress, he thought.

As a senior vice president at the largest investment firm in North America, stress came with the job and he was used to it. It was prob-

THE OTHER SIDE

ably the ill effects of that second martini last night mingling with his medication. Except for the throbbing pulse in his head, he wasn't feeling any pain but something wasn't right. Probably best to pop a couple pills, he thought. Just to be safe.

As usual, Janice was waiting outside his office, holding his latte and the daily financial highlights from the Asian and European markets. She was like clockwork. He could always depend on her to handle anything he needed and to do it efficiently. He was grateful to have someone of her caliber as his assistant. She really deserved a raise.

"Good morning Mr. Williams," she said with a wide smile emphasized by her over-applied cherry red lipstick. "I was able to confirm your nine o'clock phone conference with our Amsterdam office."

He opened his mouth to speak, but nothing came out. Janice was eyeing him, a slight hint of concern on her face. "I also ordered your daughter's birthday present," she said hesitantly. "It should arrive tomorrow, in plenty of time for this weekend's party."

She handed him his latte. His grip slipped and the cup tumbled to the floor, splashing the light brown liquid all over the lush grey carpet. *What is going on?!?* Cooper frantically thought. Confused and embarrassed, he shuffled into his office, leaving Janice outside with no explanation for his behavior. Truth was, he wasn't sure what he would tell her.

He took a deep breath and a moment to scan his office. The sun was shining through the blinds of the corner windows, projecting contrasting bars of dark and light across his mahogany desk. His desktop was empty except for three monitors displaying the latest information on the world's financial markets and a brochure for a luxury world cruise he recently booked for him and his wife. To the right of the desk, between plaques of recognition and achievement, pictures of him with heads of state, famous people, and royalty graced the wall. He would often stare at that wall, reflecting with pride on all of his accomplishments. Being that he was only the age of fifty-two, there was still plenty of time to do more.

Cooper set his leather briefcase on the desk and popped the gold clasps effortlessly, opening the case. He stared, surprised by the contents. What was his pistol doing in his briefcase? He didn't remember packing it. Let alone, why would he take it to work?

A jab of pain struck him in the head, almost bringing him to his knees. He reached into his desk drawer, removing a small orange bottle. He fumbled with the cap, spilling several small blue pills onto his desk in the process. Just the site of the pills gave him an immediate sense of calm. His addiction to the pills spanned over ten years, ever since his back surgery, and he no longer tried to resist his desire for them. Fortunately, the side effects of the medication were tolerable, but lately he was experiencing real vivid nightmares and occasionally, he swore he heard voices when no one else was around.

A flare of pain ricocheted through his head once again. He tried to rub his temples to ease the pain, but instead he watched helplessly as his hands reached out, picked up the Smith & Wesson 40-caliber pistol, and pulled back the slide. Cooper's efforts to release his grip on the pistol were futile. It was like his body was on autopilot, led by an unseen force that he was powerless to resist. Slowly, he toggled the safety off. Cooper let out an internal scream. '*Stoopppp!*'

A voice echoed through his mind in response. It was his voice, but it was different somehow, sinister and full of contempt. '*I gave you everything you desired. Wealth, prestige, pleasures... all the idols of this world,*' the voice trailed off.

What is happening to me? Cooper wondered, as he struggled to regain control of his thoughts and clear his mind.

'*Did you not expect that I would demand something in return?*' The voice was mocking him now. He almost expected to hear laughing.

His eyes fell to the pistol and he watched in horror as he uncontrollably raised his arm and pointed the gun to his head.

'Please stop. Why are you doing this?' Cooper pleaded, fully aware he was having a conversation inside his head. This had to be a dream.

A moment later, Cooper walked from his office into the hallway, the pistol now at his side. He walked casually across the hallway to his assistant's office. Janice was typing on her keyboard, busily preparing one of the many documents he needed for his call with Amsterdam. She looked up slowly, her brown eyes instantly widening in alarm. As his screams of resistance echoed silently in his head, he began to fire.

△△△

The bloody image of a woman face down at her desk faded, replaced by a woman sitting at her desk in a different office. Phasing from one location to another location in the physical realm was a benefit of his kind. He was not of the physical world after all, nor was he of the present time. His type was older than humanity, older than the world itself, immortal. He had been one of the first, and now there were thousands of his kind at work in the world. But very few were like him, and very few possessed his level of power.

He was known by many names throughout human history, but there wasn't a word in the human language for his real name. The ancient Phoenicians worshipped him simply as Baal.

Others called him Beelzebub, a prince of hell. Only beings of the spiritual world knew his true stature as Satan's second in command.

Baal often marveled at the ignorance of the Creator's greatest creation. Most of humanity still refused to believe Satan and his legion of demons existed. They remained blind to the truth of their dire predicament—that evil was an actual demonic army focused on humanity's pain, destruction, and death. That naivety allowed him and his fellow demons to thrive and succeed.

Baal dwelled for a moment on a very distant memory, his first with humans. He was there after the Fall of Man to influence Cain—feeding the man's jealousy and filling his mind with thoughts of revenge. Baal had watched amusingly as Cain had taken a rock to Abel's skull, over and over again, until his brother was dead. Most of the time that was how his kind worked, planting seeds of destruction in the minds of humans or harvesting the evil that already lay latent within. Human beings were so easy to manipulate. Their selfish nature made them weak and it was easy to bend, mold, and influence their will.

Invisible to her perception, Baal observed the woman, seated at her desk, reviewing paperwork. Natasha Ellington was extremely attractive. In her mid-forties, she retained an athletic figure and possessed the youthful face of a woman fifteen years younger. Her finger played with the curls of her dark brown hair, an unconscious habit she did when in deep thought. Baal was very proud of Natasha. She was one of his finest accomplishments.

The raspy voice booming from the phone loudspeaker interrupted Natasha's concentration.

"Madam, the Deputy Director of the CIA is here for your meeting."

"Please show him in," she said releasing the intercom button.

Baal watched Natasha place the file in a side drawer and then remove a compact from her purse to adjust her hair and makeup. He knew that she desired more than casual contact with her visitor. For several weeks, he had been stoking the flames of lust in her for that purpose.

He began to infiltrate Natasha at the age of thirty, during her divorce from an adulterous congressman. Baal had been drawn to her despair, drawn to her pain. As a result of her husband's betrayal, she became consumed with rage, hatred, and bitterness. That made her psyche open to his suggestions, allowing him to influence her thoughts and desires. Over time, as her mind became more accepting of his suggestions, he turned her bitterness into a desire for power.

Natasha quickly became obsessed as she would do anything to maintain and expand her

THE OTHER SIDE

control. As he orchestrated events surrounding her career to give her greater position within the government, she gave more of herself over to him. Under Baal's nurturing, she advanced from a deputy attorney in the State Department to her present position in less than a decade. Baal was with her the entire time, masquerading as her own conscious, whispering thoughts of encouragement, guiding her decisions, and fueling her insatiable ambition.

Now, as the Deputy Secretary of Homeland Security, Natasha could access everything Baal needed. She was in the perfect position to assist him with his plans to launch a full-scale terror assault on the United States. Crippling the country's infrastructure was a critical step to preparing the way for Satan's final victory over mankind. That was Baal's primary purpose now —to speed along the enviable collapse of society and end mankind's existence forever. *To finally destroy the Creator's most prized creation.*

Baal thought back to the scene he just witnessed in New York. Cooper Williams was also one of his pledged, but had become a liability. Normally, he would have assigned one of his lesser minions to execute the possession, but he handled Cooper's demise personally to ensure the correct dramatic effect was achieved. That was the only way to ensure Baal's master plan would not be exposed by an extensive investigation into Williams' recent activities.

Branson Schaeffer entered the office sporting his trademark bowtie. A rising politician from the South, at age forty-two, he was the youngest Deputy Director of the CIA in the history of the agency. The son of an active Supreme Court judge, Branson was single, well-educated and connected within the political and social circles of Washington. A lean frame, chiseled face, and boyish good looks contributed to his persona, but that was not what interested Baal. This man possessed aspirations and he craved power. He was not much different from Natasha, making him another perfect candidate to influence.

Infiltrating took time, plenty of which Baal possessed. The door to a human soul needed to be opened incrementally, experience by experience. Some people were easier than others, particularly if an individual was heavily medicated, emotionally unstable, or carried a secret sin that could be leveraged. None of which were readily evident with Branson. Even so, Baal was confident that Branson would turn like all the others. Everyone had their price.

"Hello Natasha," Branson flashed a brief smile that accented deep laugh lines. "It is good to see you again," he said, not being subtle as his eyes scanned her body. "May I add that you look beautiful, as usual?"

Natasha smiled slightly, extending her hand. She let her grasp linger just long enough for him to notice. They didn't know each other very

THE OTHER SIDE

well, but crossed paths on several occasions in the past three months. "It is a pleasure to see you again Branson." Natasha walked back to her desk and sat down, motioning to Branson to take a chair.

She leaned over her desk towards Branson, "I have been thinking about our conversation last week at the congressional dinner. I think you're right."

"You mean about Thereon?"

"Yes," Natasha said. "The rapid rise of that organization is disconcerting, to say the least. I plan to recommend to the Secretary that we post an alert on NTAS."

Baal chuckled inwardly at Natasha's comment. NTAS was the acronym for the National Terrorism Advisory System, a useless tool of the government designed to communicate terrorist threats to the public. It was useless for the sole fact that few in the general population even knew it existed.

"I think that is a wise move," Branson nodded, reaching into his coat pocket. "We can't afford to get caught with our pants down again," he said, referring to the fallout from the recent scandal involving the Department of Homeland Security spying on the CIA and the NSA. "Our agencies are under enough scrutiny already."

Natasha nodded in response, "I agree. Though getting caught with our pants down could be fun." She winked at Branson.

"Excuse me?" Branson said, obviously surprised by her comment.

She didn't answer him, but leaned in closer. Baal was sure the man was now experiencing the intoxicating aroma of her perfume. "So what do you have for me?" she teased, curling a lock of her hair playfully.

Branson removed a small manila envelope and waved it in his hand, appearing to contemplate if he should give it to her. That was good, Baal thought. The man was flirting with her. That meant he was interested too.

"Here is our latest briefing," Branson offered, handing the envelope to Natasha. "Burn it as soon as you read it."

Not bothering to open the envelope, Natasha placed it in her purse. There would be time to look at the contents of the folder later. Right now, she had a more important objective.

"So, do you have dinner plans?" she asked casually. "I really would like to talk after I read the report."

"Well, actually, I don't," Branson fumbled, caught off guard by her request. "Tonight is a rare night when I have some free time. My fiancée is in New York shopping for bridesmaid dresses."

Natasha smiled coyly. "Wonderful!" There was a sultry edge to her voice, hinted with seduction and anticipation. "Then I will see you at Ebbitt's at seven."

Baal watched amusingly as Branson tried to mask his excitement. Baal could hear the man's heart beating faster, no doubt a response to the possibilities that the evening may present.

Perfect, Baal mused to himself, his own excitement mounting. It was time to begin the infiltration of his next victim. Branson Schaeffer didn't stand a chance.

CHAPTER 4

Lawrenceburg, Kentucky

The patter of heavy raindrops breaking against the windshield caused Riley to look up from his reading. Overhead, a wall of dark grey storm clouds rushed across the horizon, obscuring the afternoon sun and casting a depressive sheen across the land. The darkness matched his mood after he read the latest intelligence briefing on a terrorist group he had been monitoring.

He closed the cover of his tablet, turning his attention to the entrance of the animal clinic across the street. Sandwiched between a Subway and a dry cleaner in the small strip mall, he doubted it was the type of place that dealt with repeat clientele. He glanced briefly back at the sky. Yes, a storm of terror was coming. Everything in his gut told him that.

In recent days, the chatter in the Middle East had increased indicating something big was brewing. CIA operatives only recently identified a new person of interest, Mohammad Shakim Abdul. Abdul was presumed to be the leader of Thereon, a newly-formed Islamic terrorist organization that was quickly rising to prominence in Sudan. There were no pictures of Abdul included in the briefing, only a copy of a symbol he purported to use as his signature.

Riley studied the symbol, intrigued by its detail. In the center of a circle was a seven-headed dragon. Clouds of fire shot from the mouth of three of the heads facing west. Three more dragon heads faced east with their mouths closed, and the head in the center was facing straight out. The jaws of the center head were open, revealing long, threatening fangs. A seven-headed dragon. A mark of the beast.

This same symbol was left at the scenes of recent attacks occurring in the past few months. A fact the government purposely withheld from the press and the public. It was 'need to know' information and only Riley and a select group of senior CIA officials were in possession of this knowledge.

Riley rubbed his hand through his hair and tried to ignore the bloodshot eyes staring back at him from the rearview mirror. He hadn't been sleeping well lately. Events were accelerating, placing more urgency and importance on the success of his mission.

Riley reflected on the three most recent

terrorist events, dissecting the information he knew, searching for a connection. The first event happened six weeks ago. A famous golf pro murdered his wife of fifteen years and their two small children before killing himself. Less than a week later, a bomb exploded in a Jewish synagogue in downtown Chicago, killing twenty-seven. And this week, a bank executive killed three people at a downtown Manhattan investment firm before taking his own life. In all three cases, the dragon symbol was found. Both the golf pro and the banker had the symbol tattooed on their body. At the synagogue, it had been crudely drawn on the wall of the Rabbi's office.

On the surface, Thereon's connection to these events didn't make sense. But Riley knew they were dealing with a terror threat like none encountered before. All the more reason he was selected to lead the task force. If his hunch was correct about Abdul and Thereon, Riley knew he couldn't successfully battle this threat by himself. He needed others like Noah who possessed special gifts. People like the young woman inside the animal clinic.

Picking up the mission folder from the seat next to him, he removed two copies of the *Lexington Herald-Leader* from the contents. He glanced at the first copy, dated more than fifteen years ago, and began reading the headline article. By now, he had read it so many times, he knew most of it from memory.

The headline read simply "7-Year-Old Heals Sick." The article detailed how Jessica Gardner supposedly healed more than twenty people of illness and health ailments during a church revival. The article closed with a statement that in two weeks, the same church was planning a second revival, inviting all people suffering from sickness or debilitating conditions to attend.

He shifted his attention to the second paper dated two weeks later. On the back page, next to a large advertisement for a concert featuring The Cure, was a small article containing the headline, "Healing Church Revival Goes Lame." A secondary headline stated 'Was Child Healer a Publicity Stunt?' This article was much shorter —only mentioning that more than a thousand people showed up for the church revival, most of them in need of healing. To everyone's disappointment, all left in the same condition they arrived, as the young girl was unable to help anyone.

The article neglected to provide the reader with a key insight. Jessica's aunt passed away a week earlier from injuries sustained in a car accident, a fact Riley uncovered during his research on Jessica's family. For the rest of her life, Jessica Gardner appeared to live a normal life. His research file contained her high school transcripts, copies of her timeline from Facebook, and various pictures from her Instagram account—all appearing typical for a girl who had now matured into a young woman. No miraculous healings, not even one comment or post that gave any indication that she could heal or ever healed in the past. Maybe this was a dead end. He quickly dismissed the thought. Everything led him to her.

He placed the papers back in the folder and set it next to his tablet. *Who was Jessica Gardner? Was she truly a healer or simply a pretender?* He leaned his head back and closed his eyes, purposely slowing his breathing. Methodically, he began to review all the information he had read about Jessica, all the experiences that led him to her, all the feelings, promptings, and insights he had experienced. Then he let his mind go completely blank. Ten seconds later, his mind was filled with an image of a purple flower. Riley pondered the image for a moment, not sure what it meant. *When in doubt, let go and trust,* he thought.

He checked his watch. It was near closing time for the clinic. He pulled the small cardboard box from the back seat and checked its contents. The black beady eyes of a beautiful red cardinal peered up at him. One of the cardinal's wings was bent at an awkward angle behind its head, obviously broken.

The cardinal found him that morning, wandering onto the balcony of his hotel room and pecking at the sliding glass door. Riley smiled

THE OTHER SIDE

at the memory. *The Lord always provides*. He stepped out of his vehicle and headed to the clinic entrance. It was time to find out the truth about Jessica Gardner.

CHAPTER 5

A high-pitched beep echoed through the clinic, indicating that someone just entered the lobby. Jessica Gardner glanced at her watch. It was five minutes to six. "Ugggh! Don't people know that the clinic closes at six?" she said under her breath. Well, maybe it was the UPS man delivering a package, she thought. They were expecting a shipment of antibiotics this week. She hoped that was the case. Tonight was her first date with Billy and she needed to get home to prepare.

At least this night there was something to look forward to. She hated her boring 'life is passing me by' life. If only she could get away from here and move to a big city. Any big city would do. She thought about leaving many times before, but then reality would set in. She was twenty-two years old, had no money saved, and very little work experience. If she found a job, it probably wouldn't pay enough to cover rent. Better to stay here and wait for her prince

THE OTHER SIDE

charming to rescue her from her doldrums of existence. Maybe Billy would be the one?

Jessica finished cleaning the cage and opened the adjacent one, removing a fluffy Border Collie puppy that was still sleeping off a dose of anesthesia. She placed the puppy gently in the other cage and locked it safely inside. Though it didn't pay well, her job was the only thing in her life that provided her satisfaction. Being part of the process that restored animals to health gave her purpose. The fact that it also made her feel good was an added perk.

She caught her reflection in the exam room mirror as she headed to meet the untimely visitor. Her normally free-flowing auburn hair was pulled back tightly in a ponytail, with the exception of a few curly strands that graced her forehead and occasionally obstructed her deep brown eyes. Her makeup was holding up pretty well, except for her lipstick. She hated it when her lips were their natural color, which were more white than pink. Without a deep color like fuchsia or burgundy on her lips to offset her pale skin, she looked like she was dead. Even so, the boys thought she was pretty. At least that was what they told her. *Did Billy think she was pretty?* She hoped so.

The gentleman in the lobby smiled as she entered the waiting area. His warm, inviting smile was the kind that made you want to smile back. He was well-dressed in a dark blue suit with a light blue shirt and coordinating tie. His eyes sparkled, conveying trust. Even without concentrating, she could see the man radiated an aura of gentleness and peace.

She could always see auras around living creatures, but usually she needed to concentrate on seeing them. Strangely, this man's aura seemed incomplete. Even so, it was a strong aura, stronger than any she had encountered before.

"Uh… hello," Jessica said, again eyeing the small cardboard box in the man's left hand. She noticed the fingers of the man's hand looked odd. It took her a moment to realize she was looking at a prosthetic hand. That must be why his aura seemed incomplete. She momentarily wondered what had caused the man's injury. "I thought you might be the UPS man. We close at six."

Her abruptness did not seem to faze the visitor. He continued to stare at her patiently.

"May I help you," she said, a tinge of frustration entering her voice.

"Yes, I am hoping you can," the man said, lifting the cover off of the box and handing it to her.

Jessica examined the contents of the box, a frown forming on her face. "I'm sorry, sir," she replied. "The doctor only works with dogs and cats and the occasional gerbil. Besides, he has already left for the day."

She shrugged, glancing again at the bird, noting the pain it was suffering. Translucent waves radiated from the bird in sharp bursts of red, seemingly calling to her. "I really am sorry I cannot help you and your bird. Maybe you can try the rescue shelter down on Hardwood Road?" Even though it was the truth, she felt like she just told a lie.

"Are you sure there is nothing you can do?" the man asked.

For some reason, Jessica felt compelled to help this man, but the doctor was gone for the day and of course, there was Billy. "I really wish there was something I could do," she said frowning. "I really am sorry."

The man shook his head in understanding, a pensive look forming on his face. Slowly, he removed a newspaper from his breast coat pocket. He unfolded it and handed it to her.

Confused, Jessica took the paper with her free hand and looked at the front page. Her mind flashed back in agony as she read the headline of the newspaper. Anger flared up inside of her as she threw the paper on the ground towards the man. "Who do you think you are?!?"

The man stepped back towards the entrance, his hands held up in a gesture of surrender. "Please do not be alarmed, Jessica. I am just a man who has been sent to help you."

"Help me? Are you crazy? If you don't leave now, I am calling the police." Jessica searched the pocket of her exam smock for her cell phone as a wave of fear came over her. *What if this guy was crazy?*

Her fear escalated into panic as she realized the man called her by her name. Her hands were beginning to tremble. She managed to pull her phone from her pocket with her free hand, only to drop it as she fumbled to dial 911. As she bent over to retrieve her phone, the box she forgot she was carrying turned over in her grip. The bird squealed as it spilled out of the box, tumbling across the floor. It chirped in pain as it tried to right itself, fluttering its good wing in useless fury against the air. By instinct, Jessica scooped the bird up in her hand, careful to grasp its body under the broken wing. "I'm sorry little guy," she consoled. "I did not mean to do that to you."

With the bird gingerly cupped in her right hand, she stepped towards the safety of the secured door leading to the exam rooms, her eyes locked on the stranger. The man continued watching her but did not attempt to follow her. It suddenly occurred to her that his aura remained the same the whole time. There was no deceit, no rage, and no fear—only peace and gentleness as before. Her curiosity overruled her fear. "Who are you?"

"I am not here to harm you. In fact, I desperately need your help," the man stepped forward. "But first, I need to help you."

"Help me? How?" The man took another step towards her.

"You went through a traumatic event when you were younger," the man's voice was soft and soothing, putting her a little more at ease. "Losing a family member must have been a very painful experience. I know it was for me when I lost my mother at the age of fourteen." He took another step closer. She found herself transfixed by his piercing blue eyes. It felt like having a spotlight turned on her.

He continued in the same soothing voice. "I believe you have been refusing to deal with your loss and you are harboring bitterness against others. Bitterness that you have let control you all of your life."

Painful images were coming back to her from her youth. She tried desperately to push the pain away. "I do not know why I am listening to you," she retorted. "The office is closed." She turned to open the door behind her.

"Jessica, does the word petunia mean anything to you?"

Jessica's hand froze on the doorknob. *Why did he say that?* It was a sacred word to her. Petunia was the special name her aunt called her. The woman who helped her father raise her after her mother abandoned them both just six months after she was born. The woman who died because Jessica wasn't allowed to heal her. She turned to him in a rage, "Don't you dare say that name again!"

The man took another step towards her.

He was now less than two feet from her. "She was very important to you, wasn't she?" The man reached out. For some reason, she did not resist. "Please tell me what happened?" His hand touched her arm and her world exploded.

The memories flooded back, as vivid and poignant as if she were experiencing them for the first time. Her aunt being wheeled by on a stretcher, screaming in agony. The two burly nurses blocking her from entering the emergency room. The grizzled old doctor telling her father that there was nothing they could do. If only the doctors had let her help. If only they had let her into the emergency room. She could have healed her. She knew that with every ounce of her being. *If only she had tried harder.*

Then everything went black. In the distance she heard a moaning, she didn't know it was her own voice. The only thing she felt was anger. It fed on her sorrow, taking hold of her inner being, her soul, threatening to consume everything. It demanded revenge against those who harmed her. Those who let her aunt die.

It would have been so easy to give in, to just stop thinking and let the rage control her. At that moment, Jessica almost let the anger conquer her. But strangely, there was something that restrained her. At the fringe of her perception, almost like a fleeting thought that she couldn't quite grasp, she detected a presence. There was a voice associated with the presence.

It was a calm and reassuring voice. Somehow it was able to navigate through the turmoil to reach her.

"Let it go... let the anger go. It is time to forgive and heal... *your* time to heal."

A war raged deep inside of her. Her aunt would have wanted her to love, not to hate. Above all else, she would have wanted her to forgive. But still Jessica resisted, the pain was so deep and the loss of her aunt too traumatic.

"Go ahead," a new voice said. It was the voice of her aunt. "It's time. Time to forgive everyone, including yourself. Do it now, Petunia."

Jessica clambered toward the voice. She longed for the peace that it promised. The peace that she desperately wanted. She was finished harboring her hate. She was finished wishing for a different outcome after all these years. *It was time!* With that thought, she let go of the weight that burdened her for so long. In that instant, she made the decision to forgive everyone and everything that happened. More importantly, she *finally* made the decision to forgive herself.

Jessica slowly opened her eyes, still reeling from the experience. She was on her knees on the floor of the waiting room. The man was there, kneeling next to her, his hand still holding her gently on the arm. She felt the streaks of fresh tears on her cheeks. She knew they were tears of relief. Tears of joy.

She turned to look at the man and then both

of them turned their eyes to her hand, as she slowly held it up, releasing her grasp. For a moment, the cardinal balanced itself on her palm, as if unsure of its footing. Tentatively, it began to spread its wings, similar to a phoenix rising from the flames. Together, they watched in amazement as slowly, the cardinal began to fly.

CHAPTER 6

Golden sunlight beamed across the swirling sea of maroon and orange in the overflowing stands of the football stadium. On the field below, two teams prepared to do battle, waiting for the opening kick-off. The kicker for the visiting team sent a high, floating ball into the air as a receiver in maroon positioned himself on the end zone line. As the receiver's hands touched the ball, the center of the east side of the stadium exploded in a maelstrom of fire, smoke, and burning hot debris.

Screams of terror erupted, only to be immediately silenced as a shockwave of crimson fire flooded across the field into the adjacent stands. A fiery mushroom cloud quickly rose, blanketing the stadium in darkness. When the smoke cleared, the stadium and its eighty thousand visitors were nothing but ash.

Noah woke from his dream, his breathing ragged and shallow. Sweat dripped from his forehead and his pulse reverberated loudly in his temples. *So many people dead!* His mind still held onto the images, fighting his desire to release them.

Noah tried to control the fear that overwhelmed him at the realization that he dreamt this dream before. That never happened. It was the same dream that led him to make the decision to end his life. *What did it mean?*

Sitting up, Noah concentrated on slowing his heart rate. Through the years, he worked hard to teach himself to handle the emotional aftermath of his dreams. He learned to stifle the shock of unexpected death. To suppress the terror and conquer the memories of pain. But it was difficult this time. Before this particular dream, he never dreamt of a tragedy of this momentous scale. Thousands were going to die!

He jumped from his bed, hastily throwing on the sweatshirt that he left draped over his desk chair the night before. The desk was empty except for a Bible, a tablet, and a book on lucid dreaming—all items that Riley gave him. The Bible was mainly untouched. He thought it was confusing and a little boring. On the other hand, he was eagerly embracing the other book. The concept of lucid dreaming fascinated him. The ability to become self-aware in a dream and then control the dream, like an artist wielding a brush upon a canvas, was mesmerizing. Though he practiced the recommended techniques to induce a lucid dream, so far his attempts were

THE OTHER SIDE

fruitless.

He opened the dresser door and removed a pair of new jeans. They were blue jeans, not his preferred color, but they were comfortable and they were free. It was hard to believe that only a week ago he was a homeless runaway bent on taking his own life. Now, he was living in a six-bedroom mansion in the suburbs of the nation's capital. In addition to living quarters, clothing, and food, Riley provided him with the most important thing Noah wanted. A second chance on life.

Riley was away now. Noah wondered where he was and whom he would return with this time. After they arrived from Seattle, Riley left unexpectedly, only to return two days ago with his newest housemate, Jessica. He wanted to talk to Jessica about his dream. If she really did possess the gift of healing, maybe she could fix him so he didn't have these dreams anymore.

Noah headed downstairs and found Jessica sitting at the kitchen table drinking a cup of coffee and reading her tablet. Like him, Jessica was also dressed in a sweatshirt and jeans. Must be the standard uniform of the house, he thought flippantly.

Jessica spoke without looking up. "There is coffee in the thermos on the counter. I hope you like it strong. That is the only way I drink it."

When Noah didn't respond, she looked up, her eyes going wide. "What happened? You look terrible."

Noah paused. The sheer enormity of the dream left him at a loss for words. Jessica stood up and walked over to him, touching his arm.

"I can see the turmoil you are in," she added. "Your aura is going all kinds of crazy."

"It was horrible..." They were the only words Noah could manage to say.

"Please sit down," Jessica directed, leading him to the table. "Do you want to talk about it?"

Noah hesitated. *Would she believe him?* Though he did not know Jessica well, he was already very fond of her. Jessica was not only beautiful, she was really cool. He expected her to be stuck up, like most women he encountered her age. But Jessica was different. She was friendly and really kind to him. She treated him like no one ever had. He felt accepted by her.

He took a deep breath preparing to share his dream, but was quickly interrupted by the sound of the front door opening. To both of their surprise, Riley entered the kitchen pushing a young man in a wheelchair. The man was tapping the side arm of his chair in a rhythmic pattern, but otherwise seemed oblivious to his surroundings.

"Good morning," Riley said. "Glad to see you are both still here." He paused, studying Noah for a moment, obviously detecting that something was wrong. That made Noah nervous. He wasn't ready to tell Riley about the dream. To

THE OTHER SIDE

Noah's relief, Riley didn't press the matter.

"Jessica and Noah, I would like you to meet Stephen," Riley announced, patting the man on his shoulder softly. "As you can see, Stephen is not able to walk. He has been disabled since birth." Stephen ignored Riley's touch, still intent on tapping the side arm of his chair. "Stephen also suffers from a severe form of autism."

Noah looked at Jessica. She was watching the new arrival with keen interest. She approached Stephen slowly. "Hi Stephen, nice to meet you," she said, hesitantly placing her hand on his shoulder. Stephen ignored her gesture, content to continue tapping rhythmically on the rail of his chair.

Jessica seemed taken aback for a moment. Like Noah, she had never met anyone with autism. Noah knew very little about autism, only what he read about it. He knew it was a very misunderstood condition and that people suffered from various degrees of severity. In almost all cases, they experienced difficulty with social interaction and communication, something with which Noah was painfully familiar.

"I want you to welcome Stephen to our house," Riley said as he wheeled Stephen closer to the kitchen table and then sat down next to him. "Like each of you, Stephen possesses an extremely powerful gift. Only his gift is locked deep inside of him and cannot be controlled at will." Riley looked at Jessica intently. "It is our

47

challenge to unlock his gift."

"What is his gift?" Jessica asked, studying Stephen as if analyzing him. "His aura doesn't make sense to me. I see light mixed with darkness, almost like a crisscross pattern. I have never seen anything like it."

"Stephen possesses the gift of knowledge," Riley answered, immediately noting the blank stares he received from both Jessica and Noah. "Stephen simply needs to focus on something. It can be an object, a place, a concept, or anything. It doesn't matter. When he concentrates, information and knowledge come to him."

"How is that possible?" Jessica questioned.

"How are your gifts or anyone else's possible?" Riley parried. "There are forces greater than we can imagine at work in this world." After a moment of consideration, Jessica nodded in agreement, apparently satisfied with the answer.

"Have there been others with this gift?" Noah asked, intrigued by the potential power locked inside of Stephen.

"Yes, there are examples in the Bible of people who possessed knowledge that they could not have known except through divine intervention. In one case that comes to mind, the apostle Peter confronted a husband and wife based on knowledge given to him by the Holy Spirit. The husband and wife were keeping money to themselves, despite telling everyone

THE OTHER SIDE

that they had given everything to the church. As a result of their dishonesty, they fell dead instantly."

"What?!?" Noah exclaimed. "That is crazy. Why would God kill someone?"

"That is an in-depth conversation for another time," Riley replied calmly. "Suffice it to say, everything has a purpose. You cannot judge God based on single events, you must look at the entire history of His interactions with humanity. Only then, will you gain insight into who He truly is."

Noah shrugged, not sure how to answer. He possessed very little knowledge of God or the Bible as it was, so he thought it better to keep the discussion on a level he understood.

"We don't have much time." Riley rose and walked over to Jessica. "Beginning tomorrow, I want you to work with Stephen."

Noah noticed that Jessica was visibly bothered at Riley's request. She was unsure of something. He felt the same way but for a different reason. If Jessica was busy helping Stephen, then they may not be able to spend as much time together. The thought further soured his already dark mood.

"I know you lack confidence," Riley assured Jessica. "But I know you can do it."

"I... I'm not sure," Jessica stammered. "What am I supposed to do?"

"You will need to figure that out for yourself," Riley said, turning his attention to Noah. "We have a problem, don't we? I want to know what it is."

Noah remained silent, not sure what to say.

Regaining her composure, Jessica came to Noah's side and put her arm on his shoulder in a gesture of support. "Noah had a dream and by the looks of him, I think it was a real bad one."

Riley's forehead wrinkled in concern upon hearing this. "We may have less time than I thought." Sitting back down next to Stephen, he said simply, "Tell me about the dream."

CHAPTER 7

Central Intelligence Agency, Langley, VA

Baal watched Natasha smile slightly as she made eye contact with the man seated directly across the conference table. Bill Rogers smiled back briefly in acknowledgement. Rogers was well-respected around Washington, D.C. and within his agency, having risen from humble beginnings as a field agent to the Director of the CIA. Baal's sources told him Rogers was an ethical man who was grounded in his faith. That was disappointing. Just another reason he needed to continue his efforts to infiltrate Rogers' most likely successor, Deputy Director Branson Schaeffer.

The top leadership of the other federal intelligence agencies were also seated around the table. Men and women who held secrets of state and carried the authority to direct armies of agents to execute their plans. The power represented in the room was exhilarating. Baal savored the moment. Few realized that the true power of the government was within the intelligence community. John Edgar Hoover knew that better than any human Baal had ever influenced. That man was almost as good at the intelligence craft as a demon... *almost*.

A man who identified himself simply as Riley, sat next to Rogers. Apparently, this man uncovered critical information regarding Thereon. This briefing would no doubt be interesting, Baal mused. Thereon was his creation. A terrorist organization of religious extremist bent on perpetrating evil guided by him. Humans would do anything if they believed it would lead them to an afterlife where every earthly desire would be fulfilled.

Baal studied Riley. There was something about him that was unsettling. Maybe it was his surreal calmness, in contrast to the fear and concern that radiated from those around him. Whatever it was, he would soon learn what this man knew.

Bill Rogers stood and addressed the table. "Thank you all for coming on such short notice." He turned to the man called Riley. "It is your show."

Riley stood to address the room, his eyes scanning each person seated around the table, finally coming to rest on Natasha. Riley's eyes lingered on her for just a moment too long, his face showing a barely perceptible flash of surprise. Baal immediately knew that he did not like this man.

"The information I have to share with you is brief, but the implications to our national security and the lives of tens of thousands of people are severe," Riley began. Baal noted the man's captivating voice. Each word seemed to magically hang in the air and draw those in attendance to listen intently. There had been very few others throughout history who possessed such a gift. The ability to truly inspire, influence, and motivate the multitudes through speech alone was rare among humanity.

"I lead a small team of agents and representatives of the CIA who are actively involved in tracking the activities of Thereon. As you know, this organization has been linked to multiple terrorist events on both foreign and domestic soil." He gestured to the files in front of each person.

"More recently, Thereon has claimed responsibility for a series of isolated, domestic events that would not typically be considered terrorist activities by the general population. The files that I have provided each of you provide a detailed assessment of these events," Riley paused. "We are still unsure how Thereon is executing these activities, though a strong theory is emerging."

"I will not comment on our theory at this

time," Riley continued. "What is relevant is that a trusted source has received information that a nuclear attack is eminent."

Shocked by the impact of Riley's statement, the audience listened in hushed silence, sharing concerned glances.

"The attack will be at a college football game and will involve a small megaton nuclear device," Riley said. "There is a potential casualty impact ranging from fifty to one hundred thousand."

Murmurs of shock arose from around the table as multiple conversations erupted. Everyone was talking except for Riley and Natasha. Their eyes connected for a time, again. Baal thought he observed a flash of light behind Riley's eyes, but it was gone as soon as it appeared.

Baal considered the situation, intrigued by the knowledge this man possessed. This man was very close to the truth about Thereon's plans. How much did he know? Better yet, how did he come to know it?

Riley settled the room with a gesture. The man's confidence surprised Baal. "I understand your concern," Riley assured. "And I regret that this is the balance of information that I can share at this time."

"How can you assure your data is accurate?" Natasha asked, hoping to gain insight into where Riley obtained his intelligence.

"This information is uncorroborated, but from a trusted source," Riley responded flatly.

"Who is your source?" Natasha pressed, prompted by a thought from Baal. By design, Baal had groomed Natasha to be susceptible to the thoughts he planted in her mind. Now, his suggestions were received by her as if they were her own thoughts.

"I am not at liberty to disclose that at this time," Riley deflected, shaking his head. "Disclosure of our sources could jeopardize future intelligence gathering."

Baal was becoming agitated with this man. If this man only understood the power that he was up against. Baal decided against urging Natasha to ask another question. Better not have her come off as too challenging. After all, the CIA and the Department of Homeland Security were supposed to be on the same team. What Baal really needed was Natasha to get closer to this man. He needed to know more about Riley and who he was.

Martha Coolridge, the Director of the Federal Bureau of Investigation, took advantage of the lull in the conversation. An extremely analytical woman, she earned the nickname, the Thinker, owing to her lack of vocal engagement in meetings. When she would speak, she always said something very relevant and poignant. "If we go forward on the assumption that an attack, as you describe, is going to occur, I calculate we have less than two months to prevent this catastrophe."

"How do you figure?" asked Nathan Dietrich, the Director of the National Security Agency. Nathan was a short, stocky, charismatic man. A recently retired Navy Admiral, he held his current position less than a year. Baal knew that Nathan suffered from depression, despite his outward personality. Baal also knew that depression was not the only demon plaguing the man, just the one that was most active and influential at the moment.

"Simple," Martha confidently responded. "The first game of the upcoming college season is going to be played right outside of Washington, D.C. during the last week of August. The actual attack could occur at any time during the season or at any game, but we should assume it will be during the opener. A terrorist event like that so close to the nation's capital would have severe ramifications domestically and throughout the world."

After a few more questions to Riley, which he answered vaguely, the meeting ended. With Baal's persuasion, Natasha immediately pulled Riley to the side of the room for a private conversation.

"Nice job," Natasha offered, hoping to appear genuinely appreciative of Riley's efforts. "I am sure you and your team have been working diligently. It's O'Connor right? Riley O'Connor?"

THE OTHER SIDE

"Yes. It is a pleasure to meet you, Deputy Secretary. I do appreciate your compliment," Riley said humbly. "This is a tough situation that we have been placed in and we really have our work cut out for us." He looked squarely at Natasha with a slight smile on his face.

Prompted again by Baal, Natasha asked Riley, "If you don't mind me asking, how long have you been an analyst in the CIA?"

"My entire career. The job has always fit what I was made to be."

"Lucky you. Very few people find that in life."

Riley looked at her oddly, forcing Natasha to speak, "Is something wrong?"

"No, I apologize," Riley said. "It's just that... for a second, you reminded me of someone."

Natasha chuckled, "I get that all the time. People often tell me that I remind them of a more mature Kate Middleton."

Riley nodded his head. "Yes, the Princess. Maybe that is it." But he didn't look so sure.

At that moment, Bill Rogers, interrupted their conversation. "Excuse me Natasha, may I borrow Riley for a moment?"

"Sure thing, Bill," she said respectfully. "As it turns out, I have to leave now for a meeting across town." She turned to Riley and extended her hand in parting, "It was a pleasure to meet you. Expect a call from me first thing in the morning as I will be assigning a special liaison from our office to work directly with you and your team." Without waiting for a response, Natasha exited the room, leaving the two men.

Baal observed Bill and Riley converse for a few moments, hoping to gain additional information that he could use. He saw that flash in Riley's eyes once again. It was a subtle, barely detectable light, but it was unmistakable. The intensity of the light shifted constantly, as if Riley's eyes were lit from within by a candle flame dancing against a sudden breeze. The implications of this revelation disturbed Baal. It had been many centuries since an Anointed One walked the earth. The apostle Paul was the last. A man with tremendous powers given to him by the Creator. If Riley possessed even a shadow of that power, Baal knew Thereon's mission was truly in jeopardy.

Baal immediately phased out of the physical realm, the office and the two men dissolving before him. He expected to encounter resistance to his plan, but definitely not this soon and not by an Anointed One. He needed time to rethink his strategy in the light of this new development.

There was no doubt that Riley O'Connor and his team, whoever they were, needed to be stopped. Failure to do so could delay his master's return by years or maybe even decades. That was a scenario Baal wanted to avoid at all costs. Anything other than success meant he would bear the brunt of his master's fury... and that was a punishment worse than hell itself.

CHAPTER 8

"Why did you decide to go with Riley?" Noah asked Jessica. The two of them walked slowly down a concrete path, headed towards a small clearing in the lush green woods that surrounded the park. The park was surprisingly peaceful, an oasis in the middle of a bustling mega subdivision. It was Jessica's idea to come to the park and Noah was glad she suggested it. He enjoyed spending time alone with her. Well, technically they weren't alone since Stephen was with them.

Noah pushed Stephen in his wheelchair slowly, making sure he was comfortable with the bumps caused by the small indentations in the concrete that created the impression of a brick walkway. Noah hoped Stephen was enjoying the experience, but most likely, Stephen was unaware of his surroundings. In Noah's opinion, Stephen appeared not to notice anything at all.

Jessica shrugged, "I really am not sure. I prob-

THE OTHER SIDE

ably came with Mr. O'Connor because I want to do something more meaningful with my life."

"Like what?" he asked.

"I have always felt that I was destined for something bigger. That somehow I was going to make an impact that mattered to this world," Jessica paused. "I guess I wanted a change and Mr. O'Connor gave me this opportunity. My life in Kentucky was *sooo* boring."

She gave Noah a curious look. "Why did you come?"

That was an easy question for Noah to answer. "Riley said he would help me solve my problem," he said simply.

Jessica stopped abruptly beside Noah. "What you can do is not a problem. It is a gift. Please don't think of your gift as a burden."

Noah grimaced, her response bothered him. It seemed to be such a shallow response because it ignored all the pain that he experienced. It ignored all those people who had suffered. "I wish I looked at it that way, but I don't," he retorted sharply. "What kind of gift lets you see people suffer and die? It is not like your gift, Jessica. Your gift helps people."

They walked in silence for several moments. Noah was beginning to fear he was being too harsh. Deep down, he knew Jessica was just trying to encourage him.

The path ended at a clearing overlooking a small pond. A swarm of dragonflies crisscrossed the lush brush and flora that grew along the water's edge, in search of insects. Their small metallic bodies created a shimmering effect in the air, amplified by the afternoon sun reflecting off of the water. Jessica sighed and took a seat on the bench of a nearby picnic table. "I'm not so sure that I help people," she admitted, her voice devoid of its normally upbeat tone. "I thought my gift was gone. I'm not sure I can help or heal anyone."

"What do you mean?"

"Mr. O'Connor thinks I just need to figure out how to use my gift. He is positive that I still have it." She looked at Stephen. "I know Jesus and his apostles healed people, but I'm not Jesus. I don't know what makes him think I can do it."

Noah understood Jessica's confusion about Riley. He felt the same way. Riley was cryptic about so many things, but Riley was adamant that Noah and Jessica would both help people. He wondered what made Riley so confident about their abilities. It wasn't normal.

Despite his mysterious personality, one thing was sure, Riley kept his word. He was currently training them to understand the nature of their powers. Last night, Riley introduced them to the biblical origin of spiritual gifts. Riley cited several passages from the Bible that referred to powers that were granted to the apostles by Jesus, among them the gifts of healing, prophecy, and Stephen's gift, knowledge. Noah wasn't fully convinced that seeing the future was a gift. It had always been a curse and he had not seen any evidence to the contrary. At least not yet.

"If it means anything to you, I think you can do it," Noah said. He didn't look at her, continuing to stare at the ground.

"That is really sweet, Noah," Jessica said, smiling at him. He still didn't look at her. "Wow! You're pretty shy, aren't you?"

Noah didn't answer. Of course he was shy. Being a freak did not lend itself to inspiring self-confidence. Fear, yes. Self-confidence, no.

"It's ok to talk to me, Noah," Jessica insisted. "You, Stephen and I... we all share something that is unique. That means we have a special bond."

"You think?" Noah responded, not knowing what else to say.

"Yes. In fact, I'm really looking forward to the future."

Noah perked up at her comment. "You're not scared about the future?"

"Hardly, life is meant to be lived," Jessica responded cheerfully, raising her hands into the air as if giving the sky an imaginary hug. "There is so much I want to do. We are young. We have our whole lives ahead of us. Why would I be scared?"

Noah frowned, "Nothing is guaranteed, Jessica. Not even life."

Now it was Jessica's turn to frown. "Boy, you really are dark on the inside, aren't you?"

Noah was not bothered by her comment, it was the truth. "If you could see what I have seen, you would be cynical too."

"Perhaps... but if you could see broken and hurting people restored through healing, then you would realize good things happen in life as well."

"Maybe," Noah said, his voice only a whisper.

"That is why I am optimistic about trying to heal Stephen, even though I am unsure of how I will do it or if I even can. I have hope that I will and hope makes all the... "

"...difference," Noah finished her sentence, remembering what Riley told him the first night they met.

They sat in silence for several minutes staring at the pond, watching a flock of baby ducks swim hastily after their mother. The ducklings bobbed and weaved amongst each other, each one trying to be the closest to its mother. Even so, they managed to maintain a fairly uniform line, moving swiftly in whichever direction their mother led them.

"I wonder how they learn to fly," Noah pondered.

"I think it's instinctual. Animals just know how to do things because of their instincts," Jessica said confidently.

Noah thought about Jessica's comment for a

moment. Perhaps she was on to something. "So maybe our powers are like that. Maybe we will learn to use them instinctively."

"Now, that is an interesting thought," Jessica said. "That makes me think that I have been approaching the situation with Stephen from the wrong perspective. I have been agonizing over a process or formula to heal him, but maybe there isn't one? Maybe I should just try and it will happen naturally."

Noah could tell she was lost in thought as she analyzed the possibilities. Slowly, a devilish grin formed on his face. He stood up, grabbing Jessica's hand and raising her to her feet. "There is only one way to find out if you are right," Noah said, his voice rising in excitement. "Now is the time to give it a try."

CHAPTER 9

The residence was dark and empty when he entered. That was odd, Riley thought. He wondered where the others were so close to nightfall. It crossed his mind they may have decided to flee, but he quickly dismissed the thought. They were nearby, perhaps exploring the neighborhood. At least their absence would provide him a chance to think without any distractions.

Though this morning's meeting at the CIA headquarters had gone well, he couldn't shake the feeling that something was wrong. That somehow, another chain of events was now set in motion that could impact his plans. The image of Natasha's face flickered across his mind. There was something about her, something dark and deceptive. He would need to be cautious with her.

Riley opened the refrigerator, retrieved a slice of day-old pizza and began gnawing on the crust, his mind deep in thought. Perhaps the real thing bothering him was his team was incomplete and unprepared. If they truly had less than two months before a massive terrorist attack, he was in trouble. Bill was understanding of his situation, but still wasn't giving him any grace. Lives were at stake. A great deal of them. He needed more time.

Riley removed his phone from his pocket and scanned a recent email he received from headquarters. One of the junior analyst monitoring health care admissions just stumbled across a bizarre case. A college student voluntary checked herself into the psychiatric ward at John Hopkins University claiming she was seeing ghosts.

Duke sauntered into the kitchen, inspired by the sound of the refrigerator door closing. Riley patted the German Shepherd on the head and broke a piece of crust, tossing it casually towards the dog who caught it easily between his gaping jaws. Duke had been a constant companion since the accident, a gift from his brother who operated a service dog academy. During his recovery, Duke gave him both physical and emotional support that he sorely needed. He watched as Duke pulled on the towel wrapped around the refrigerator, opening the door. A moment later Duke returned to the table, the pizza box grasped between his jaws.

"Ok, just one slice," Riley said laughing. "But no bedtime snacks tonight, ok?" Duke ducked his head, giving the impression that he was nodding in agreement. He gently took the offered slice in his mouth, retreated to a large cushion in the corner of the room and began gnawing on the pizza, much like his owner. Riley loved that dog. He couldn't imagine facing each day without him.

The sound of the front door opening jarred him from his thoughts. Duke let out a brief bark in protest, not liking the interruption to his meal, and returned to eating his pizza. To Riley's surprise, he heard the unmistakable sound of laughter coming from the hallway. A moment later, Jessica appeared, trailed by Noah pushing Stephen.

"Welcome back," Riley said, eating his last bite of pizza. "I trust you all enjoyed your day." He couldn't help but notice that both Jessica and Noah were visibly excited.

"We did," Jessica replied. "We took Solly for a walk... I mean jaunt... I mean wheel," she blushed in embarrassment at her own comment. "Anyway, we were at the park."

"Solly?" Riley asked a little bewildered.

"Stephen is too formal of a name," Noah interjected, walking over to pat Duke on the head. The dog ignored him, his jaws still tightly wrapped around the pizza crust. "We decided to give him a hipper nickname. Jessica suggested we name him after Solomon, the wisest man in history. So we came up with Solly."

"I am not sure Stephen will be happy with his name change," Riley frowned.

"Come on, Mr. O'Connor, loosen up a little. You're always so serious." Jessica scrunched her forehead pensively and pretended to tighten an imaginary necktie in painfully deliberate movements before checking her watch and repeating the motion. Noah laughed hysterically at her imitation of Riley.

Riley chuckled. He knew she was right, but he found it hard not to be serious when he knew the things he knew. "You got me on that one, young lady," he said. "Just remember, this is a serious world. There are things happening around us that you could not fathom."

"But, you still need to take time to enjoy life, Mr. O'Connor," Jessica said.

"Go on, Jessica," Noah interrupted. "Tell Riley what you discovered today."

There was an excitement in Noah's voice that was unusual. Riley considered that Noah might actually be having fun. Whatever the case, Noah definitely connected with Jessica and that was promising.

Jessica placed her hand on Stephen's shoulder. Stephen stopped his tapping on the rail of his chair and seemed to warm to her touch. "I think I can heal Stephen—his legs anyway."

"Tell me what happened," Riley responded, not surprised by her statement.

"I can't even remember how I healed before,

it was so long ago," Jessica said, taking a seat next to Riley. "I have been convinced that I lost the ability."

"Why do you think you were able to heal that bird?" Riley asked.

"I don't know," she frowned. "It just happened, but I think you helped me somehow."

"Maybe," Riley said.

"Today, Noah suggested that I allow my instincts to take over. So I tried to focus on one thing and one thing only... healing Stephen."

"What happened when you did this?" Riley probed, eager to hear what Jessica discovered about her ability.

"Nothing." She looked at Noah, a slight smile forming on her face. "Then Noah suggested I touch Stephen."

"It was cool, she went into a trance," Noah marveled.

"It is hard to describe," Jessica said. "I could feel everything that he felt. When I focused on an area of his body, it was like I was looking at a CT scan, but at the cellular level. When I focused on his spinal cord, I knew right away the reason he was paralyzed. His spinal cord is undeveloped and there are no nerve connections below his waist."

"What about his autism?" Riley asked. Healing Stephen's paralysis would be a miracle, but not the miracle they needed. They needed Stephen's brain.

Jessica shook her head, looking discouraged. "I couldn't read his brain. It was like a black spot on the CT scan. When I concentrated on that part of his body, I was overcome with this horrible sense of..." she paused searching for the right word. "Wrongness. I had to let go of Stephen, it was horrible."

Riley took a deep breath, contemplating this revelation. Jessica's explanation was not what Riley expected to hear. Healing flesh and blood was one thing. Healing the taint of evil was an entirely different matter.

"Thank you for your efforts and the update. I need you to keep working with Stephen while we are away," Riley said, rising from the table. "You need to strengthen yourself to face that wrongness. It is the only way to heal Stephen." He started to walk towards the door and paused, turning to Noah. "Are you coming?"

"Me?" Noah asked.

"Yes, you," Riley stated. "You need to pack a bag. We are going to be gone for a few days."

"Where are we going?"

"First, to a psych ward in Baltimore," Riley said, noting that Noah looked apprehensive after his comment. "No, I am not going to commit you, Noah. I will need your help with someone there."

"Ok, sounds cool," Noah said, shrugging his shoulders. "Then where?"

Riley didn't answer. He really wasn't sure

where they were going after Baltimore. The only thing he could trust was his path would eventually lead him to the missing team members. He unmistakably knew they were out there, somewhere. He just hoped that by the time he found them, it wasn't too late.

CHAPTER 10

Baltimore, Maryland

Riley scanned the large red brick building, his eyes coming to rest on the engraved stone above the main entrance. It read 'Henry Phipps Psychiatric Clinic 1912'. The building stood in contrast to the many modern facilities surrounding it. Situated less than a mile from the bustling downtown of Baltimore, the John Hopkins Medical Center was a city unto itself. The massive campus consisted of more than eighty buildings constructed at various times since the late nineteenth century. This particular building had been an active medical facility serving the mentally ill for more than a hundred years.

Riley turned to Noah, "This is the place. Now, before you go in..."

"Wait a minute," Noah protested, interrupting him. "Aren't you coming with me?"

"I can't. Not this time," Riley said, staring at the building.

Noah pushed himself back into his seat and folded his arms in defiance. "I am not going in alone. Have you looked at me?"

It was a fair question. For the trip, Noah donned the same black street clothes that he wore when Riley first met him. Though he was not wearing make-up, his nails still bore the traces of black nail polish and his hair was even more unkempt than before. Based on his appearance, he wasn't exactly prepared to create a warm and friendly first impression.

"Noah, I need you to listen to what I am about to tell you. It will help you to understand why I need you to do this... why I need you, and Jessica, and others." Slowly, Noah turned to look at Riley.

"We are at war," Riley said, staring off into the distance.

"That is crazy, Riley," Noah argued. "Who are we fighting?"

Riley turned to Noah, his eyes demanding undivided attention, "We are fighting in a war between angels and demons."

Noah was silent for a long while, absorbing the enormity of this information. Riley noticed Noah's feet beginning to fidget nervously, indicating his uneasiness with this new reality.

"Do angels and demons actually exist?" Noah gulped, turning to look at the ominous building.

"Yes, they really do," Riley responded. "And they have been at war with each other since before the creation of humanity." He peered at the horizon, as if looking at something very far away. Riley could recite from memory several verses of the Bible dealing with the war between angels and demons. The earliest battle was recorded in the opening chapters of the Old Testament. He also knew there were more than eighty references to demons and even more references to angels in the New Testament alone. Yes, angels and demons were very real. He could vouch for it. He had seen them both.

"Now, this spiritual war is spreading into our physical world and it is manifesting itself in acts of violence, hate, and terrorism," Riley continued. "That is why I need your help," he turned back to Noah. "You were given your gift for this precise purpose."

"You're telling me that I can see the future so I can serve in some invisible war?" Noah scoffed, not believing. "How can I fight something I can't even see?"

Riley pointed at the building in front of them, "I believe there is a person inside that building who can see this war. I need you to convince her to join us."

"You mean someone who can see angels and demons?" Noah asked, shaking his head in disbelief. "This is getting crazier, Riley. It reminds me of one of those cheesy sci-fi reruns on late-night television." He pushed his long bangs away from his face and stared at the brick building. "What if I don't want to fight this war?"

Riley considered the question for a moment. "You are free to walk away. But something tells me that is not what you are going to do. Still, it is a decision you must make."

They sat in silence for several seconds, lost in their own thoughts. Riley knew the truth was going to be difficult for Noah to believe. If Noah only knew what Riley experienced. As if reading his mind, Noah asked, "What happened to you?"

Riley knew the question would come up eventually. They would all ask him, and they should. It was important that they really understood who Riley O'Connor was. Jessica asked him the same question the first day she arrived at the residence.

Riley stared at the artificial fingers of his left hand, his mind jumping back to that night on the boat. The storm had come upon them unexpectedly. There was nothing they could have done. He looked at Noah.

"Three years ago, my wife and I were caught in a freak tornadic waterspout off the coast of Maine," he began slowly. "We were able to send a distress signal, but a few minutes later, our boat was flipped upside down as the spout hit us directly. My left arm was smashed between the mast and the deck of the boat causing me to be pinned. I was underwater for more than an hour before help arrived."

Noah was staring at him with his mouth gaping in horror. Riley chose his next words carefully. "I met God that night."

"Really, you met God?" Noah said doubtfully.

"Yes, along with his angels," Riley paused. "I was dead and I went to Heaven."

Noah shook his head, unsure of what he was hearing. "What happened next?"

"I woke up in a hospital room the next day. My legs were broken and my arm had been amputated. Even though my memories of being in Heaven were very vague, I vividly recall the presence of God enveloping me." Riley would never forget that moment. It was like his life flashed before his eyes and he saw how everything that ever happened to him was for a purpose. "God orchestrated everything, including my accident, to bring me to that very point."

"Did God say anything to you?"

"He simply said *Follow Me*." Riley gripped the steering wheel tightly with his good hand for support, "It was shortly thereafter that I began to receive promptings of the Holy Spirit. Over time, as I obeyed these promptings, I began to discover that I was now blessed with certain abilities. I also came to understand that God was calling me to do something for him, but I didn't know exactly what that would be. Now I do. My purpose is to fight the spiritual war against the demons... here on earth."

"Wow!" Noah exclaimed, "That is an amazing story." Noah paused thinking for a moment.

"What happened to your wife? Is she ok?" Noah asked.

Riley closed his eyes for several seconds, his head drooping. When he looked at Noah, a stray tear rolled slowly down his left cheek. "She died in the incident. We never found her body." Riley released his grip on the steering wheel, trying to relax. His wounds were still fresh. Even after all this time, he missed Charlotte so much.

They stared in silence for a few moments, then Noah unbuckled his seat belt. "So what is this psycho girl's name?"

Riley inhaled deeply and took a moment to regain his composure. It was always difficult to share that story, but it was also somewhat cathartic. It reminded him that life is meant to be enjoyed and cherished. That life on earth is temporary and it must be used to make a positive impact in the lives of others.

"Her name is Marie Bennett. She is twenty years old and a student at John Hopkins University. She checked herself in voluntarily two days ago requesting observation and counseling. That is all I know at this point."

"Why can't you go in?" Noah asked.

"Because of what has happened to me, I am not like everyone else," Riley said. "If Marie sees me through her spiritual lens, she is likely to flee as she won't know what to make of me. That is why you must do this."

Noah considered this information while he adjusted his hair in the vanity mirror. "Ok, Riley, I am going to trust you," Noah's voice trembled slightly. "What do I do when I get in?"

"Ask the nurse to see her," Riley said, removing a small folded piece of yellow paper from his jacket. "But first, ask the nurse to give her this note."

"That's it? Then what?" Noah questioned, expecting more information. Riley didn't need his heightened sense to see that Noah was petrified of his assignment. He couldn't blame him.

"That is the easy part. The next part will be more difficult." Riley placed his hand on Noah's shoulder. "Noah, it is very important that we get Marie to join our team. You have to succeed."

Noah gulped in response. "How do I do that?" he finally asked.

Riley smiled, knowing his request, though simple, would prove challenging for Noah. "I want you to make a friend."

CHAPTER 11

Noah unfolded the worn piece of paper and read the small inscription that Riley had written in block letters.

"FOR WE ARE NOT FIGHTING AGAINST FLESH-AND-BLOOD ENEMIES, BUT AGAINST EVIL RULERS AND AUTHORITIES OF THE UNSEEN WORLD, AGAINST MIGHTY POWERS IN THIS DARK WORLD, AND AGAINST EVIL SPIRITS IN THE HEAVENLY PLACES."

-EPHESIANS 6:12

Riley also included a short note under the inscription. It read, 'I know what you see. There are others like you.'

Noah hoped the woman would know what it meant because he was still a little unsure. Was there really a battle between good and evil beings going on around them? It was crazy to believe such a thing.

Noah approached the reception desk where a rather chubby nurse was reading a magazine. She gave him a disapproving frown as she scanned him with bored brown eyes. "May I help you?" she huffed, as if Noah was interrupting her in the middle of something important.

"I need to meet with Marie Bennett."

"Do you have an appointment?"

Noah hesitated, "No, but I have an important message for her. Would you at least give this to her?" He handed the paper to the nurse who snatched it quickly from his hands.

"Wait here," the nurse said, pointing to a chair along the wall. Noah sat down on an old wooden chair that looked like it belonged in the Smithsonian. Even just sitting in the lobby gave him the creeps. He couldn't imagine working here, let alone being a patient.

His mind drifted to Jessica. He missed being around her. Her acceptance of him, and who he is, was something he never experienced before. He wondered how she was progressing with Stephen. It would be amazing if she truly could heal him.

A few minutes later the nurse returned. "I need you to sign in," she said. "She will meet you in the visitor's room. Down the hall, third door on the left." She handed him a clipboard and promptly returned to reading her magazine.

As Noah headed down the hallway, he took long deep breaths, trying to remain calm. His stomach felt like it was turning inside out. What was Marie Bennett going to think of him? Worse, what was she going to say when he told her that he wanted her to go with him? The more he thought about it, the more it made sense to him. He belonged in this place. He was no doubt insane.

Noah opened the door and entered the visitor's room. The door closed behind him with a sinister thump and he heard the click of an automatic lock. Noah shuddered, there was no turning back at this point.

The room was stark and plain, but large. The concrete cinder block walls of the room were painted a pale blue, but the color failed to induce the stress-free environment that was intended. Instead it made the room feel even more confining. There were two plastic tables surrounded by plastic chairs on each side of the room. There was nothing else in the room except for a buzzer and a sign located next to the door he just entered. A young woman with black hair sat at the far table, her head down, staring at the floor.

He approached the table hesitantly, "Are you Marie?"

The woman nodded but did not say anything as she continued to stare at the floor. Noah took a seat across from her. "Hi, my name is Noah." Still, she gave no response—not even an acknowledgement that he was there. Noah was beginning to panic. This woman wouldn't even look at him.

"Why won't you look at me?" he finally asked

THE OTHER SIDE

after a period of silence that felt like a decade.

"I am frightened of what I may see," she said cautiously.

"You see angels and demons, don't you?" Noah asked, purposely keeping his voice hushed. There was no one else in the room, but Noah didn't want to take any chances that his conversation would be overheard. "It's ok," he reassured her. "I believe you. Please look at me."

Gradually, Marie raised her head, her face slowly relaxing as she looked at him. Noah was immediately struck by her beauty. He guessed she was a few years younger than Jessica, closer to his age, but there was a sophistication to her that he could not describe. Her straight black hair was shoulder length with slight curls at the ends. She had deep red lips, accented by the soft flush in her rounded cheeks that complemented her Hispanic complexion. Chocolate colored eyes, almost solid in color, searched him with an intensity that he could not describe, making him feel exposed. He immediately thought this woman would know if he were telling a lie, simply by looking at him.

Marie continued to examine him in silence. It almost seemed to Noah that she was looking through him, not at him. The intense scrutiny was making him nervous. *Who wouldn't be*, he thought, trying to calm himself. *This woman's stare would make a drill sergeant sweat.* "See, no spirits around me," he finally said, holding his arms up for inspection, not sure what else to do.

"You may not have spirits around you, but your appearance is still a little shocking," Marie said seriously. "Who are you?"

Noah ignored her comment. "I'm just a messenger," he said. "But I am like you. I have a gift too," he insisted.

"You see them too?" she asked, peering intently at him.

"No! That would drive me crazy," Noah blurted.

Marie shot him a glance that caused his face to turn red in embarrassment. *Oops*, he thought. *He was really screwing this up.*

"I'm sorry," Noah apologized, "I didn't mean to offend you. I do that sometimes when I get nervous. You know, speak without thinking." Marie didn't seem to be accepting his convoluted apology, so he kept rambling.

"I am used to talking to myself. I haven't really had many friends before..." he trailed off realizing he wasn't helping his cause. Marie simply stared at him with those intimidating eyes. He thought about ducking under the table. At least then, she wouldn't be able to see him.

"Enough!" Marie stated. "What do you want?"

Noah looked down at the floor and then back to Marie. She was staring at him with a look of leeriness. "I want you to check yourself out of here and come with me," Noah held his breath, waiting for her answer.

"Come with you?!?" she exclaimed. "You must be crazier than half the people in this place. I don't even know you."

"It's very important," Noah pleaded. "I can't explain it all. I just need you to meet Riley. He is somebody who can help you."

"I don't understand. Why doesn't this person come here and speak to me himself? I don't believe that you are telling me everything."

"Well, I know it sounds crazy, but he said you would know why when you saw him."

"I think this conversation is over," Marie said, the disappointment evident in her face. "It was nice to meet you, Noah. You seem like a nice guy, a little weird, but nice." She rose to leave.

"Marie, please wait!!!" He couldn't let her leave, he couldn't let Riley down. He reached out and grabbed her arm. As soon as he touched her, the room faded away, replaced by an image of a lush, forested park.

Noah examined his surroundings. He knew this park. It was the park that he just visited with Jessica and Stephen. He watched as three people and two dogs crested the hill in front of them. He didn't recognize the person walking one of the dogs, but the two other people he knew. The first person was himself and the other was Marie.

"That's me?" Marie gasped.

Noah hadn't realized he was still holding

onto Marie. She was next to him, her face a kaleidoscope of shock, fear, and awe at what she was seeing. He was feeling the very same emotions because this was a new experience for him too.

Marie unintentionally moved closer to Noah, now gripping his arm in return. "What is happening?"

"You are seeing a vision of the future," Noah said confidently. "This is my gift."

Marie watched in silence as the three people approached them. Noah could hear himself talking to the man walking Duke as they passed by, "I disagree on this one. I think Riley is wrong." The man didn't respond, but for some reason, the future Marie burst out laughing.

In attempt to follow the group, Marie let go of Noah's arm and broke contact with him. Instantly, they were both back in the visiting room of the hospital.

Marie's shocked expression caused Noah to burst out in laughter. It was probably a nervous release of energy, but still he couldn't help himself.

Marie scowled at him, "What just happened?" Frustrated, she threw a punch at Noah that landed on his shoulder. "And why are you laughing?"

Noah responded between fits of laughter, "It's just, well, you look like you have seen a ghost."

Apparently, the humor of his comment was not lost on Marie, as her pout turned into a small smile. She sat back down at the table. "Was that really the future?"

"I think so," Noah nodded. "My dreams haven't been wrong yet, but --"

"But what?" Marie asked, concern clouding her face.

"That has never happened to me before. I usually have dreams. Never a vision and never has there been anyone else with me." Noah shook his head in confusion. "This is all a little weird and shocking for me as well."

"Me too," Marie agreed, looking a bit more comfortable. "At least it's nice to know that someone believes me. I would never have believed you could see the future if I hadn't experienced it for myself."

The door to the room opened and an elderly woman entered followed by an old man in a white gown. The man's frail, wrinkled hands were tied in front of his waist with plastic bands. A muscular orderly followed the pair to the other table and positioned himself between the man and the door. Marie let out an audible shriek and immediately closed her eyes.

"What is it?" Noah asked.

"That man. I have seen him before in the hallways," Marie said, turning her head toward the opposite wall so the man was not in her field of vision. "He is always with an orderly and he is always handcuffed. I asked one of the nurses why and she said it's because he is prone to random bursts of violence. She also said that he has been here for twenty years."

"That's very sad," Noah offered.

"What is even sadder is that woman is his wife. She visits him every day, but he never says a word. He doesn't even seem to acknowledge her."

"I wonder what is wrong with him."

"If you could see what I see, you would know," Marie said, nodding her head for emphasis.

"What do you mean?"

"He is plagued by one of those creatures."

Noah stared at the man. He couldn't see anything out of the ordinary. "You mean a demon? I will have to take your word for that. He looks fairly normal, if you call being handcuffed in a mental institution normal."

Marie paused, thinking for a moment. "You know, you gave me an idea. Close your eyes." She grabbed his hand. "Now open them."

Noah opened his eyes and looked at Marie. "Ok, now what?"

"Look at the man," Marie directed.

Noah shifted his eyes to the man. Only there was no longer just the man. Emerging from the man's back, almost like a second torso, was a muscular grey creature with small black horns peppering its back. The creature's head reminded Noah of an alligator, with beady black eyes and a scaly appearance, only the snout was much shorter and the creature's front fangs were the size of butcher knives. What was even more disturbing was the creature's hands were buried deep inside the man's head. The sight was so alarming, Noah jumped out of his chair in fear, losing contact with Marie. The image of the man returned to normal in an instant.

Noah looked at Marie, his eyes wide in terror. "What in hell was that?" he said, which earned him a glaring look from the orderly.

"Did it work?" Marie asked excitedly. "Did you see what I see?"

"It was horrible! That terrible creature—all evil and scary and funky looking. I can't describe or even understand it." He sat back down, but only after moving his chair to the other side of the table next to Marie, as far away from the possessed man as possible. "Is that what you see?"

"Yes, and I see them many places, though not always as nasty as that one. Now that I think about it, coming to a psych ward was probably not the best idea. They seem particularly vile here."

"That was crazy," Noah said, shaking his head in disbelief. Maybe his eyes were playing a trick. He had to be sure. "Can we try that one more time?" Noah asked.

Marie laughed, but didn't say anything. Maybe she was finally warming up to him.

"I'm serious," Noah insisted.

"You must be a sucker for punishment," Marie responded. "But have it your way." She grabbed his hand again. Together, they both turned to look at the man.

The man's wife was now reading to him from a worn leather Bible. The man stared at the wall, blind to his surroundings. The creature on the man's back appeared to be laughing at the man's wife.

"Is that thing laughing?" Noah asked.

"Yes, I think it is," Marie said bitterly.

For some reason, watching the creature laugh in pure delight as it tortured the man and his wife filled Noah with a burning sense of injustice. Marie must have felt the same outrage he did because she shouted at the creature, "Leave that man alone! Go back to hell where you belong!"

The orderly immediately turned around at her outburst. "Is there a problem?" he barked.

Noah and Marie ignored the orderly. Their eyes were both locked on the creature, who was now staring at them intently. Noah wasn't sure, but he thought he detected an alarmed expression on the creature's face. A moment later, the creature disappeared.

"It's gone!" Marie gasped.

"I said, *is there a problem here*?" The orderly barked again approaching Noah.

"No sir," Marie replied. "I was not talking to

you."

"She was talking to me!"

They all turned to see the old man. He was now standing, a small smile breaking on his face. "Thank you!" the man said humbly. "Whatever you did... thank you."

Marie, Noah, and the orderly watched in disbelief as the man turned to his wife and knelt at her feet. He placed his head and bound hands gently in her lap and began to sob. Noah couldn't hear what the woman was saying in response, but mixed with the man's cries, he heard the words 'I love you' repeated again and again by both of them.

Marie looked at Noah, her face echoing the amazement that was evident in his own. No words could describe what they both were feeling.

Marie was the first to speak, breaking the odd silence between them. "So, on the assumption that I believe what you are saying and I go with you, why is this person so important?"

Noah had been expecting the question. "Like you, he has seen things from the spiritual world." Marie's face brightened. Knowing she was now interested, he waited a moment before delivering the knockout punch. "But what is even cooler is that he has met the angels in Heaven and lived to tell about it."

CHAPTER 12

Jessica forced herself to swallow against the bile that was slowly inching its way up her throat. The harsh taste was becoming familiar to her, a subtle reminder of her failure. Reluctantly, she tried one last time to penetrate the darkness that clouded Stephen's brain. It was like pushing a nail through a brick wall with her bare hands. She couldn't pierce the darkness directly, only scratch it, ripping it away black strand by black strand. She finally gave up. The darkness was just too strong.

She released Stephen's hand and fell back onto the couch, defeated. She massaged her temples, trying to release the pressure that was thumping in her head. She didn't know which was worse, her frustration at not being able to heal Stephen or the pain she was feeling from the effort. Everything she tried failed.

Jessica expected that healing Stephen's brain would be a challenge, but didn't anticipate she would also fail with healing his paralysis. She

THE OTHER SIDE

did everything she could think of—from visualizing the regrowth of cells to picturing Stephen walking. She even tried to massage his spinal cord directly and commanding him to be healed, but that proved awkward with Stephen sitting in his chair. Not to mention she felt like a TV evangelist. Each failure only served to create more doubt in herself and her ability to heal. She didn't know how she healed people before. It just happened.

"Ugghh!!!" She yelled with a final burst of frustration. *Maybe healing the bird was a fluke after all? Perhaps her power truly was gone?*

Visible disturbed by her outburst, Stephen began to thrash back and forth violently, banging against the plastic tray that kept him securely in his chair. Concerned for his safety, Jessica moved to his side, grabbing his chair to stop it from rocking.

"I am so sorry, Stephen," she soothed. "I didn't mean to upset you." She patted him gently on the back, not sure what else to do. "I just wish I knew how to heal you," she said in desperation.

As if in response to her plea, Stephen began to move his right hand in a random pattern on the tray of his chair. After several seconds, he began grunting loudly. Jessica was not sure what to do.

Stephen's grunting continued as he began moving his hands in more dramatic motions in a faster more deliberate pattern on his tray.

She began to realize a distinct pattern to his motions. Was Stephen trying to write? She observed him for a few more seconds before it hit her. Stephen was not trying to write. He was trying to draw.

Jessica raced to her bedroom, snatching her journal and a pencil from her desk. Her heart racing in excitement, she returned to find Stephen still making motions on the tray. What was he trying to communicate to her? Maybe he knew how to help her. It made sense that he would. Riley believed Stephen possessed the gift of knowledge. Could it really be true?

Stephen seemed to feed off of her excitement and began emitting a series of short high-pitched yelps. Jessica tried to hand Stephen the pencil, but he wouldn't hold still. Not knowing what else to do, she placed the open journal and the pencil on the tray. Stephen immediately grabbed the pencil, making a fist with it, and set the pencil tip down on the page.

Stephen's noises subsided as he began to trace on the paper, slowly at first and then quickly. She watched in amazement as a picture began to take form. At first it seemed to be a vague outline, but shortly, finite details began to emerge.

After a few intense minutes, Stephen released his grasp on the pencil, letting it drop to the floor. He immediately closed his eyes and dropped his head. Jessica wasn't sure what was happening to him, though it appeared he was now asleep. Careful not to disturb him, she gently removed the journal from his tray and studied the picture.

Jessica was amazed by the image on the paper of a beautiful woman, the shading of the drawing making the woman appear three dimensional. She was on her knees at the foot of a large cross, her arms lifted upward with her hands clasped. The woman was wearing a checkered shirt and her hair was tied in a long, braided ponytail that was pulled over one shoulder. Above the cross, in the upper part of the sketch, small figures appeared to be watching the scene from the sky above.

Jessica placed the drawing on the table, pondering what it meant. She began pulling absentmindedly on her braid as her mind jumped from one possible answer to the next. She stopped mid-pull, noticing her hand on her braid and the checkered cuff of her shirt. *The woman in the picture was her!*

Suddenly, she vividly recalled that day at the church when she healed those people. The pastor had asked the members of the congregation to lay their hands on an elderly woman and pray for her healing. The woman suffered from a viral eye infection that left her blinded in one eye and was now threatening the other. There was nothing modern medicine could do to help her.

Jessica remembered wanting to touch the

woman too, but her aunt wouldn't allow her. After the service, Jessica approached the woman. She didn't understand why she did it, but she felt compelled by some internal sense of purpose. She took the woman's hand, knelt, and began to pray.

A moment later, she felt a warmth of energy flow from her hand into the woman. The woman dropped to her knees in response and began sobbing, her tears mixed with shouts of joy and praise. "I can see! Oh my Lord, thank you Jesus!"

Was prayer the answer? Jessica mulled this revelation. If her ability to heal was truly a spiritual gift from God, it would make sense that it would occur under such circumstances. She read enough of the Bible to know the apostles healed people, often in conjunction with prayer. Perhaps that was how it worked. Maybe she was only a conduit for God's power, not the originator. She just needed to open the door to let Him work.

Energized by this revelation, Jessica knelt in front of Stephen who was still asleep. She gently took his hand and concentrated. Instantly, her perception was transported into Stephen's body, to the area of his damaged spinal cord. Slowly, purposefully, and from her heart, she began to pray out loud.

"Father in Heaven, it has been a long time since I have prayed to You. I have chosen to live my life without You. I was angry and bitter that

You took my aunt from me. I understand now I was wrong to feel that way." Jessica felt a little embarrassed to pray in the presence of Stephen. When in fact, she felt embarrassed to pray period. It had been so long.

"Please forgive me. I know now that I need You more than ever in my life. I need Your forgiveness, I need Your power, and I need Your grace." Stephen began to stir in his chair, probably awakened by her voice. She continued, "Father, this man needs Your power to heal him. He needs Your touch to restore him. Please God, I beg of You, please heal this man. For Your honor and for Your glory. In the name of Jesus, I pray."

As the last words left her lips, Jessica felt her hand turn ice cold, only to become burning hot instantly. The sensation was like nothing she ever experienced. Her hand felt like it was going to explode. She didn't know what to do, only that she wanted to release the pressure in her hand. She felt something flow from her hand into Stephen. It was similar to the pressure one felt when holding a water hose, only stronger.

Through her enhanced vision, she watched in astonishment as Stephen's spinal cord began to grow, basked in a bluish light. Miraculously, cells, nerve endings, and sinew appeared where there was none before. Blood vessels branched out in a web pattern connecting to existing vessels around the spine. She felt more power flow from her hand into Stephen as blood began to flow into the newly generated tissues. Her skin tingled as she sensed the electrical current of nerve impulses now traveling up and down Stephen's spinal cord. The sheer amazement at what she was observing was mesmerizing. Seconds later, the blue light faded, like a breeze extinguishing the flame of a candle, leaving only the small glow of the wick. Then the light disappeared along with her enhanced perception.

Exhausted from the effort, Jessica opened her eyes, but all she could see was darkness. She wasn't sure just what happened. Where was the light? She was dizzy. In addition, her head was throbbing even harder than before, making it difficult to get her bearings. She tried to stand up, but stumbled, too weak from her labors. A hand reached out and caught her before she fell to the floor. She grasped the hand tightly, steadying herself. Gently, she was pulled to her feet.

Slowly, the room began to brighten as her vision returned. She blinked her eyes, but they were still out of focus. Gradually, the blurriness in her eyesight cleared. Stephen's tray lay overturned on the floor at her feet. He must have knocked it out during another episode of thrashing, she thought, her head still reeling. The pounding in her head was making it difficult to do much of anything. It took her a moment to realize Stephen's chair, sitting in front of her, was empty.

She felt a firm squeeze on her hand. Her

breath caught in her throat as her gaze landed on Stephen. He was standing next to her, his head still staring down at the floor. There was an odd smile on his face. For some reason, she understood what it meant. The realization brought a smile to her face as well. Despite her doubts, despite her fears, she achieved the impossible. She finally healed again.

CHAPTER 13

Riley steered the SUV into a tight curve, tossing the occupants in the back seat into a tangle of arms and legs. Riley caught the look of apprehension in Marie's eyes through the rearview mirror as she positioned herself back into her seat. No doubt she was having second thoughts about her decision to join him and Noah.

"I am sorry," he apologized. "I'll try not to let that happen again. But make sure that your seatbelts are securely fastened, just to be safe. We still have a ways to go."

He had only known Marie less than an hour, but he liked her already. There were aspects of her personality that reminded him a little of himself. She was direct, no nonsense, and quite opinionated. That was good because it was exactly what he expected from a person with the spiritual gift of discernment.

When he and Marie first met, she just stared at him intently, studying him. After several seconds of examination, she smiled and extended her hand in greeting. "Whoever you are, whatever you are—I know I can trust you," she said. "Tell me what I need to do."

Noah quickly interrupted, "How do you know that? What do you see?"

"He is bathed in pure white light," she responded, still looking at Riley. "I have seen beings bathed in the same light, but only a few times. When I have, they were carrying a sword and fighting against demons."

"Angels," Riley remarked, to no one in particular.

Minutes after Marie checked herself out of the clinic, Riley received an urgent call from Bill Rogers at CIA headquarters. There was an active shooter on the campus of American University and casualties were being reported. Even more concerning, the shooter was tweeting images from the campus library with the hashtag #Hail-Thereon.

Normally, incidents of this nature were the jurisdiction of the FBI. But if Thereon was involved, he needed to investigate. The most current information from campus police, local law enforcement, and the FBI was instantly being transferred to his mobile phone from the CIA's communication center. As he drove, he managed to glimpse a few of the photos from Twitter. What he saw made his heart hurt. The scale of death was appalling.

By the time they arrived on campus, the situation had stabilized and rescue efforts were underway. Members of a specialized SWAT team killed the shooter, but only after a nasty confrontation. According to preliminary reports, the shooter was a Caucasian woman, heavily armed with automatic weapons and explosive devices. There were severe casualties on all three floors of the library and several areas of the building were destroyed from explosives she detonated.

Riley grimaced while processing the latest casualty report. The overall death toll, including members of the SWAT unit, exceeded fifty. Several bodies were found decapitated.

Riley pulled the SUV alongside of the curb and cut the engine. He couldn't get any closer. Before him, a wall of police cars, ambulances, and fire engines blocked traffic on Massachusetts Avenue in both directions. A large crowd of bystanders and media had already formed along one side of the street, vying for the best position to observe the chaos before them.

A hastily constructed barricade of yellow tape created a perimeter around the main entrance to the University's library. Riley watched as a SWAT team exited in formation, followed by two paramedics wheeling out an injured woman. She was obviously one of the lucky ones.

"Leave everything and follow me," Riley

ordered.

"You want us to go with you?" Noah asked, the color draining from his face. "That's a crime scene," he gulped. "What if there are dead people in there?"

"There are dead people," Riley responded, exiting the car. "You need to get used to it. Let's go."

Riley flashed his credentials to an officer standing at the barricade and ducked under the yellow caution tape. Marie and Noah followed suit under the disapproving eye of the officer. Riley didn't care that he was breaking protocol by bringing civilians into the crime scene. He needed them to see this. Even more important, he needed to know what Marie could see.

The lobby of the library opened into a large reading area crowded with tables, couches, and desks. Several items were overturned and displayed the ragged scars of bullet holes, as if they had been used as barricades. Deep crimson splatters marked much of the furniture and several pools of blood stained the carpeting. Riley quickly counted eighteen bright yellow body bags scattered throughout the room. Chilling markers of the carnage that had occurred. It was a massacre.

Riley turned to Marie, "Do you see anything?"

Marie hesitated, "No. Whatever was here is gone. But I still feel its presence."

"Describe what you are feeling," Riley pressed.

"It is difficult to explain. It feels really cold," she offered. "It was something very powerful and very evil." Riley sensed the evil as well, but not exactly the same way that Marie did. For him, it was more of an awareness versus an actual feeling.

The room was a buzz of activity as police, fireman, and paramedics were darting to and from all areas of the building. In the center of the room, a man that Riley presumed to be a detective, hurriedly wrote notes as he interviewed three young women. The faint stain of blood could be seen soaking through a bandage applied to the arm of one of the women. Riley made his way over to the small group, and introduced himself to the detective, curious about what the man uncovered.

"CIA?" the man studied Riley for a moment, a quizzical look on his face. He shrugged his shoulders, "Not normally your turf, but I can use all the help I can on this one." He extended his hand in greeting. "I am Frank Gillian, special investigator for the FBI."

Frank appeared to be in his mid-fifties and struck Riley as a man who had seen more than he bargained for during his career. The man's eyes were bloodshot and his face unshaven. Riley smelled a slight hint of stale alcohol on the man's breath. In spite of his less than polished

THE OTHER SIDE

first impression, there was something about the detective that intrigued Riley.

"What information can you share?" Riley asked, hoping the detective would be forthcoming.

"None of my information has been corroborated, but what I do have, I can't explain," Frank said, rubbing the stubble on his chin. He pointed his thumb at the woman with the bandage. "This woman claims the shooter lifted a grown man with a single hand and threw him twenty yards." The woman nodded in agreement, but didn't say anything.

"The other woman said that the shooter moved with lightning speed, quickly jumping from one area of the room to another in an instant." The detective scanned his notes. "I have crazier stories from other witnesses. I am not sure what to make of it."

Riley considered the detective's comments. A person possessed by a demon could manifest unusual abilities such as superhuman strength, telekinetic abilities, or unusual intelligence. Given what he knew and the scope of the carnage around him as well as Marie's assessment, Riley knew with certainty this attack was demon-inspired.

"Riley, something is wrong with Noah!" Marie shouted from behind him.

Noah was standing just a few feet away, his face frozen, his eyes wide open, staring off into the distance. Riley knew instantly what was happening, though he never observed it before. Noah was having a vision. He moved quickly behind Noah and placed his hands under Noah's armpits to support him.

A few seconds later, Noah began shaking his head, disoriented. "Hey, what are you doing?!?" he cried, surprised that Riley was holding him.

"It's ok, Noah. What did you see?"

"There is a second shooter!" Noah exclaimed, recalling his vision. "He's here in this room!"

"You mean now?" Riley said, surprised by Noah's statement. He pulled his XD-9 pistol from his shoulder holster. Like all CIA agents, he completed extensive firearm training annually, and had proven to be a decent shot at long range. Under ten yards, he was deadly accurate.

Noah nodded affirmatively and began to look around the room, his face a mask of fear.

"What does he look like?" Riley demanded, as he was scanning the room.

"I couldn't tell. In my vision, the shooter was already firing," Noah responded. "People were diving for cover, many were getting shot, and some were shooting back. It was complete chaos."

Riley reached for Marie. "I need you to be my eyes. Tell me if you see something unusual."

"Drop the weapon!" Detective Gillian barked, his gun focused on Riley. Riley ignored

THE OTHER SIDE

him. Around the room, more people took notice of what was happening, many officers also raised their guns toward Riley. Riley kept his gun lowered, but in front of him, ready to fire. He waited for Marie to give him the signal, his uneasiness rising by the second.

Across the room, a large group of policemen appeared through a side entrance, trailed by two paramedics pushing a gurney. A third paramedic followed carrying a bright orange duffle bag with the first aid insignia prominently displayed on its side. On the opposite side of the room, two firemen were smashing down the remains of a door that was damaged by an explosive. No one around the perimeter appeared to be aware of the standoff in the center of the room.

"There!" Marie yelled, pointing towards the side entrance. "The paramedic with the bag!"

Instantly, Riley began running through the crowd of people in front of him, towards the far side of the library. The paramedic was on his knees, removing something from his bag. Before Riley could get a clear shot, the paramedic was on his feet brandishing an assault rifle. Within seconds, he was firing into the crowded room.

Riley exchanged fire as he dove behind an overturned couch. He scrambled to his right as bullets ripped through the springs and padding of the couch, leaving several gaping holes. That was too close, he thought.

Riley came up from the other side of the couch, pistol ready. The shooter was still twenty yards away, but momentarily turned his attention to the other side of the library, peppering the room in a wide arc, maximizing his target range.

The library erupted in greater chaos as people scrambled for safety. Many were able to find protection behind tables or other wooden furniture. Others were not as fortunate, caught in the shooter's spray of bullets. From behind him, Riley heard other shots as the police returned fire. Riley took aim and fired again toward the shooter.

His bullet struck the paramedic in the shoulder. Except for a momentary shudder from the impact, the shooter appeared unharmed and continued shooting. Riley fired again, this time sending a bullet into the shooter's stomach. The shooter didn't even flinch. As if annoyed by Riley's vain attempts to stop him, the shooter trained his gun on Riley. A wicked smile formed on the shooter's face, as if he recognized Riley, and knew who he was.

Before Riley could react, three rapid shots sounded from directly behind his position. The shooter fell to the ground, lifeless. All three shots had found their target in the shooter's head.

Riley turned to see Detective Gillian lowering his weapon. The detective made eye con-

THE OTHER SIDE

tact with him. "Thank you," Riley said appreciatively, holstering his weapon before extending his hand. "You saved my life."

"I can say the same. If you hadn't acted quickly, when you did, I and many others may not be alive," the detective responded gratefully. "How did you know about the second shooter?"

Riley looked at him and then across the room. Noah was helping Marie up to her feet. The two had taken refuge behind an overturned bookcase. To his relief, they both appeared unharmed.

With a slight smile breaking on his face, he turned back to the detective as a cherished verse of scripture came to his mind. "Just as you do not know the path of the wind, or how the bones form in the womb of a pregnant woman, so you do not know the work of God who makes everything."

Without another word, Riley turned and headed towards Noah and Marie, leaving the detective scratching his head in confusion.

CHAPTER 14

Moraine Lake, Banff National Park, Canada

The sunlight danced brilliantly off the snow capped peaks, reflected by billions of tiny diamonds of ice. A stiff breeze pushed an occasional snowflake across his path, stirred up from the mounds of snow that blanketed the land. The cold air didn't bother him, even in physical form. He couldn't feel it. He couldn't feel anything.

Baal surveyed the valley below. This place was one of the few on earth that he liked to frequent. One of the few that reminded Baal of Heaven. He knew that he would return to Heaven one day. It was not a question of how or if he would return, it was only a question of when.

"I will never understand why you like this place." The voice surprised Baal. He thought he was alone. He turned his gaze away from the scenery below and towards the voice, knowing who he would find. Asherah was standing several yards away, watching him with a skeptical look on her face.

He looked at Asherah, admiring her beauty. Like him, she had assumed a physical image, which was typical for their meetings on earth. She was dressed in a low-cut Egyptian tunic that more than displayed her adequate cleavage. Her hair was soft red, wavy, and fell to her waist. Wide brown eyes with dark lashes gazed at him intently, beckoning to him. Her plump lips were formed in a pout of disappointment. She looked ravishing, as she always did.

Consorts since the beginning of their creation, they chose to follow Satan during the first wave of fallen angels, forever changing the course of eternity. That was eons ago, before the dawn of humanity. Since then, Asherah had become his most trusted advisor and confidant. One of the strongest demons in her own right, she was loyal to him and no other, except Satan himself.

In the early age of humanity, Asherah was known to humans as the Mother Goddess who held the power over fertility. At that time, angels, demons, and humans interacted in the physical plain on a daily basis under the vigilant eye of the Watchers. Baal chuckled at the memory of those days, so long past. The irony of what occurred was still amusing to him.

The Watchers were angels sent to protect humans from the schemes and influence of Satan. Only Satan was able to coax some of the Watchers to his side, creating in many of them lustful desire for the very beings they were sanctioned to protect. This led to the second wave of fallen angels, called the Grigori. In all, a third of God's angels had chosen to follow Satan and rebel against the Creator.

That was when the war between angels and demons truly began. A war over the future of humanity. Fortunately, the demons had allies on Earth, like the Nephilim, to assist them in the destruction of humankind. Nephilim were the offspring of the Grigori and human women. They were giants—half-human, half-demon beings with unique abilities and powers. Baal fought alongside many of the Nephilim who were now revered as gods in the mythology of early civilizations. They were truly powerful creatures. So powerful, the Creator had no choice but to destroy them.

Abhorred at the transgression of the Grigori and the Nephilim, the Creator banished the Grigori to eternal imprisonment in the Abyss. Then, God brought forth the Great Flood to rid the world of the Nephilim, their tainted bloodline, and all of humanity. The only exception being the prophet Noah, who gained the favor of God and survived in an ark God instructed him to build.

THE OTHER SIDE

The flood did have its benefits, Baal mused. The physical world was now inhabited with the evil spirits of the dead Nephilim. The spirits willfully submitted in servitude to Satan, as their only hope for redemption lie in the overthrow of the Creator.

"This place reminds me from where we came," Baal said reflectively, walking off the ledge of the hillside to inspect the valley. Directly below him, a greenish-blue lake surrounded by lush forest reflected the mountains that encircled it. He imagined himself diving deep into the lake, the piercing cold of the water taking his breath away. How he desired to feel alive once again. He envied humans for that reason alone.

"Foolishness!" Asherah sneered. "It is a waste to dwell on this place. When our time comes, we are going to rebuild Heaven. We cannot even imagine the beauty of what we will create." She appeared next to Baal in the air and peered down into the valley. "It will be grander than anything before, anything now, and anything imaginable."

"You are always the pragmatist, Asherah," Baal replied coolly. "I am glad you are here. There is an urgent matter we must discuss."

"Is there a problem?" she asked, walking back onto the ledge.

"Problem? No, no problems," he paused. "Only interesting developments."

"Of what type?" Asherah inquired, reclining casually in the air. Her movement caused her tunic to shift around her midsection in a manner that exposed what it originally covered.

"The Anointed has others working with him. A healer, a truth-seer and surprisingly, an oracle."

"An oracle?" Asherah said in disbelief. They both knew the last oracle to walk the earth died more than two thousand years ago. "Are you sure?"

"Yes, my eyes observed a divination of the oracle through a domestic," Baal affirmed. Domestics were lessor minions of the animal kingdom that he and other demons controlled for the purposes of eavesdropping. His domestic of choice was a common household fly due to its size and relative invisibility, but rats and crows proved just as adequate.

"I expected the Anointed to arrive at the university to investigate our little party. In fact, that was part of my plan," Baal said, recalling the events at the library. "To my dismay, his two companions thwarted my fun."

"How so?"

"I intentionally planned a second shooter for two objectives. Primarily, I wanted to kill the Anointed. My secondary objective was to create additional terror and death." Baal rose and began pacing in the air.

"The oracle foresaw the events and warned

the Anointed," he continued. "The truth-seer was able to identify my minion before the plan could be executed. It was all very disappointing."

"That is interesting," Asherah agreed, her tunic shifting form to that of a black lace negligee. Her hair was now blond and curly. "It appears you are faced with a real challenge," she cooed.

Baal looked off in the distance pretending not to notice her wardrobe change. It was hard not to behold her beauty. He desired her and she knew it. Baal pushed the thought out of his mind. Consorting with her was not the distraction he wanted. Human flesh was what he desired above all else, only that was technically forbidden.

To ensure the fallen angels would never interfere so directly with humanity again, the Creator imposed restrictions. In addition to limiting all but the strongest demons from crossing over into the physical world without a host body, directly consorting with humans would initiate immediate imprisonment in the Abyss. That was why Baal and the demons craved possession of a human. Sexual interaction with humans was only possible through possession of another human.

"So how can I help you?" Asherah asked, her eyes turning deep blue.

"The oracle is not unknown to us. One of

Satan's scouts has a stronghold established that we can leverage," Baal said. He was pleased with this important discovery. A stronghold was a valuable tool to his kind.

Centuries ago, demons learned to use the sin nature of mankind, inducing humans to sin. Overtime, repeated sins of the same type made a human more susceptible to that sin, building a stronghold which could be leveraged to make the individual commit additional sins. Just as in battle, once an invading army establishes a stronghold, it can be used as a base to attack the enemy in other areas.

"Oh, this is intriguing," Asherah exclaimed, floating into the air to stand next to him. "What type of stronghold?"

"Despair," Baal responded darkly. "The oracle was planning to take his own life the night the Anointed found him. The Anointed must be strong, because the spirit has been cast out and unable to access the stronghold. It appears the oracle has been shielded. That is why I need you."

"But despair is not my specialty," she said, grimacing in confusion. "You must have something else in mind?"

"I need you to focus on what you do best," Baal smiled. "You are strong. Almost as strong as I am. You should be able to easily overcome any defense that the Anointed has set up around the oracle."

"For what purpose am I tempting this young man?"

Baal approached Asherah and gently touched the side of her head, sliding his hand through her hair. "I need you to create dissension in the ranks of the Anointed," he said. He let his fingertips graze the nape of Asherah's neck and glide slowly down her arm. "We first need to divide his team before we conquer them."

She blushed purposely in response to his gesture. "Sounds delightfully dangerous," she said softly. "I am eager to work on this young oracle."

"Be gentle," he laughed, beginning to cross over. There was somewhere else he needed to be. A vital meeting with an old friend he had not seen in decades.

Asherah began to fade as well, but not before he heard her tease, "Do I have to be?"

CHAPTER 15

*T*he pinpoints of pressure created by the splatter of liquid pounding on his head was an odd sensation. He glanced upward toward the heaven. It had never rained on the earth before. That is until now.

The normally placid vapor that separated the earth from the sky was billowing in all directions, expanding across his entire view. Lightning bolts shot from dark areas of the firmament, crashing into the earth in streaks of bright white. In the distant horizon, sheets of grey moved in chaotic patterns, buffeted by strong winds from the east. The rain was falling with such intensity that he could not see twenty yards in front of him.

A deep rumble sounded from the core of the earth, accompanied by a heavy tremor. To his left, a large plume of steam burst from the ground, sending an arc of liquid thousands of feet into the air. So the Creator has finally made good on his promise, Baal thought. It has begun.

Baal turned his attention to Ahijah, the leader of

the Nephilim. He noted the fear that radiated from the giant's eyes. Baal had never seen him afraid. Mostly human in form, Ahijah stood more than twenty feet tall. His massive arms spread nearly that length. He possessed enormous strength, able to lift objects that would take a team of a hundred men. He used that strength to defeat many of the human armies in battle. Now, few opposed him. But strength wasn't Ahijah's only talent. Ahijah could control the elements of metal. Shape them to his will and unleash them with brutal force.

"What is your plan?" Baal asked, studying the ice cold wetness that now coated his hands.

"Head to Mount Hermon and climb as high as I am able," Ahijah bellowed, scanning the horizon. In the far distance, a mountain towered high above the others surrounding it, its peak obstructed by the swirling storm clouds. Mount Hermon was special. It was where the angel Azazel and the other Grigori first arrived to take human females as lovers and wives. Azazel was Ahijah's father.

"What about your son, Og?"

"Og is going to try to gain access to the prophet Noah's ark. If that fails..." The giant looked towards the sky, not bothering to finish his sentence. Og did not possess the strength or talents of Ahijah, but was still a giant by human standards and one of the strongest Nephilim warriors. But that didn't really matter now. Not when every living creature on the world was in imminent danger of being destroyed.

"This is not the end," Baal assured.

"How can you be sure?" Ahijah roared so his voice could be heard above the increasing winds. "The Grigori are already banished. This flood is meant to end us all."

"Maybe," Baal acknowledged. "But remember, you are a special being. Your flesh may die, but your spirit will live on." With nothing else to offer but words, Baal hoped to provide the giant encouragement.

An explosion burst from the earth below their feet, sending the giant hurling into the sky. Baal phased into the spiritual realm instantly, letting the debris pass. He reappeared next to the giant, who landed hundreds of yards away. Ahijah rose to his feet and stepped out of the crater his body left in the damp earth. The look on Ahijah's face surprised Baal. No fear—only determination.

"I have to go," the giant said. "Come find me when it is over."

Baal watched silently as Ahijah ran towards the mountain range in the far distance. Each stride from the giant covering twenty yards or more as he leaped from side to side to avoid the exploding earth around him. Baal knew it was the last time that he would see his friend alive.

Baal rubbed his fingers slowly across the gleaming metal bar, imagining the sensation of the soft metal gliding across his skin. He remembered what it felt like to touch gold. A memory that was now only a figment, almost forgotten.

THE OTHER SIDE

He surveyed the vault around him. Hundreds of gold bars, stacked in orderly blocks. It was a beautiful sight. Too bad it was wasted.

This vault was identical to the fifty others situated in the underground facility. Each vault housed gold or some other precious metal. This area was off-limits to humanity, with the exception of a few chosen to protect the vault contents. Those with that responsibility lived in fear because they knew the vaults were haunted.

It was common for these humans to find bars of metal on the floor or even whole pallets overturned with no apparent cause. Some had seen an apparition or an unexplainable mist rolling through the corridors. Baal knew why. It was his old friend.

Around him, bars of gold began to rise from the stacks and float, weightless in the air. Good, Baal thought, Ahijah is here. In front of him, Baal watched as a form took shape. It started as a shimmer in the air, then gradually became a translucent cloud resembling a giant human.

"Good to see you, comrade," Baal said. "It has been a long time."

"Sacred One," a voice replied as the figure knelt before Baal. "For what purpose do I owe you submission?"

It was the correct question to ask, but the implications still bothered Baal. As penalty for their rebellion, the Creator decreed that the spirit of the dead Nephilim would roam the

Earth. It was a torturous punishment. Baal felt sympathy for their situation. How could he not? Before the flood, he broke bread and drank wine with many of them in freedom. Now, imprisoned on Earth, there was no choice but to be servants of Satan.

"The final battle is imminent," Baal proclaimed. "Satan is not far from making his grand appearance on Earth." It was a statement of fact. Everything was in motion to bring about the fulfillment of the prophecies. "We have only to set a few more pieces of the strategy in place," Baal added.

The room remained silent. Baal expected a different response from Ahijah. Support in the best case, subtle resistance in the worst. But not silence.

"Have you anything to say, Ahijah?" Baal probed, somewhat guarded.

There was a long pause. "Forgive me," Ahijah said. "I grow weary with this existence."

That was odd, Baal thought. Something was not right with Ahijah but he decided against pushing the matter. There were more important priorities to address. "Perhaps a change in venue is in order," Baal offered.

Ahijah remained silent, his form hovering motionless. The gold bars settled slowly to the floor, as if in surrender.

After his death in the flood, Ahijah established his spiritual kingdom in the same location of his Nephilim kingdom, though the land was now covered by ocean. He lived for centuries undisturbed until the exploration of the new world occurred during the sixteenth century. In retaliation for disturbing his domain, Ahijah lashed out periodically, using his power to create, control, and destroy metal, causing destruction of those who trespassed. Over time, this area became known to humanity as the Bermuda Triangle. Seeking isolation from the expanding world, Ahijah eventually abandoned this area and retreated to the solitude of one of the most impregnable fortress ever built, Fort Knox.

"What would you have me do?"

"How would you like to do battle against an Anointed?" Baal offered.

"It would be my honor. Where do I find him?"

Baal quickly relayed the information to Ahijah along with a description of the Anointed. As he concluded his instructions, Ahijah fell to one knee and bowed.

"You do not need to kneel for me, old one." Baal said, surprised.

"It is not for you, great one," Ahijah responded, his head still facing the floor.

Baal turned, his defenses at the ready. Even though he knew what to expect, seeing the brilliance of an angel of the Lord was always a mesmerizing experience. The angel's body was like that of a polished bronze statue, magnificently formed and radiating light from within. The angel wore a stark white tunic, secured at the midsection with a rope whose strands were of gold. Slowly the angel raised his head, revealing piercing white eyes that burned with a bright inner fire.

"Raphael!" Baal seethed. He stepped backward creating more space between himself and the archangel. Raphael was one of seven great angels who possessed immense power and shared command for God's army of angels. Raphael was the angel chosen by God to bound the Grigori and lock them in the great Abyss until the Day of Judgment.

"Leave us!" the angel's voice echoed in the small chamber. Immediately, Ahijah blinked into nothingness.

"What business do you have with me, Oyeb?" Baal said, using the ancient Hebrew name for one's personal enemy. He assumed a defensive posture to protect against a sudden attack by the angel. Baal carried a great deal of respect for Raphael—a worthy adversary, but not invincible. Their last meeting was decades ago. Both left the confrontation wounded.

"I bring warning to you from the Almighty," Raphael said, his voice booming like a canon through the vault. "Desist your pursuit of the Anointed. The Almighty is not going to allow your activities to continue without retribution."

THE OTHER SIDE

It was difficult for Baal to hide his satisfaction at the angel's comments. The Creator was concerned. Concerned enough that He was willing to risk direct confrontation.

"You risk much, Raphael," Baal responded. A twelve-inch roman dagger appeared in Baal's hand, the blade glowing crimson red. It was the same dagger used to decapitate John the Baptist. The blade was forged with the essence of evil in the fires of Hades itself. It could cut angel flesh just as easily as human.

Raphael pulled his sword from a sheath on his back. Pure white flames enveloped the blade and leapt at Baal expectantly. Baal didn't hesitate. He attacked the angel, his dagger moving in a stunning flurry of red. He had been waiting for this opportunity for a very long time.

CHAPTER 16

McLean, Virginia

"That was a remarkable feat you pulled off the other day," Natasha said, sounding generally impressed. "Your actions saved many lives."

"Thank you, but I can't take all of the credit. It was a team effort and the FBI actually took the terrorist out," Riley said. He was surprised to receive a phone call from Natasha about the events at the university since he had not yet debriefed the CIA. His intuition told him to be careful about what he shared.

"I am curious... who are the civilians you brought to the crime scene?" she asked casually.

Riley paused before answering. She was fishing for something. "Civilians?" Riley played dumb.

"The young man and woman who were with you," Natasha clarified. "The CIA doesn't have any records of a man and woman matching their descriptions under your employment. In fact, I discovered your intelligence unit doesn't even officially exist under the agency."

Riley pretended to be surprised by her comment. "My unit? I am not sure what you are talking about," he deflected. "I suggest you talk with my superior."

"Listen, Agent O'Connor," Natasha said, a slight hint of frustration entering her voice. "I want and need to be in the know. Your mission is far too important to both of our agencies to have any screw-ups. We cannot afford to have a clandestine group of agents working without authority on a case of this significance."

Riley chuckled, "Trust me, Natasha. I am working under the ultimate authority."

"This is not a laughing matter, Agent O'Connor," Natasha chided. "If something goes wrong, or worse, we fail, the public will demand accountability. Many people, including you and me could lose our jobs."

"Is that what this is really about?" Riley asked incredulously. "You're concerned about your job? With all due respect, I don't have time for this."

"Don't test me," she warned in response. "I want to know who these people are and what you are doing with them. Otherwise, I will do everything in my power to shut you and your activities down." There was an edge in her voice that Riley could feel, more than hear.

"Goodbye, Natasha," Riley said flatly, ending the call, knowing that he was leaving the Deputy Secretary fuming in anger.

Riley stared blankly out his bedroom window, reviewing his conversation with Natasha. She apparently could access specialized information from other sources. She was also willing to force her way into his operation. He knew he needed to be very careful. She was not to be trusted. After a few moments of reflection, he decided he would deal with Natasha later. Right now, he needed to share some important news.

Riley headed downstairs to the living room where he found Marie, Jessica, and Stephen. Stephen's wheelchair lay vacant in the corner, no longer of any use. He stared at the chair in awe as a series of memories from years before cascaded over him. *Stephen could walk!*

Marie and Jessica were looking through a magazine of designer clothing, sharing comments on the styles they liked or disliked. Upon meeting each other, they hit it off immediately. Riley was pleased to see them bonding because he knew that they were going to need each other a great deal in the coming weeks.

"How are my two favorite young ladies doing?" Riley said as he walked over to check on Stephen. Stephen sat by himself on the far side of the couch, his blue eyes staring absently at the television screen that flickered silently above the mantle of the fireplace. "Hello Stephen," he added, placing his hand on Stephen's shoulder affectionately. "What are you watching?" He asked, not expecting a response.

"Hello, Mr. O'Connor," Jessica said. "We are just taking a little break. I've been sharing with Marie my experiences with Stephen."

"It is really fascinating what she was able to do," Marie said. "In fact, everything that is happening is amazing."

Riley agreed. He often thought about what it must have been like to witness the miracles of Jesus and the Apostles. Now he was witnessing the miracles of the Holy Spirit first hand.

Marie rose and said to Riley, "Thank you, Mr. O'Connor."

"For what?" Riley said, taken aback.

"For saving me. I thought I was truly going crazy." She looked at Jessica and then at Stephen. "I don't know how I know, but I know I am supposed to be here."

"Me too!" Jessica echoed.

Riley nodded in agreement, smiling because he knew they were together because of divine providence.

"So any suggestions on how we heal Stephen's brain?" Jessica asked, changing the subject.

"Actually, I do," Riley said. He had been thinking through a conversation with Noah about what happened in the mental hospital. "I have a theory that I need you and Marie to test out."

Marie and Jessica looked at each other and then at Riley. "Ok," they both said at the same time.

"I think Marie is blessed with another gift besides discernment."

"Another gift?" Marie asked, confused.

"Noah told me what happened to you both in the clinic. Somehow you were able to experience each other's gifts."

"Yes, I was able to see the future," Marie nodded, remembering Noah's vision. "It was cool and creepy all at the same time."

"Then at the university..." Riley continued. "Noah's vision was like none he ever experienced before. It was a vision of the immediate future. He was standing next to you when it happened."

"So, what does all of that mean?" Marie probed.

"I believe you also have the gift of helping," Riley responded, knowingly. A smile breaking on his face.

"The gift of helping?" Marie asked, a little unsure. "What does that mean?"

"A spiritual gift that manifest in different ways," Riley answered. "In your case, I think you have the ability to intensify the power of other people's spiritual gifts."

Both Marie and Jessica looked at him expect-

THE OTHER SIDE

antly, waiting for more information. "Let me expand," Riley continued. "I think Marie can make you a stronger healer. Together, you may be able to cure Stephen."

Jessica, now excited by the possibility, pushed Riley. "How do we make this happen?"

Riley didn't answer, but only smiled in response and turned his gaze to Stephen.

"Ok, I get it," Jessica said, crossing her arms slightly annoyed. "We have to figure it out for ourselves."

"Just how do you know that Stephen is gifted?" Marie interjected. "He can't even communicate." She crossed her arms as well. "And the way you look at him, like you know him. What are you not telling us about Stephen?"

Yes, she was good, Riley thought. Marie had seen beyond the obvious. He took a seat on the couch next to Stephen, who now appeared to be listening to the conversation.

"During my experience in Heaven, Stephen's gift was made known to me," Riley said, his blue eyes twinkling in reflection. "At the time, I was not sure what it meant or what I was to do about it. Now I do. That is why I need you to heal him."

"But how in the world did you ever find Stephen?" Marie asked. "Did God tell you where he was?"

Riley laughed softly for a moment as he patted Stephen on the knee, almost as if the two were sharing an inside joke. "Knowing where to find Stephen was the easy part."

Marie and Jessica looked at each other again. They turned to Riley, eager to hear his explanation.

Riley stared at Stephen for a moment, his eyes expressing a fondness that only a parent could. "I knew where to find Stephen because Stephen is my son."

CHAPTER 17

"You're so sweet," Jessica said, clasping the rose next to her breast. She leaned towards him, her lips approaching his. Noah waited expectantly for the kiss, not quite believing what was happening. Jessica actually wanted to kiss him.

Their lips touched for a long moment. Then the roar of the crowd erupted, causing Noah to flinch. On the field, a football team in blue was preparing for the opening kick-off. The fans all around them, were beginning to jump in their seats, chanting and whistling in anticipation. In the deep recesses of his mind, he knew this exact situation happened before. But he couldn't recall exactly when.

Now, Jessica was jumping along with the crowd, the rose no longer in her hands. In fact, Noah didn't see the rose anywhere. The kicker positioned himself for kick-off, raising his hand in the air. As Noah watched, he knew something bad was about to happen. Not knowing why, he felt the urge to run, but there was nowhere to go.

The kicker sent the ball into a high arc to the end of the field where a player dressed in a white and gold waited to receive it. Suddenly, Noah remembered—the bomb! "Noooo!!!" he shouted.

Everything froze—the football lay motionless, suspended in the air, only seconds from the open arms of the receiver and the massive destruction that would ensue. The crowd around him were now statues, stuck in a myriad of poses, some with arms held up or waving small signs, others caught in the middle of a high five. Next to him, Jessica was frozen, a curious look imprinted on her face, as if she were deciding if he were real or a figment of her imagination.

A gigantic wave of realization exploded over him as it occurred to him what he was experiencing. For the first time, he was awake in his dream. He was finally lucid!

Noah examined his hands, rubbing his palms together. He pinched himself, just to be sure. He felt the pressure of his fingers on his skin as he squeezed. His hands looked and felt just like they did when he was awake. The sensation was the same. The thought that he was dreaming was insane—it felt too real.

With wonder, Noah gazed around the stadium. Everything appeared like he was in the real world. The sun was shining brightly in the light blue sky, illuminating a sea of colors in the stands. He even felt the coolness of a fall breeze blowing against his face.

Each person, seated to his left and right, were distinct and different, though he had never seen any of them before. He noted each individual's hairstyle and color, as well as the texture of their clothing. Even facial characteristics, like dimples or moles, were observed. He couldn't believe what he was seeing. He was experiencing a realistic dream world created by his brain, but at the same time, viewing it with the full capacity of his consciousness, aware that it was not real. It was amazing!

His eyes settled on the field and the player waiting to receive the ball. He knew what was next—destruction. He needed to get out of here. Suddenly, the world around him leaped into motion. He turned to Jessica. He needed to save her too, only now, she was gone. Had he unconsciously changed the dream so she was no longer in it? He wasn't sure. It didn't matter, time was up. The ball landed in the receiver's arms, causing a roar to circulate through the stadium. Noah jumped, wishing with all his heart to fly away from the scene. Seconds later, he was hovering hundreds of feet above the crowd, floating in the air.

The bomb exploded, sending a mushrooming cloud of fire hurling towards Noah. He tried to outfly it, but the wave of fire was too fast. It engulfed him in flaming darkness. Noah began to scream...

Noah woke from his dream, still screaming. He instantly heard footsteps racing down the hall. The door opened and Riley rushed in, concern etched across the deep creases in his forehead.

"Noah, are you ok?" Riley said, sitting on the end of the bed. "Was it another dream?"

Noah nodded, feeling slightly embarrassed that he was a grown adult having nightmares. He kicked the covers away and went to the closet to retrieve his sweat suit. At least it was Riley, he thought. If Jessica found him like this, he would have hidden himself under the covers, too embarrassed to look at her. If it had been Marie, he might as well have jumped out of the window. She would have teased him about nightmares for the rest of his life.

He reflected on his dream for a moment. He wondered if it would feel the same to kiss Jessica in reality. It felt so real in the dream. Then again, he never kissed a girl before, so he wasn't sure.

"So tell me about it," Riley said, as Noah took a seat at his desk.

Noah shrugged, as if acting nonchalant about the whole thing would somehow change the end result of his dream. He knew it wouldn't. People were still going to die. "It was like before."

"Look at me Noah," Riley demanded, his voice taking an unusual tone of authority. "I need you to tell me everything you observed— *every detail*. It is extremely important."

Noah was surprised by Riley's odd reaction. Startled, he was tempted not to tell him anything, then thought better of it.

Folding his arms across his chest and leaning against his desk, Noah proceeded to tell Riley about the dream, purposely leaving out the part about Jessica. Riley seemed impressed that Noah became lucid during the dream, though Noah wasn't sure why.

"That's it, Riley," Noah finished. "It exploded just like before." Noah heard movement outside of his room. Someone else was up.

Riley studied Noah for a moment longer. "This is not a joke, Noah. Lives are at stake. What are you not telling me?"

Jessica popped her head into the room, surprised to see Riley. "Oh, I am sorry," she said. "I saw the light on. I was worried something was wrong with Noah. Is everything ok?" She was dressed in a pair of pink designer pajamas. Even with no makeup, Noah couldn't help but think she looked gorgeous.

"It's fine!" Noah said sharply, hoping she would leave them alone. He tried not to look at her. He couldn't look at her.

"Please come in, Jessica," Riley motioned for her to sit on the bed next to him. "Noah had another dream. He was just telling me the details." He turned back to Noah.

Embarrassed, Noah's face turned flush red. It was one thing to tell Riley he had a dream about kissing a girl, but to have the same girl hear it for herself was downright creepy. It would blow any chance he had with Jessica, slight as that chance might be.

"Noah, what's wrong? You can tell me," Jessica said, placing her hand on his knee to reassure him. Her eyes showed genuine concern. He forgot she could see his aura. Between Riley, Jessica, and Marie—there wasn't any hiding of anything. He might as well be on a reality TV show. He let out a long breath, seeing no other option.

"In the beginning of the dream, Jessica was with me." Noah murmured.

Jessica look startled and quickly removed her hand from his knee as if touching something extremely hot. "Me?" she asked, looking to Riley for an explanation.

Riley continued to concentrate on Noah. "Go on."

Noah didn't want to lie, but he didn't want to tell the truth either. After a long moment of silence, Noah turned to Jessica. "I am sorry, I don't usually dream of you this way... I mean at all... I mean ever," he stammered. *Crap!* He was making a fool of himself. He should just shut up now.

"What happened Noah?" Jessica pleaded.

Noah could tell she was genuinely concerned. The last thing he wanted was for her to worry. He didn't want to hurt her in any way.

THE OTHER SIDE

"I was kissing you," he blurted, hanging his head in shame.

Both Riley and Jessica relaxed. A moment later, they burst out into laughter. Noah wasn't sure what to make of it. Why were they laughing at him?

"You're not angry at me?" Noah said, looking at Jessica.

Jessica rose and plopped a light playful kiss on his forehead. "No Noah, I am not angry at all. I am actually flattered," she smiled. "I am just glad you are all right." She headed for the hallway. "I am going back to bed. You should do the same. Just don't have any more dreams of me, or any of us dying, or anything like that, ok?"

Noah nodded slowly. He wished he could promise her that. At least she wasn't angry with him. That meant there was still hope.

Riley got up and followed Jessica out of the room. He stopped at the doorway and said to Noah, "There is a purpose for everything that happens. Jessica was in your dream for a reason, though we don't know exactly why." He turned and left the room, leaving Noah alone.

Noah continued to stare out the window in silence for the next several minutes, contemplating the twists his life had taken in the past weeks. He wondered what the next several weeks would reveal as he and the others pushed further down the path as a team. Where would it lead? Was there any way to stop the evil, death, and destruction?

Unbeknownst to Noah, resting peacefully on the ledge of the windowsill above, a small moth watched him intently, having observed everything that transpired. A moment later, it flew into the air and out into the hallway, heading towards Riley's room. Somewhere in the spiritual realm, a woman laughed in delight at what she just learned. Not only was her assignment going to be fun, it was now going to be a great deal easier than she had anticipated.

CHAPTER 18

CIA Headquarters - Langley, Virginia

On a rare occasion, like the advent of a total lunar eclipse, Bill Rogers became angry. To Riley's chagrin, this was one of those times. In fact, Bill Rogers wasn't just angry. He was furious.

Being summoned to an urgent meeting with the Director was never a pleasant experience. It typically meant something was very wrong. It was a fitting way to end a long morning that started hours earlier with Noah's nightmare. Riley hoped this trend of unpleasantness would not continue into his evening.

"What the devil got into you?!?" the Director shouted, slamming his fist down on his mahogany desk with a commanding thump and leveling a stare at Riley that would melt steel. "Why did you hang up on the Deputy Secretary?!? Do you know what you have started?"

Riley knew he deserved every bit of the tongue-lashing he was receiving. Disrespectful behavior with an individual of higher rank always led to punishment, at least in the federal government.

"Well, do you have anything to say for your actions?" Bill demanded, sitting down in his chair to catch his breath. Riley perceived Bill's heart rate was much faster than its normal pace, not a good situation for a man his age, who had survived two previous heart attacks. The pupils of Bill's eyes were also constricted. Riley knew he needed to defuse this situation quickly, primarily for Bill's sake.

"Bill, I am truly sorry," he apologized. "I know that I overstepped my bounds with my actions." He was being truthful. He knew the second he hung up the phone with Natasha that he crossed an imaginary line of protocol. "You know the last thing I want to do is jeopardize our mission."

"You sure have a brilliant way of demonstrating it," Bill said, still fuming. "What got into you?"

Riley knew he needed to choose his next words carefully. Bill understood Riley's gifted nature, but seldom observed it in action. Bill was ruled by logic and procedure. "I don't trust Natasha Ellington," Riley said methodically.

"What? Are you kidding me?" Bill asked, dumbfounded by Riley's comment. "What

THE OTHER SIDE

grounds do you have not to trust her? For Pete's sake, you don't even know her. You just met her last week."

"Only a strong gut feeling," Riley said, shaking his head. He wished he could validate his feelings further, but that would mean spending more time with Natasha, and that was a prospect that he did not want to consider.

"Well you know, as well as I do, that your gut feeling is not going to fly with the Department of Homeland Security." Bill leaned forward on his desk, the color in his face changing from deep crimson to a softer red. At least his vitals were returning to normal. "Natasha Ellington is a senior officer and therefore demands your respect and cooperation. Are we clear?"

"Crystal!" Riley said, holding Bill's gaze.

"Now I expect you to be overly accommodating to any of her future requests—for the good of your mission and for our agency."

Riley knew what that meant. Natasha must have threatened Bill in some manner. Probably the exposure of his clandestine team of super agents. After a longer than normal pause in the conversation, Riley asked, "What is she asking of the agency?" He had a good idea of the answer, but he wanted to hear it directly from Bill.

"She wants the standard stuff," Bill replied, wiping the perspiration from his forehead with a handkerchief he produced from his shirt pocket. "Personnel files, mission charter, budget requisitions—nothing out of the ordinary."

"And if we don't comply?"

"She threatened to inform the Senate Intelligence Committee about you and your team."

"We are the CIA. Why do we have to give that information to DHS?" Riley retorted, his frustration mounting.

"Technically, we don't. But Natasha made a strong argument that it was important to verify the credentials of anyone working on a mission of this importance and magnitude. Congress has been informed of the potential threat to the nation, but we are purposely keeping it from the press to avoid a major panic." He opened a file on his desk and scanned the documents briefly. "How well did you research the backgrounds of these people before adding them to your team?"

Riley shook his head slowly, consenting that he was not in a position to win this debate. "Not as thoroughly as the agency requires," Riley admitted.

"See, Natasha has a point. I have to agree with her on this one. Even though I trust your judgment, we have processes that must be followed."

Riley sighed inwardly, logic and procedure had once again won over faith and belief. The last thing he needed was the bureaucracy of another federal agency interfering with his activities. He knew Natasha would start digging deeper when she realized that, on paper, his team was just a group of ordinary people. Somehow, he needed to figure a way to satisfy her demands and stall the release of this information.

"Can we create a reasonable delay in providing this information to her?" Riley asked. "I still have one last member to locate. I am worried that DHS could interfere with my efforts."

"How much time?"

"Thirty days."

Bill exhaled loudly, considering Riley's request. "Riley, you know I believe in the spiritual war that is going on around us. But we are in the minority. I read the FBI report from Agent Gillian and he couldn't logically explain how you knew about the second shooter. It is that type of situation that will raise suspicion about you and your activities."

Bill was the only person in the CIA who Riley fully briefed on the events that occurred at the library. Even though they both anticipated there would be questions from other agencies, Bill made a decision to run with a watered-down version of Riley's statements, purposely leaving out any references to spiritual powers and demonic forces. A formal debrief with the agency's executive team and key analysts was scheduled later that day. It was a meeting that Riley was not looking forward too.

Finally, Bill shook his head and answered, "Natasha's request is routine. To delay it would cast more suspicion on you and the team."

"Then give me the time to create the proper cover stories for my team," Riley offered.

Bill stood up and began pacing, thinking through Riley's request. "You have two weeks. That's all I can provide."

"I'll gladly take it," Riley agreed. It was not what he wanted, but he would make it work. "Hopefully by then, we will have a better handle on the threat from Thereon and my team will be fully functional. Which reminds me... have you approved my other requests?"

"Yes, I have approved boot camp for your team at Camp Perry."

"What about security?" Riley asked. Early in the week he submitted a requisition to Bill for a small team of armed military soldiers to protect them during actual engagements. They may be fighting a spiritual battle, but it involved real danger.

"That request is still in process," Bill responded, "but I am sure it will flow through Internal Review with no questions."

"Thank you," Riley said, rising to leave. "One last request," he added, knowing he had already asked for too much.

Bill looked at him expectantly.

"Be very careful with the information you share with Natasha. As crazy as it sounds, anybody can be an agent of evil."

"Are you implying that Natasha has been compromised?" Bill appeared pained by the ac-

THE OTHER SIDE

cusation. "What proof do you have?"

"None. As I said, it is only a hunch," Riley said, shrugging his shoulders. "If I am wrong, then there is nothing to worry about."

"Then let's hope you are wrong," Bill said.

Riley stood, preparing to leave. Bill motioned him to remain seated. "We're not done yet." Bill slid a bright red folder across his desk toward Riley.

"What's this?" Riley asked.

"Your next assignment. I need you and your team to head south to Richmond this weekend."

"Is there a threat from Thereon?"

"Maybe, or something much worse..."

Riley quickly scanned through the first few pages of the brief. "This looks like a domestic issue for the FBI. What would the CIA have to do with investigating a church organization?"

"The Bureau has been monitoring this church for several months. They recently identified a significant amount of money transferred to the church from an organization linked to Thereon. They have asked for our help."

"What do you need us to do?"

"You will be teamed with a select unit from the FBI. At this stage, we only want to get someone inside to observe and to identify key church leaders. Since the church is a private organization, details of their leadership are protected from governmental agencies, like the IRS. We need to know who we are dealing with."

"Sounds simple enough," Riley said, closing the file. "I would like to work directly with Agent Gillian on this one."

Minutes later, Riley steered onto the scenic George Washington Memorial Parkway headed towards McLean. He zigzagged through the mid-morning traffic of slow driving sightseers, eager to get back to the manor. Jessica and Marie were going to work with Stephen this morning. The thought of Stephen being healed brought tears to his eyes. To have an actual conversation with his son, after so long, would truly be a gift from God.

As he drove into the subdivision, doubt slowly inched into his mind, dampening his enthusiasm. Even with Stephen healed, there was so much to do to prepare his team to engage the enemy. Not having clarity as to the location of the last team member was just frustrating fuel on the fire. It could take weeks to locate the individual without clearer direction and he was running out of time. His concern was mounting that he could fail at his mission.

Riley glanced into the rearview mirror attracted by something on the edge of his peripheral vision. For a split second, he could have sworn a faceless form with fire red eyes had been staring at him from the back seat.

He felt a chill wash over him, then quickly recede, leaving him feeling exposed and vulnerable. There was no doubt, the enemy had just paid him a visit. Nothing dramatic, nothing flashy. Just a brief but terrifying glimpse to let him know they were watching.

Riley pulled into his driveway as a new concern entered his mind. If the enemy found him, then the other members of his team were vulnerable as well. That meant only one thing. They were all in danger.

CHAPTER 19

"It's all wrong," Marie said, referring to Stephen's brain cells. "It is like nature got mixed up. The cells are corrupted. I am not sure what else to say."

Jessica sensed the wrongness too. Stephen's mind was not damaged or deformed, she was sure of that, but it was corrupted. The darkness appeared to originate in the chromosomes of Stephen's brain, coating the cells with random black stains, like mold growing on a piece of bread. She attempted to examine the stains directly, but she was repulsed by what she felt. It could only be described as evil. Pure, unbridled evil.

With Marie's assistance, they set out to probe the darkness surrounding Stephen's brain. Diligently working together, they managed to penetrate into the blackness. It was like pushing their way through dark, oily sludge.

Oddly, the experience reminded Jessica of a time when she helped her aunt to bake molasses cookies. She had dipped her finger into the molasses, pressing deep into the thick liquid. It took some effort to remove a small taste. The long tendrils of the molasses followed her finger to her mouth and settled on her clothes and in the locks of her hair. The darkness was very similar, it seemed to cling to her despite her efforts to free herself from it.

"I am not sure what we can do," Jessica hesitated, studying the taint of evil that covered another cell. "Even with your help, I don't think we are strong enough."

"Let's try again," Marie said, eager for the challenge. "What do we have to lose?"

"Just my breakfast," Jessica remarked, knowing what was about to come. At least it was comforting to have Marie with her this time.

It hadn't taken long for Jessica to decide she liked the sassy and bold woman. She didn't remember consciously making the decision, it just happened. What probably sealed the friendship was their shared affection of the three most important tenets of life—fashion, cuisine, and politics. They both also desired something grander in life.

Marie was studying to be a lawyer, a role that was perfect for her personality. Quick-witted, intelligent, and opinionated. That was Marie. Unlike herself, there were no shades of grey in Marie's world, only black or white. Jessica wished she possessed that clarity to life.

Concentrating on a cluster of Stephen's brain cells, Jessica focused on a specific area that was overpopulated with dark stains. She let the power flow from her, a beaming light of white that smashed into the darkness. Immediately the taste of bile filled her mouth, only this time it was intense, like she swallowed a rotten habanero pepper. She wretched involuntarily and felt Marie's grip on her arm tighten as she experienced the same reaction. Jessica didn't know how long they could last.

Before their eyes, the darkness seemed to take form, as if preparing to mount a counterattack against the intruding light. Waves of undulating black pulsed against the light, repelling the power. The physical strain on Jessica was tremendous. From the excessive exertion, Jessica felt perspiration spread across her forehead. They were not getting anywhere.

"On the count of three, push harder," Marie said. "One... two... three..."

A momentarily burst of intense power erupted through the stream of light and into the darkness. It seemed to Jessica she could hear the agonizing wail of the darkness against their assault. After a moment, the darkness exploded into millions of tiny particles, a fireball of black heading towards her. Jessica gasped as a wave of cold darkness spread over her. A moment later, the cloud of darkness receded back towards the cells, reforming into a mass of emptiness that was still very much alive.

"It didn't work," Jessica cried. "It's just too strong." She didn't have much energy left. They were going to fail. As if sensing her doubt, the darkness began to crawl up the shaft of light, slowly encircling it in a sheath of black, consuming it inch by inch.

"Jessica... let go!" Marie shouted.

She barely heard Marie's cry, her world was turning black all around her. All she could do was watch the darkness slowly expand towards her. A molten flow of death. Patches of black began to form in the center of the beam of light as the darkness continued to consume it. Someone was moaning in pain. It was Stephen. Oh no! She thought. *What was she doing to Stephen?*

Jessica tried with all her might to stop the flow of energy, but it was too strong. Fueled by her doubt, panic set in. She didn't know what to do. As if sensing her distress, the darkness sped towards her in an arching wave, preparing to crash into her. "Help!!!" she cried desperately.

Through the blackness and cold, she felt a strong hand on her shoulder. It instantly radiated warmth into her body. On the outskirts of her perception, barely audible, she could hear a man praying. Then everything begin to change.

As if doused with a bucket of ice-cold water, she felt a charge of energy course through her body. Waves of faith, hope, and love filled her to the point of overflowing emotions. She then felt a sensation that she never experienced before. It was if there was another living presence inside of her. Her fears and doubts were instantly displaced. There was no room in her soul for anything else but the spirit that was welling up inside of her. She couldn't contain its power. With a final effort, she willed everything she was, everything she contained, towards the darkness.

The beam of power sizzled brilliant white in response, easily melting through the darkness. Everywhere Jessica focused, darkness transformed into light. Once stained cells emerged free of the black corruption, completely healed of the foulness that had befallen them. In seconds, the light expanded to encompass Stephen's entire brain. Stephen's moans of pain went silent, extinguished like the darkness.

"It's working!" Marie exclaimed, the amazement hanging in her voice. "The darkness has almost disappeared."

With one final surge, the power left Jessica. Stephen convulsed violently in response. There was a dazzling flash of light and then everything around her went black.

CHAPTER 20

Asherah felt his longing for the girl. She savored his deep desire that was transmitted through the bond established earlier with the oracle. She relished what she felt for a moment, letting it feed her own lust. It was addictive. She craved more of the feeling, and with greater intensity. Sadly, to deepen the experience, she would have to possess the oracle, but that was not an option. At least, not an option at this time.

Bonds were a spiritual thread connecting a demon to a person's stronghold. Since strongholds built upon a person's deep-set emotions and desires, a bond allowed a demon direct access into a person's psyche. Using a bond to inflict thoughts and desires into a human, as she was doing with the oracle, was not the same as possessing someone. When a demon possessed a human, both the emotions and physical sensations could be felt. But through a bond, the experience was only an echo of the feelings. Still, it was enough.

The oracle was oblivious to her presence as she hurled darts of despair and worry through the bond. Asherah wasn't worried about being detected, even by the truth-seer. That was the advantage of utilizing a stronghold to infiltrate a person. It could be done from the spiritual realm —slowly, overtime, and at leisure.

She watched the events occurring in the small bedroom through the eyes and ears of another minion. This time she chose a field mouse. It lay crouched under the corner of the dresser, virtually undetectable.

She sent the emotion of fear through the bond and watched.

Noah kneeled at Jessica's side, taking her hand in his. "I was so worried about you," he said.

"He really was," Marie affirmed. "He has been standing guard over you all afternoon."

Jessica looked at Noah, "I don't know what to…"

Try as she might, Asherah couldn't resist admiring the healer. What she accomplished was extraordinary. Few had ever been able to do it. Even the apostles of the One failed at times to vanquish evil spirits from the possessed. Somehow, this young healer managed to remove the very essence of evil itself.

Evil was not a bad thing, Asherah mused. It was only the absence of the Creator. Soon, the Creator would be replaced by the Master. She

THE OTHER SIDE

longed for that to happen so evil would become the unifying presence of this world. Darkness would finally cover the light, for all eternity.

"Looks like someone has risen from the dead," Riley interrupted, suddenly appearing at the doorway. Asherah used the disruption as an opportunity to shoot a dart of disappointment at the oracle. She watched the oracle frown in response to the untimely entrance of the Anointed One.

"Someone has been waiting all day to meet you," Riley said proudly. He stepped from the doorway into the room. Behind him Stephen entered, a wide smile on his face.

"Hello, Jessica," Stephen said. His deep harmonious voice echoed off the walls of the small room.

Jessica leaped from the bed, breaking Noah's grip, and wrapped her arms around Stephen, giving him a strong hug. "Stephen, I am so glad you're ok!" she cried. "I was so worried I hurt you."

Stephen returned the hug affectionately. "I could say the same about you," Stephen replied.

Asherah couldn't have asked for a better scenario to occur. She fired a flurry of barbs at the oracle. Anger, betrayal, jealousy, and pride exploded into Noah's mind.

Noah rose to his feet, his face contorted from his pain. He collided shoulders with Stephen as he exited the room, knocking Stephen slightly backward into the desk. A few moments later, the sound of the front door slamming shut boomed down the hallway.

"What's up with him?" Marie asked.

"I don't know. His aura was a mix of all kinds of things," Jessica said. "I am sure he will be fine. He is moody, after all." She returned her focus back to Stephen and the two engaged in small talk.

Asherah noticed there was now a pensive look on the Anointed's face and he was scanning the room. As if noting his concern, the truth-seer began to do the same. Asherah wondered if they detected her presence.

Just to be safe, she severed her link with her minion, but only after she scrambled the tiny brain of the mouse, killing it instantly. She would leave no trace of her intrusion into their world for them to find. She never did.

Pleased with her success, Asherah sent a summons to Baal. He would be very interested in her progress. The oracle had proven easy to manipulate. Now it was time to turn the oracle against his team.

She considered her options, the dull echo of anger still smoldering through the bond. Yes, before she could proceed, the proper stage needed to be set. She sent a couple of new thoughts and desires to the oracle before releasing the connection. She smiled inwardly as the remnants of the bond faded away. The last emotion she sent was her all-time favorite. It was the root of all things destructive. Bitterness.

CHAPTER 21

Department of Homeland Security – Washington, D.C.

Natasha dialed the number written on a small piece of paper left on her nightstand days before. A moment later, she heard the now familiar voice of Branson Schaeffer.

"Hello?"

"Hey, it's me," Natasha said, not bothering to identify herself.

Branson paused before answering. "Natasha?" Branson said, taking a guess. That irritated Natasha, she didn't like sharing her lovers.

"Have you heard anything else about the American University massacre?" She asked, hoping for a positive response. "We reviewed the reports from the FBI, the CIA, and the campus police, but things are not exactly adding up."

"I agree with you," Branson said. "Only there isn't anything else I can add. You probably know as much as I do, or more by now."

"Can you tell me anything about Riley O'Connor and his activities? The CIA Director told me it would be more than two weeks until I can review the personnel files for his unit."

Branson sighed, "Only that Riley is the director's little pet project. Honestly, he has kept me and the rest of the agency in the dark about Riley's assignments."

Natasha clicked her long nails on her desk, disappointed by his response. She couldn't wait that long for those files. She needed Branson to push the matter with his agency, not passively wait for information to come to him. It was urgent that she understand as much as possible about Riley and his team.

"Did you like the other night?" she said amusingly, playfully changing the subject. She heard a slight chuckle on the other end as Branson stalled.

"Yes... yes I did. It was amazing," he said finally.

"I thought so too," Natasha said. Branson was quite capable in many ways and he was proving to be one of her more enjoyable trysts. "Would you like to do it again?" she teased.

"I have been replaying our evening in my head. Of course I would."

"Then I have a favor to ask of you," Natasha breathed softly.

"Sure, anything," Branson said, a hint of excitement in his voice.

"I need Riley O'Connor's personnel file and those of his team. Now, not later."

Branson's response was immediate and argumentative. "No way! I can't do that. There are formal channels to follow. Giving those files to you would place us both at risk."

Good, Natasha thought, at least he has a spine. She liked a man with fortitude. Still, this was business. She didn't miss a beat as she went in for the kill. "Do you think what we did the other night was out of protocol? What would happen if someone found out about us?"

"Who is going to know? Besides, you wouldn't be able to prove anything," Branson challenged.

"Let's just say I have some pictures of us that your fiancée would not be happy to see. If you want them, then I suggest you do what I ask."

There was dead silence on the other end. She knew she had him.

"Call me as soon as you have something worth talking about. Then maybe we will get together again." She hung up the phone.

With that minor task completed, Natasha turned her attention to the small brown folder on her desk. She quickly reviewed its contents, finding several files and an official requisition for her signature. The request was to reinforce key oil and natural gas pipeline facilities throughout the country with additional se-

THE OTHER SIDE

curity. Approving the requisition would mean the reassignment of more than one hundred DHS agents and hundreds of state troopers from within various states. Only her signature was necessary to authorize the order.

She leaned back in her chair contemplating the implications of signing the requisition. With a simple stroke of her pen, she could change the world. People relocated, families impacted, hundreds of thousands of dollars spent, the list went on and on. She relished for a long moment the feeling of power she possessed.

She considered her options. Even withholding her signature on the requisition created implications. Not signing it would enable the planned attack to proceed. Though the threat on the natural resource infrastructure had not been officially validated, she knew it was real. It was like the myriad of other threats that existed, but so far only appeared as vague generalities, empty whispers, and unsubstantiated claims to the intelligence community. The world was oblivious to the activities that were occurring as part of the larger war that was underway.

She tossed the requisition onto a pile of other sensitive documents that rested on the credenza behind her. After a moment of consideration, she picked up the entire stack and walked to the far corner of her office where a large industrial shredder waited patiently for its next meal.

She would wait a few days to report the accidental shredding of the document and then the signature process would start over. Another requisition would eventually appear on her desk for signing, but only after several weeks had passed. As slow as the government moved, it could be months before resources were actually reassigned in the field. That was more than enough time. She set the papers into the shredder, but was distracted by a news flash scrolling across the television screen on the adjacent wall.

Security forces at the Dome of the Rock just thwarted a bombing attempt by a small group of Jewish extremists. She shook her head in amusement. Those Jews were unknowingly helping her cause, no doubt believing that rebuilding the Jewish Temple would usher in the Messiah.

That was nonsense. The Messiah had already come, but rebuilding the temple was important in the larger picture. Before her Master could return, the temple needed to be rebuilt on that exact spot. Then the Master would enter it and finally claim himself the god of all.

She hoped she lived to see that day. She turned her attention back to the shredder and pressed the button. The documents and the requisition disintegrated into nothingness.

CHAPTER 22

Richmond, Virginia

Large iridescent banners surrounding the coliseum batted back and forth in the steady breeze, flashing vibrant colors at each twist and turn. The air seemed energized in anticipation for the upcoming worship service, charged by the thudding beat of a contemporary worship song that blasted from a pair of large speakers.

A Summit of Light service was not likely to be described as ordinary. To call it this would be similar to describing a manned mission to Mars as a routine airplane flight. It wouldn't make any sense. Services at Summit of Light were truly out of this world.

Birthed a decade ago by Pastor Anthony Jessup, Summit of Light was the rock star of progressive megachurches. The envy of all others. The nondenominational church skyrocketed to stardom along with the explosion of social media, landing it securely as the largest megachurch in North America in less than five years. In addition to a vast online presence, Summit of Light built and acquired brick and mortar churches in major population centers throughout the continent. It now boasted more than one hundred and fifty satellite churches, a main educational campus under construction in Seattle, and a corporate headquarters facility in Dallas.

With more than one million members, including politicians, pro athletes and members of the Hollywood elite, the church was an economic powerhouse. Conservative estimates placed the church's weekly revenue from offerings alone at more than ten million dollars. The real wealth of the church, however, was generated from its unique business model which included vast real estate holdings, a global merchandising channel, and a financial arm that provided commercial and personal loans made exclusively to church members.

Riley watched from his sedan in the parking lot as the four members of his team disappeared into the frenzied crowd waiting entrance into the coliseum. They would be out of contact for the next two hours during the worship service. That made him uncomfortable, particularly because Stephen was with them so soon after his recovery. He bit his lip and tried to relax.

"Well, nothing to do but wait," Riley said to

THE OTHER SIDE

the FBI liaison seated next to him. Riley was glad to have someone to converse with and keep his mind off Stephen and his team. "What do you think about all this?"

Frank Gillian chewed on the tip of his pen a few seconds in silence, watching the spectacle before him. "I don't get it. Not any of it," he said wearily.

"You mean the connection to Thereon?" Riley asked.

"Well, that makes no sense at all. Why does a church that makes more money than most large companies need any form of financial help? Even if there was a need, why would they seek help from a terrorist organization?" Frank scribbled something on his pad and then placed the pen back in his mouth. "But this whole megachurch thing, it's got to be a scam. People can't be that ignorant."

"So I take it you are not a religious man?" Riley ventured.

The detective shook his head negatively. "I think religion is a racket. Just look at the throngs of people at this event. All of them trying to make themselves feel better about their state of life." The pen crackled in protest as Frank clenched his teeth. "Worse yet, lots of people barely have enough money to live, yet these churches are shaming them into giving what they don't have."

"You have a very pessimistic attitude," Riley

remarked.

"I mean no offense, if you're into the religion thing," Frank offered. "But I have seen too much in my years to make it possible for me to trust in any religion of man."

Riley conceded the detective had a point. Man has exploited organized religion throughout history for personal gains. Summit of Light was a prime example of a religious group that far exceeded the boundaries of being an institution of worship. The real question was how far did the exploitation go?

"What kind of things have you seen?" Riley asked, genuinely curious.

"Fifteen years ago, I busted an Archbishop of the Catholic church who was running a sex ring in my old neighborhood," Frank grimaced at the thought. "The bastard was a pillar in the community. He was even close with my parents. To her deathbed, my mother refused to believe he was guilty and hated me for my role in his prosecution." The pen Frank was chewing broke in two, apparently giving up the ghost.

"I am sorry to hear that," Riley said, watching Frank's reaction. Frank discarded the remains of the first pen and was now gnawing on a fresh red pencil.

"What else?" Riley probed, detecting there was more to Frank's experience than he was sharing.

"You name it, extortion, slavery, child

THE OTHER SIDE

abuse, embezzlement, adultery... the list goes on," Frank shared. "All crimes committed by people who are supposed to be spiritual role models. It is so hypocritical, it's laughable."

Frank shrugged his shoulders and stared blankly into the distance. "I can't make this stuff up. It is everywhere. People chasing a false dream of hope, prosperity, and happiness. They waste their money, time, and energy toward an ideal that always disappoints." He finished with a loud crunch on the pencil. "It's really sad. If God truly existed, why would he allow so much pain and suffering in this world?"

Riley took a measured breath as the revelation settled on him. So, that explained Frank's animosity. Only it wasn't just animosity towards religion, it was actually anger towards God himself.

"So how long ago did you lose them?" Riley asked. It was not the question he planned to ask, but it was what came out.

Frank stared at him strangely for a moment before answering. "Eight years ago," he huffed, dismissing the question. "I'd rather not talk about it."

Riley was silent, appearing to contemplate how to proceed in the conversation after hitting a dead end. Happy with the impasse in the conversation, the detective returned to chewing his pencil, his mind on a distant memory.

When he first met Frank, Riley sensed the

detective would be integral to his team's future success. Initially, this was the reason he requested Frank to be the liaison for this mission. Now, he realized there was a greater purpose. One involving divine intervention.

Riley's intuition also told him Frank was ready to hear the truth about his team. But for some reason, he knew not to share anything about his own talents. Perhaps that was a secret for another day.

A minute later, Riley broke the silence, his words heavy with reflection. "At the university's library, you asked me how I knew about the second shooter. Before I tell you the answer and expand on the real battle we are fighting, would you listen to a story I feel you need to hear?"

The detective stopped chewing on his pencil and turned to Riley, his interest piqued. "What story?"

Riley settled back in his seat. "It is the most important story in the history of humanity. It is about a man who walked the Earth more than two thousand years ago. His name was Jesus."

CHAPTER 23

The urge to let go and be swept away by the flow of music was getting stronger with the sound of each new chord. Even though her body was responding to the music, Jessica forced herself against waving her hands and singing along. Above the stage, a massive Jumbotron displayed the song lyrics in a dazzling brilliant light, illuminating the immense crowd that swayed in rhythmic motion below. Jessica didn't want to give any indication to the others, but she was having fun.

Before entering the coliseum, Noah suggested they split up and pretend to be boyfriend and girlfriend. It was a good idea. There were several young couples in the crowd and they would fit right in. For some reason, Noah was adamant that Jessica accompany him, and Marie and Stephen be the other couple. It didn't really matter to her. They would all be together anyway.

Shortly after identifying themselves as visitors, she and Noah found themselves in a private suite overlooking the coliseum floor below. There were other visitors there, but somehow they had been separated from Marie and Stephen. That made Jessica a little nervous.

A stylish man dressed in designer jeans and a sports coat soon introduced himself as Derrick, their personal concierge for the event. If there was anything they wanted or needed, he was there to help them. His role was also to make sure they were introduced to as many church members as time allowed.

The worship service was more like a rock concert. In the short intermissions between the music, various speakers took the stage providing brief motivational speeches based on verses of the Bible. As if by magic, each speaker seemed to elevate the energy of the audience, almost to the point of frenzy. It was as if the crowd was becoming its own life force, one massive presence waiting in eager anticipation for the main event.

It did not disappoint. The arrival of Pastor Anthony Jessup was accompanied by a crescendo of blaring music, flashing lights, and even a brief pyrotechnics display. Waves of applause erupted from the crowd, as the lights went dim and the Pastor's face filled the Jumbotron.

The stunning handsomeness of the pastor immediately gripped Jessica. Hazel green eyes gazed at her from a chiseled face that belonged on the cover of GQ. In his mid-forties, the pastor was still a vibrant image of youth, betrayed only by the soft streaks of grey that highlighted his dark hair. Jessica was captivated by him, as well as the entire experience unfolding before her.

The pastor's sermon was engaging and uplifting, but it perplexed Jessica that it was broadcast instead of presented in person. Considering this was the church's annual membership conference, it would be normal to expect the pastor to be present. After brief reflection, she decided it didn't matter. Pastor Jessup possessed a very genuine manner that made her want to believe what he preached. Words from his inspirational sermon still echoed in her mind as she and Noah followed Derrick to a VIP tent constructed on the main floor.

The tent was lavishly decorated with flowers and ribbons. Several tables with white linen tablecloths, small dinner plates, and silverware were quickly filling with other visitors, who eagerly sampled food from an extravagant buffet. At the far end of the tent, two men stood watchfully in front of a door. Jessica observed a man dressed in a suit walk through the door, but only after showing his credentials to the men.

"What's through there?" Jessica asked Derrick, pointing to the exit door.

"Oh, don't mind that," Derrick quickly responded, handing Jessica a plate. "That leads to the hallway and main conference room. There, we are hosting a special luncheon for our leadership and the people who have helped build the church over the years. Our annual conference is packed with a variety of meetings, training events, sermons and, of course, good food and fun." He gave her a napkin roll containing silverware and ushered her and Noah into the buffet line.

When she was sure that Derrick was out of hearing range, Jessica whispered to Noah, "We need to get into that conference room."

Noah looked surprised by her comment. "We are not secret agents, Jessica," he argued. "Riley wants us to scope this place out, not eavesdrop on some church meeting."

Something about Noah's tone bothered her. His voice carried an edge of anger. *Why was he being so moody?*

"Hey guys!" Marie said, appearing in the buffet line behind them. "Was that service something or what?" she exclaimed. She and Stephen were holding hands, obviously trying to look the part. Jessica stifled a momentary pang of jealousy. She really didn't know why she felt it. She wasn't attracted to Stephen. Maybe it was just the intimacy of the healing experience they shared.

"Pretty amazing," Jessica agreed, dismissing her thoughts about Stephen. She needed to focus.

"Well, what's next?" Stephen asked. He was smiling from ear to ear, obviously still marveling at everything he was experiencing. Stephen said it best himself after his healing. With God's help, he had been reborn and was now a new creature. Everything was a new experience for him.

"I have an idea to help us collect some intelligence for Riley," Jessica said. She quickly shared with Stephen and Marie what she learned about the leadership luncheon. "Are we in agreement?"

"I'm game," Marie said.

"Me too," Stephen added.

"Ok... I guess I'm in too," Noah said, though he didn't sound very sure. "But I want it on record that I think you guys are crazy," he added.

"Great, now we just need a distraction," Jessica said. "Any thoughts on what to do?"

As a group, they all turned to look at Stephen expectantly. Jessica smiled inwardly. If anyone knew, it would be him.

CHAPTER 24

"It's ironic and slightly funny, but I really do not know how my ability works," Stephen said smiling. "But let me try something." He turned his focus to the two men at the other end of the room and concentrated. His eyes brightened for a moment, as he thought of a brilliant idea. "Wow! It worked!"

The group huddled around Stephen, eager to hear what he discovered. "It turns out one of the security guards is also an EMT," Stephen said assuredly. "I have a plan that will get the two of you through that door." He pointed at Marie and Jessica.

"Are you sure?" Noah questioned, a skeptical look on his face. "What if they get caught?"

"I thought of that too," Stephen replied with a wide grin. "Trust me."

Five minutes later they were casually eating at a cocktail table near the exit door, pretending to engage in trivial conversation. Prompted by a pat on the back from Stephen, Noah began to convulse, his eyes wide in terror.

Jessica screamed, "Someone help, he's choking!" Marie and Jessica moved away from the table, pretending to be afraid. Strategically, they positioned themselves near the security guards, their eyes still locked on Noah.

Stephen grabbed for Noah, purposely pushing the cocktail table over, sending a spray of plates and silverware onto the floor in a crash. Noah fell to the floor, still convulsing. "Help! Is there a doctor here?" Stephen yelled, motioning to the security guards. "This man is choking!"

A few bystanders surrounded Noah to provide what assistance they could, giving Stephen the opportunity he needed. Jessica watched as one of the security guards raced towards Noah, leaving the other one at the door. A moment later, Stephen was in front of the second security guard, causing another distraction.

"We need to call 911! Do you have a cell phone?!?" Stephen grabbed the security guard's arm, pulling him towards Noah. "Please, he's my best friend!" The guard tried to push Stephen away, but Stephen was hanging on the man's arm with all his weight.

With the second security guard preoccupied with Stephen, Marie and Jessica slipped through the exit door and closed it quickly behind them. They waited a few seconds to see if anyone followed, but no one came through the door. For the moment, they were safe.

"Ok, now what?" Marie asked.

Jessica inhaled deeply, smelling the air. "I don't need Stephen's power to answer that one. Let's find the food."

After a few minutes of traversing the service corridor, they found an entranceway that led to a small balcony overlooking a large atrium. On the atrium floor, a large assembly of men and women were dining, while staff in white and black uniforms attended to them. At the far end of the room, three men and two women sat at a rectangular table where a seat in the middle of the table was empty.

"I bet that is the executive leadership table," Marie said. "I wonder who will sit in the middle seat?" As if answering her question, a distinguished looking man on the far end of the table stood up and tapped his fork on his water glass, sending a clinking sound through the room. The conversational buzz settled to a whisper, as everyone turned in attention.

"Distinguished donors, welcome to our twelfth annual leadership meeting," the man said, a large smile on his face. "Before we get started, I would like to introduce the Summit of Light leadership board." One by one, the individuals stood as their names were announced.

"Henry Farson, CEO of iConnect, one of the largest social media companies in the world," the speaker said as a young man dressed in a crew shirt with a sport coat raised his hand and waived at the group.

"Senator Sheila Banter, ranking member of the Senate Intelligence Committee," the speaker continued, as a tall slender woman with blond hair smiled and winked at the crowd. She sat down as a frail looking man with large spectacles stood.

"May I present, Dr. Michael Phillips, Dean of Religious and Philosophical Studies at Harvard University," the speaker announced, pointing to the dean.

"Are you getting all of this?" Marie asked. Jessica nodded, recording a video of the event with her phone.

"Last, but not least, let me introduce Marcia Conrad, Global Director of Finance, Chase Manhattan Bank, the largest international banking institution in the world." An attractive older woman stood and bowed her head in acknowledgement.

"There you have it. The Summit of Light leadership team!" the speaker enthusiastically said as applause erupted from the attendees.

"But, I am not done yet," the speaker said, interrupting the applause. "Ladies and Gentlemen, I have a special surprise." He motioned towards a nearby door. "Making a rare, in-person appearance... I present our leader, Pastor Anthony Jessup!"

Screams of delight and applause filled the room as the door opened to reveal the unanticipated guest. The pastor waived enthusiastically as he entered the room. At that exact moment, Marie let out a blood-curdling scream.

Everyone turned towards the unexpected sound, their eyes landing squarely on Marie and Jessica. Immediately several men dressed in black suits scrambled towards their position in the balcony.

"Let's get out of here!" Jessica yelled, grabbing Marie by the arm, only Marie was not moving. She was in a complete daze, her eyes locked on something below.

"Marie!" Jessica yelled, tugging on her arm. "Snap out of it!" Jessica finally stepped in front of the unresponsive Marie, trying to pull her to her feet.

Instantly, Marie was shaking her head as if trying to clear it. "What happened?" she moaned, placing her hand on her forehead.

"We have to go now!" Jessica urged, forcibly pulling Marie to her feet. Together they scrambled towards the doorway.

"Stop!!!" a voice yelled from behind them.

Jessica pushed Marie in front of her as a hand grabbed her shoulder from behind, spinning her around. She felt another hand engulf her wrist and clamp down like a vice.

She found herself facing a burly-looking man with a security badge on his breast pocket. "Let me go," she demanded, "You're hurting me." She grabbed the man's hand, trying to free herself. In response, the man's grip tightened on her wrist.

"You're not going anywhere little lady." The man began pulling her forcefully towards the stairwell.

Jessica didn't know how she did it, but she felt power flow from her into the man's hand, only it felt different than before. Instantly the man's hand turned deep red as bright blisters erupted and spread up his forearm. He howled in pain as he released her from his grip. Seizing the opportunity, Jessica turned and fled through the door, leaving the man clutching his hand in obvious pain.

With Marie in the lead, they sprinted down the corridor towards the door that would lead back to the coliseum. They heard the sound of footsteps behind them in pursuit. Together they burst through the exit door into the VIP tent, passing the stunned security men who had resumed their post. Noah and Stephen were nowhere to be seen. Jessica stopped for a moment, worried about their safety, only to be pulled back into a sprint by a firm tug from Marie.

Marie led her into the main area where throngs of worshippers were mingling with members of the church band. Jessica ventured a look behind her and saw three men and one of the security guards burst onto the main floor. Her pursuers stopped for a moment, scanning the crowd of hundreds before them.

"Duck," Jessica yelled. Both her and Marie

fell to their knees and scrambled across the floor, now obscured by the throng of worshippers around them. At the far end of the room, Marie stopped for a moment, not sure which direction to go. Jessica looked behind her, but all she could see was a mass of legs and feet.

"What are you two doing?" a voice yelled from above. *Oh no!* Jessica thought, believing for a moment they were caught. Hesitantly, she looked up, only to relax when she saw Derrick, her concierge, standing over her.

Slowly, Marie rose to her feet, clutching her stomach, "Please get me to the nearest exit. I don't feel well. I think I am going to be sick."

With both Derrick and Jessica hovering over her, the group shuffled towards a nearby exit door. As soon as they were outside, Marie and Jessica dashed into the parking lot, leaving Derrick in confusion.

As quickly as they could, they headed towards the pick-up zone, ducking between cars as they walked. Marie suddenly stopped and keeled over, vomit spewing from her mouth.

"Are you ok?" Jessica asked, her concern spiking. Marie didn't respond. She did not look well. Her face was pale and her skin was clammy.

"What happened in there? Why did you scream?" Jessica asked, scanning the area behind her to make sure no one was following them. Fortunately, they were shielded by a large SUV. In front of her, just fifty yards away, was the

THE OTHER SIDE

pick-up zone and the mini-van. It comforted her to know that inside was a team of agents, fully armed and ready to protect them.

"I'm not sure," Marie said, still appearing dazed. At least the color was beginning to return to her face. "I couldn't control my reaction. If you hadn't blocked my view of Pastor Jessup, I don't know what would have happened."

Jessica looked at Marie oddly. "What did you see?"

Marie's dark brown eyes leveled on Jessica. Jessica could still see the remnants of fear reflected from whatever Marie witnessed.

"He's a demon, Jessica," Marie said, shaking her head as if she couldn't believe her own words. "I don't know how it is possible, but Pastor Anthony Jessup is a demon in the flesh."

CHAPTER 25

McLean, Virginia

"**M**any times, you have heard me say we are at war." The tone of Riley's voice demanded immediate attention. He needed them to understand and to embrace the seriousness of the commitment he was asking. To engage in direct battle against Satan was not to be taken lightly. It was a matter of life and death. Around him, his team listened with keen interest. Everyone except for Noah.

Jessica and Marie were huddled together on the sofa, sharing a fleece blanket. A rare arctic front currently enveloped the region, plunging the normally tepid summer temperatures into the thirties. Noah appeared to welcome the weather, sporting a black t-shirt and his blue jeans. He sat by himself on the far side of the room, a disinterested look on his face.

Stephen sat on the floor in front of the sofa, gently caressing Duke's head. The dog was sprawled on his back beside him, obviously enjoying the attention. Duke always provided a calming effect on Stephen. Now, due to his miraculous healing, Stephen was finally able to return the favor.

The team spent most of the day relaxing after returning from Richmond late the night before. Riley was very pleased with the team's performance over the weekend. It was a huge breakthrough that they were able to identify the true leaders of the Summit of Light organization. Agent Gillian and the FBI were already putting the information to good use.

However, Marie's discovery about Pastor Jessup was extremely unsettling. Riley wasn't sure what he would do with the information for now. No one, not even Bill Rogers, would believe the pastor was not of this world.

Riley opened the black book in his hand and began to read out loud. "Be sober, be vigilant; because your adversary the Devil, as a roaring lion, walketh about, seeking whom he may devour." He closed the Bible. "A warning from the apostle Peter about our enemy, the prince of darkness."

"You mean Satan?" Jessica clarified, snuggling closer to Marie.

"Yes. By choosing to join this team, you have crossed an imaginary line and chosen sides. Because of this, Satan is aware you are fighting against him. That means he is now plotting to undermine you, to cause harm, and to destroy you."

Jessica inhaled deeply, startled by the implications of Riley's statement. "Can Satan really hurt us?" she asked. "I mean physically?"

Riley nodded affirmatively. "I recruited you to work with the CIA because we need your extraordinary abilities to fight this war. Like you, our enemy has unique powers—powers that can hurt, destroy, and kill. Powers that he will use to defeat you." Riley paused to let the severity of his statement make its intended impact.

"How is he able to do this?" Stephen inquired with a genuine element of concern in his voice. Riley knew why. Earlier, Stephen expressed his fear that his healing could be reversed after learning what Jessica did to the security guard at the conference. Riley didn't think so, but then again, the array of spiritual powers was vast.

"Satan is a super genius whose methods are subtle and cunning. Remember, he is a master of deceit. He is also an expert on human behavior. He has been studying humankind since the creation of Adam and Eve."

"But how can he harm flesh and blood?" Stephen repeated for clarification. "Satan is of the spiritual realm."

"His methods are infinite and are different for each person. For one, person his attack could take the form of an addiction that leads to a health issue or even death. For another, he uses his powers of influence to lead a person to make a destructive decision that causes harm to themselves or others."

Stephen nodded, "I think I understand what you mean. His attacks are not direct, or even immediate in nature, but the long term impact is the same."

Riley nodded in agreement. "Harm does not have to be physical. It can manifest in the loss of a relationship, financial debt, or another way. Yet, there is a more direct form for which we must be most on guard—demonic intervention."

"Like at the university," Marie affirmed. "Those were real bullets shot at us. We could have been killed by that possessed man." She shivered at the memory and pulled the blanket closer to her chest.

"Yes," Riley agreed. "One of the most frequent miracles performed in the Bible by Jesus Christ was the exorcism of demons and evil spirits from people who were possessed. The devil has an army of demons, spirits, and possessed people to execute his attacks. That army is now hunting you."

"How did these people become possessed?" Noah asked, suddenly taking an interest in the conversation.

"I don't know," Riley admitted, glad that Noah was listening. "I believe in some cases, it occurs gradually. In others, people invite Satan to do it."

"Where did Satan come from?" Jessica interrupted.

"He came from Heaven," Riley replied. "The Bible says he was the most beautiful angel ever created by God. Satan was a master musician tasked with leading the rest of the angels in worshipping God. He is the most powerful of the angelic beings. Even the archangel Michael, the general of God's army of angels, cannot stand alone against him. Satan was cast out of Heaven because he believed himself to be greater than God and used his position to influence other angels to rebel against God by joining him."

"Why doesn't God just destroy Satan and the demons and end this battle, once and for all?" Marie asked.

"A good question! The Bible prophesies that God will eventually cast Satan, his followers, and those who reject God into an eternal lake of fire, forever to be separated from God and Heaven. As for now, he has chosen to let the devil roam."

"I don't understand," Marie challenged. "If I were God, I would just be done with Satan. Why would God allow Satan to continue to cause harm?"

"Another good question. We don't know the mind of God. We only know that he does allow Satan to work openly and freely here on Earth. I can only take solace in the fact that God does everything for a purpose, even though that purpose may not be revealed to us. For now, it is a battle."

"And we are the soldiers," Stephen said defiantly.

Riley smiled. "Yes. You are the soldiers." Riley paused, looking beyond the physical to assess each person's state of mind. There was apprehension, but he did not detect any fear. That was good. "Now that you know the enemy and the danger before you, does anyone want out?"

There was complete silence in the room. Riley looked at each person. He needed to know if they were fully committed. To his relief, only Noah was wavering in his commitment, evidenced by his downward stare. Riley pursed his lips, resisting the urge to confront Noah in front of the others. He decided it would only create concern amongst the team.

"Tomorrow you will begin basic training at the CIA Academy at Camp Perry," informed Riley.

"They're going to train us to be agents?" Marie asked. Riley could tell she was excited at the prospect. Both she and Jessica looked thrilled.

"You are going to get extensive training which includes field tactics, weapons use, defensive driving, hostage rescue, first aid, and a host of other important skills," Riley replied.

"That is too cool!" Jessica and Marie bumped

fists together.

"A transport will be here at seven tomorrow morning and will take you to the academy. The training will last the entire week."

"You're not coming with us?" Stephen asked.

"No, I have somewhere else to go," Riley responded. His voice was distant. "There is someone who needs my help." Riley did not elaborate any further. He couldn't have, even if he wanted to. He didn't know much else about the situation before him. The only thing he was sure of was that it was someone important to their mission. Someone who was about to do battle with agents of evil, perhaps even the devil himself.

CHAPTER 26

The mile markers flashed by in an unending blur, reflecting the last rays of the setting sun. Riley had been on the road since seven that morning, driving north with no particular destination in mind. In an hour, he would reach Boston. He grimaced at the thought of returning to that city—too many painful memories. Memories he would never forget and would always struggle to suppress. It was there where he and Charlotte started their fateful voyage.

The ride was uneventful, a welcomed rest from the chaos of the past week. He was enjoying the opportunity to think, to plan, and to pray. He desperately needed this time to recharge. Even so, he felt a pang of anguish at leaving his team behind, in particular, Stephen.

Stephen's divine healing was a miracle beyond Riley's greatest expectations. God had shown great mercy to have answered a prayer that Riley prayed every day since Stephen's birth. There were no words to describe how grateful he was. To have a second chance with his son was a dream come true and he planned to take full advantage of it.

During their free time, he and Stephen were inseparable—getting to know each other on a completely different level. But what Riley learned about Stephen surprised him. He expected an attitude of bitterness, or at the very least, regret for the years spent confined both mentally and physically. Instead, the opposite was true. Stephen was full of joy, expectation, and sensitivity to the world around him.

Riley marveled at Stephen's outlook on life. Stephen knew what was important and what was not. Stephen possessed a unique ability to put everything in perspective. Stephen most certainly understood what others could not. That life was not to be taken for granted. Like an oasis of water in the desert after a rainstorm, each drop is to be relished and enjoyed because there is no guarantee it will be there tomorrow. Likewise, each moment was to be treasured and valued to the fullest, for life could change at any time. Riley experienced that truth first hand when he lost Stephen's mother, Charlotte.

A bright green road sign attracted his attention, breaking his train of thought. The sign displayed the words 'Halifax College'. He didn't know why, but those words felt familiar to him. He let the feeling pass. His mind jumped to the problem he was wrestling with during the past

THE OTHER SIDE

few hours.

How does he expose the truth about Anthony Jessup? A records search of the pastor came up with nothing of significance. He did not possess a driver's license, a passport, or even a social security number. Anthony Jessup may as well have been from another world, which was not far from the truth.

He passed a sign indicating an upcoming exit for Halifax College. With a prompting flooding over him, he was sure of it. This was his exit. He turned onto the ramp and followed the signs. In a matter of minutes, he was on a vacant two lane road headed towards the small town of Eastford, Massachusetts.

An incoming call from Agent Gillian came as a welcomed distraction to the monotony of the drive. He heard Duke fidget in the back seat from the interruption to his sleep. Riley was so absorbed in thought he forgot Duke was in the car.

"Hello Frank. Good to hear your voice," Riley answered. The last time they spoke was in Richmond. For a moment, Riley wondered if Frank believed what he told him about the spiritual war against humanity, but his gut told him no.

"Hello, Agent O'Connor. Is all well?" The detective's voice sounded unusually cheery.

"Yes it is. How are you?"

"Better than I deserve. Today has been a good day. We have a new break in the Summit of Light investigation."

193

"Glad to hear that. What's up?"

"The large money transfer we discovered from Thereon to Summit of Light... we had it wrong."

"What do you mean?" Riley asked, intrigued by Frank's declaration.

"Our junior analyst researching the transfer made a rookie mistake and misread the transaction code. It was actually a money transfer from the church to Thereon."

No, that couldn't be right, could it? Riley thought. *Why would Summit of Light transfer such a large sum of money to a terrorist organization?*

"That doesn't make any sense," Riley replied, analyzing the implications of the detective's findings.

"The rabbit hole goes deeper," Frank added.

"Deeper? How so?"

"We found several other money transfers dating back three years, all bearing a similar three digit suffix. We think the suffix was used for internal tracking purposes by the church."

Riley knew from prior investigations that each electronic money transaction was coded with a variety of information. A common transaction contained data that identified the entities sending and receiving money, the accounts the money was being transferred between, as well as more mundane data such as the time, date, and amount of the transfer. In some cases, special comments or tagging information would also be added. The combination of all the information resulted in a code that uniquely identified each transaction.

"Now get this," the detective's voice escalated in excitement, "We are looking at more than eighty million dollars in money transfers."

"Eighty million?!?" The enormity of the amount shocked Riley. "Did it all go to Thereon?"

"No. We are highly confident there was only a single payment to Thereon, but this is where it gets interesting. We found Summit of Light made sizable money transfers to more than fifty other organizations and in some cases, directly to individuals. You might find one of these individuals particularly interesting." The detective paused, eagerly waiting for Riley to respond.

"I'm listening," Riley said, not much for drama.

"There was a transfer of two hundred and fifty thousand dollars to an offshore bank account registered to Roberto Flores."

"Who is he?"

"Roberto Flores is the brother of Rita Flores."

"Rita Flores, the university shooter?" Riley was struggling to make sense of the connection.

"The one and the same."

"Do we know why the fund transfer was made?"

"We are not sure. We can't contact Roberto Flores to ask him about it for multiple reasons."

"Why not?"

"Primarily, he has been in a medically-induced coma for the past twenty-six months at Georgetown University Medical Center. Apparently, this guy has a rare blood disease that is systematically shutting down each of his major organs. In fact, he was scheduled to be removed from life support this month as his insurance stopped paying his bills. That was until the hospital received a payment large enough to cover his expenses and then some." The detective was quiet for a moment.

"So what is the connection to Summit of Light?" Riley pondered out loud.

"Oh, that one is easy. Rita is one of the founding members of the church."

"So was this large amount of money payment for what she did at the university?"

"Maybe," Frank acknowledged. "We don't know for sure. But that is our primary theory at the moment."

A hypothesis started to form in Riley's mind. "Frank, would you send me the autopsy report for Rita Flores?"

"Sure, there is not much left of her. She was shot up pretty bad. What's up?"

Riley wasn't sure he knew the answer. "Just a hunch," he said.

"Fair enough. Let's plan to talk tomorrow."

"Take care, Frank." Riley ended the call, his mind lost in thought about the information he

THE OTHER SIDE

just learned.

Minutes later, Riley pulled through the entrance gate to Halifax College and headed up a sloped road towards a complex of buildings. A faded wooden sign with bold block lettering directed him into a central parking area. He surveyed the parking lot as he pulled to a stop. The lot was almost full, which was odd for this time of day. Classes should have ended hours ago. There must be a special event tonight on campus, he thought. He decided to check it out.

A few minutes later, Riley found himself in the rear of a small auditorium. There were several empty seats, but a good crowd for the show. On stage, a man dressed in a tuxedo was snapping his hands in a rhythmic motion in front of a young woman. Behind him, two students sat playing patty cake and another student danced in a circle to imaginary music. The man stopped snapping his fingers and made a motion with his hand. Instantly, the woman began to howl like a wolf, generating hysterical laughter from the audience.

Riley ignored the theatrics and focused his gaze on the man in the tuxedo. This man seemed to sense he was being watched and turned to face the audience, his eyes intently searching the crowd, periodically stopping on certain individuals. His eyes finally came to rest on Riley, a look of surprise forming on his face as they made eye contact. Riley nodded in acknowledgement before taking one of the empty seats, still holding the performer's gaze. Riley knew at that moment his journey was over. He was staring into the shocked eyes of his next team member.

CHAPTER 27

Halifax, Massachusetts

Long ago, Darius O'Malley came to the conclusion that the human race was diseased. People were so self-focused, carrying around countless thoughts of worry, anger, jealousy, hurt, and of course, sexual deviation. He had not met a single person who did not harbor a dark secret, a sorrowful regret, or a malicious desire. He knew that if everyone knew what everybody else was truly thinking, the world would explode in fear. Fortunately, Darius was not like everyone else. He didn't think or act like other people. How could he? Very few people, if any, could do what he could.

It never went unnoticed by others that Darius was cocky. Darius' unique ability gave him a sense of pride bordering on supreme arrogance. He couldn't help feeling that way. Not when he possessed the power he did. Scientists called him a telepathic. New agers called him enlightened. He called himself lucky. The ability to read other people's thoughts was a gift that saved his life more times than he could count.

For as long as he could remember, Darius knew the thoughts of others. His ability had always been there, just like his other senses. For him, it was as natural as hearing or seeing. It was not until he was a teenager that he discovered his telepathy could be controlled and that his ability went beyond reading minds. With concentration, he could probe deep into the mind of an individual, exposing memories, secrets, and in some cases, influencing their actions.

His fascination with understanding his talent and how he could leverage it plunged him into deep research on mind control, hypnotism, and a host of other fringe sciences. He soon learned that he could easily hypnotize people at will, making them his puppets. People, and their secrets, were now his to exploit. Their bodies, his to control.

Darius stared at the man in the rear of the auditorium, filtering out the chaotic noise of the hundreds of other thoughts occurring in the room. Darius tried to push into the man's mind, but was immediately stopped, as if his probe encountered a mental brick wall. His heart skipped a beat. Something was wrong. He pushed harder, sending a mental fist against the barrier, but it bounced off harmlessly. That

THE OTHER SIDE

never happened before. The man's mind was impenetrable.

The man seemed to know what Darius was doing and even smiled in acknowledgement of his feeble attempt to read him. The man nodded and then took a seat in the back row, continuing to stare at Darius with a look of satisfaction on his face.

A distant memory entered Darius' mind. When Darius was five years old, he witnessed a violent attack on his mother, committed by an unknown individual with a random motive. Unprovoked, this stranger violently attacked his mother, all the while screaming vulgarities and other nonsense. The assailant would have possibly beaten his mother to death, except for the intervention of an off-duty police officer. Darius vividly remembered being terrified, not only because of the attack, but this was the first and only time that he could not read an individual's thoughts.

His mother was an illegal immigrant from Honduras who married his father only because she became pregnant. She didn't love Darius' father, she never did. But Darius's father did the honorable thing. Together, they raised Darius in a basement apartment in the center of one of the toughest neighborhoods in New York City. It was not ideal, but it was all they could afford.

As a youth, Darius quickly learned how to handle himself. His ability enabled him to confidently look in the eyes of those who threatened him without fear. Growing up in in this brutal community, where fist fights, violent crime, and the occasional killing were as common as baseball and apple pie, you either fought with bravery or you fought with fear. Either way, you fought to survive.

Early on, Darius learned how to exploit confrontational situations. His ability gave him a freakish advantage over his peers. As a young teen, he mastered the art of information gathering, leveraging hidden secrets for favors, money, and protection. He lived by a simple formula. First survive, then thrive. And that was exactly what he did.

After graduating high school and coming of age, Darius spent his next few years scouring the casinos of Atlantic City, looking for victims to strip of their wealth and dignity. Poker wasn't much of a game when you knew what your opponents were holding. After padding his bank account with plenty to spare, he decided to pursue a more legitimate profession and one that was a great deal safer. He had made many enemies at the poker table, and he knew that the people he crossed, if given the opportunity, would not have a second thought of gunning him down in a deserted alley as retribution. Yes, being a mentalist was a much more stable profession.

Now, as Darius stood on stage, staring at the

man in the back of the auditorium, he felt an unfamiliar emotion creeping into his mind. He tried to fight it, but logic was not going to conquer emotion this time. After all these years, Darius O'Malley felt fear again. The worst kind of fear he could imagine. Fear of the unknown.

CHAPTER 28

While waiting backstage for Darius to appear from his dressing room, Riley studied the two-page program he was given when he entered the auditorium. On the back page, there was a small photo of Darius O'Malley. Darius was a handsome guy, despite having a large nose. His black hair was finely curled and cropped squarely around his head. His jaw line was his most pronounced feature, square and strong. It complimented a magnetic smile that beckoned engagement.

A brief bio under the photo told him that Darius resided in a small resort community in Cape May, New Jersey. There must be more to Darius, Riley thought. He wondered how an entertainer, typically performing on small college campuses, could afford housing in that oceanfront community.

The verse from the book of Matthew entered his mind again, first coming to him in a thought earlier that day. It was a short verse, one he hadn't even realized he memorized. *'Jesus, knowing their thoughts, said, "Why do you think evil in your hearts?'*

It was common for the Spirit to bring a verse of the Bible to his attention when he was in need. Though examples exist in the Old Testament of God speaking directly to people, that didn't happen now. Now God spoke to his people through the verses of the Bible, through circumstances, and through the counsel of others. That is what made discerning God's will so unclear. He wished God would make an exception now and speak directly to him. At the very least, God could send him a text message once in a while to tell him he was on the right track. With a sigh, Riley pushed his musings aside and cleared his mind, meditating on the verse of scripture.

At first, Riley thought the Holy Spirit was rebuking him. It was true he was frustrated. Despite the success his team was experiencing, the truth was they were no closer to preventing the stadium attack than when they started. The possibility of failure and the magnitude of the resulting deaths was beginning to plague him. He needed results and he needed them fast. Not only that, he was beginning to place blame on others for his lack of success. Thoughts like these were dominating his mind with increasing frequency, making it difficult for him to focus on the task at hand.

After a few moments of concentration, he

knew that his first interpretation of the scripture was incorrect. He had missed the meaning relevant to his situation. The message was not about evil in his own heart. It was a clue to help him understand Darius O'Malley.

The door to the dressing room opened, revealing a much more casual Darius. He was wearing jeans, a faded blue t-shirt, and a New York Yankees hat. He did not look surprised to see Riley. In fact, he smiled warmly.

"I was expecting you would be here," Darius said, making sure to keep an arm's-length away. "Is this a friendly call or are you and I going to have to fight it out in the parking lot?" His accent was thick, typical of a lifelong New Yorker. Even though Darius appeared calm, Riley knew Darius was prepared to fight.

Riley held up his CIA badge and quickly closed it. Just enough for Darius to see the badge, nothing else. "My name is Riley O'Connor. It is urgent that I speak with you."

"You a Fed?" Darius asked, the surprise evident on his face. He took a step backward but retained his defensive posture.

Riley shook his head, his eyes locked on Darius. He felt that subtle pressure in his head again, as if something was trying to push itself inward.

"Who are you?" Darius demanded. "What do you want with me?"

Riley could tell Darius was struggling with the conversation. Asking questions was easy when you knew what the other person was thinking. It was apparent Darius had relied on his ability for much too long.

"Take it easy, Darius. I am going to give you the answers you seek," Riley assured him, he stepped closer to Darius. "But first, I need to show you something." With that, he opened his mind and let Darius O'Malley inside to learn his secrets.

CHAPTER 29

Washington, D.C.

"Yes, I just received the files but I have not reviewed them yet." Natasha glanced at the brown envelope on the corner of her desk. Branson delivered on his promise only an hour ago.

She listened intently for a moment. "I understand your concern. I thought that would be the case. That is why I wanted to inform you of the investigation." Natasha only learned about the investigation by the FBI and CIA that morning. It frustrated her that she did not have more access to what was going on in the other federal agencies, particular the CIA. She wondered if Branson was purposely holding back on her.

A few moments later, she burst into laughter. "I wholeheartedly agree," she offered in response. It was funny how some people were skilled with the ability to make other people

THE OTHER SIDE

laugh. She didn't have that gift. She was way too serious about everything.

"Peace and love be with you too, Pastor Jessup," Natasha said. "I will be in touch." She hung up the phone.

Her eyes fell back onto the envelope. She picked it up, measuring its weight. It didn't seem like much. She opened the envelope and began reading. A black and white photo of an attractive young woman graced the first page. The file was not very thick and did not contain much information on the woman. After a few minutes of casual reading, it was apparent that Jessica Gardner was as vanilla as they come. No prior residences except her current address, a mathematics degree from the University of Kentucky and no spouse or children. She did not even have a passport. The only other documents in the file were a college transcript, an I-9 employment verification form, and a hiring justification submitted by Riley O'Connor just three weeks prior.

She read the justification, hoping to glean more insight into the woman that Riley had been so adamant was not part of his team. The only factor that stood out was that she was apparently a mathematics genius with a specialty in cryptanalysis. That was a dead end, she thought. The CIA was always hiring code crackers. She tossed the file to the side and picked up the next file.

The next file contained similar information

as the first file, minus the college transcript. It appeared Noah Walker did not attend college. He was listed as residing at the same address as his parents, which struck Natasha as odd. Riley's justification was even stranger. Noah was a master hacker. The justification cited several incidences of corporate hacking that were attributed to Noah. What did Riley need with a master hacker? It didn't make any sense.

There were two additional files in the envelope. She choose the thicker file and examined the name typed in small black letters on the tab. It belonged to Riley O'Connor. She reviewed his file in detail for several minutes. It appeared that Riley was a model agent. There was not a blemish on his record in more than twenty-seven years of service with the CIA. Riley received positive performance reviews each year, experienced normal levels of promotion, and only recently rose to his current position working directly for the Director. The rest of the file contained the routine papers any file would contain on an agent of the government. She scanned these documents quickly, not seeing anything of interest.

Becoming frustrated with her lack of success in uncovering something useful, she flipped to the section of the file reserved for personal data on family members. Though it was not publically shared, it was common practice for the CIA to conduct routine background checks on all immediate family members of an agent. To her dismay, the section contained only a few items on Riley's wife and son. There was a copy of an obituary for Riley's wife, a coast guard accident investigation report, a copy of a psychological analysis performed on Riley's son and a photograph.

Natasha reviewed the analysis of Riley's son first and was surprised to learn Stephen was paralyzed and suffered from severe autism. That must have been difficult for Riley and his wife to raise him, she thought. She picked up the accident report and briefly scanned the summary. Again Natasha was surprised to learn that the body of Riley's wife, Charlotte, was never recovered from the ocean. Natasha suppressed a momentarily pang of compassion for Riley. It was hard not to feel sorry for him. Lastly, she studied the photo taken of Riley and his son, Stephen. Riley sat with one arm around Stephen, his other arm resting on the top of the coffin. Riley's face looked haggard and pained.

She pondered the information she just read. No doubt Riley had experienced a great deal of adversity. It suddenly occurred to her that Riley might have a weakness after all. Coping with the care of a disabled person and the loss of a spouse would take a severe toll on anybody. Most people were not equipped to deal with that much distress and difficulty. In those situations, people developed coping mechanisms to help them escape from the reality of life, usually a destructive habit such as drinking, drugs, or gambling. Riley O'Connor could have a secret vice too. It wasn't much of a theory, but it was a possibility.

She reviewed the picture once more, this time studying the details of the photo. There was something familiar about the young man in the wheelchair. She had seen him before, but she couldn't place when or where. She let the thought fade. She would have remembered meeting an autistic boy in a wheelchair.

The door to her office burst open. Gerome Downes, the Secretary of Homeland Security stomped into her office. Gerome was a large man who sported a receding hairline and his trademark antique spectacles. Gerome was well-respected by his peers and harbored the devotion of his employees. Even Natasha liked the man, despite the fact that she coveted his position.

"Have you heard the news?" Gerome bellowed.

"No, what's going on?" Natasha said, appearing alarmed.

"Grab everything you have on Thereon. We are heading to the war room. Now!" His tone of authority made Natasha jump to her feet.

"Sir, what has happened?" she asked, scrambling to collect a set of files off the credenza.

He began shaking his head side to side, his face contorted in agony. "Ten minutes ago, the

U.S. suffered a massive attack. I don't have all the details, but the attack hit us at multiple locations across the country." His eyes leveled on her, conveying the seriousness of the situation. "The United States is now at full alert. We are at war."

CHAPTER 30

Cape May, New Jersey

"I am on my way back as we speak," Riley exhaled in frustration. "ETA to Langley is four hours." Riley turned on the radio to scan through the channels.

"We will keep you updated. Hurry back," Bill Rogers said.

"I do have to make a drop-off at the residence, then I am coming in," Riley responded. Bill knew Riley had been hunting, but did not know yet about his catch.

"You found another?"

"Yes," Riley answered, stealing a glance at Darius beside him. "I will brief you on the situation when I arrive. See you then." He hung up the phone and turned his attention back to the radio, finally finding a news station.

"I don't need to read your mind to know something is very wrong. What's up?" Darius asked.

"There has been a large scale terrorist attack. Right now, we need to listen." He turned up the volume of the radio. The anxious voice of a reporter broadcasting live from the location of one of the incidents filled the vehicle.

Above, the sun was just beginning its descent, ushering in the blanket of dusk. The sky was slowly transforming into a palette of deep silver blue colors with orange and purple hues. Under different circumstances, Riley would have enjoyed the majestic spectacle before him. Only he couldn't. Not when a war was raging across the country.

Riley stepped on the gas, easily exceeding the forty-five mile an hour speed limit of the country road they traveled. He wished he were already on the interstate heading south, only there was no easy way to get to the interstate from Cape May. Four hours was a long time when the world was crashing down all around them.

After spending the night in a hotel near the college, he and Darius embarked on their trip back to Langley earlier that morning. As part of his agreement to join Riley, Darius demanded they travel to Cape May to pick up his best friend, Spencer. When Riley learned Spencer was a yellow lab, he didn't have a choice but to agree. He knew far better than most the kinship that one could have for a loyal companion. In fact, Duke appeared to be enjoying his new riding partner. They were both curled peacefully in the back seat.

Riley reflected a moment on the events of last night. Shortly after Darius probed Riley's mind, Darius had fallen to his knees, sobbing. The memories Riley chose to share with Darius changed everything Darius believed. Riley skillfully knew they would have that impact.

Most go through a similar experience when faced with a crisis of belief, at least those who choose to accept their new reality. In Darius' case, he did not believe God was real. He always held an ironclad belief he was accountable to himself and no one else. That he was the only person in the universe he could trust. A glimpse of his Creator crumbled his self-relying belief into powder.

Darius' new understanding was a key motivator in convincing him to join Riley's team, but it wasn't the only reason. Darius was a passionate patriot. He loved his country. He welcomed the opportunity to be part of something bigger. Riley's insight told him Darius also had another motive. Darius was eager to spend time with other people who were gifted and would understand who he was and what he could do.

Riley directed the car into a blind turn only to slam on the brakes moments later, bringing the car to a screeching halt.

"Whoa!" Darius yelled. Just yards ahead of them, the road was draped in sickly, yellow fog.

THE OTHER SIDE

It was so thick that the sedan's headlights reflected directly back at them, forcing them both to shield their eyes.

To the side of the road, at the edge of the fog, Riley noticed the embankment sloped steeply. He could see a brackish substance at the bottom of the embankment. It was water.

Riley shot a glance at his map app. He was about to cross a short bridge that also served as a dam, blocking one of the many tributaries that fed into the bay. The lake was not large, but no doubt it was deep. He needed to be careful. "We should be ok, just some fog from the lake," he said, trying to put Darius at ease. As Riley eased the vehicle slowly into the fog, Duke began to growl in a low guttural tone. He was quickly joined by Spencer.

He scarcely driven a hundred feet when the piecing sound of static crashed through the speakers of the car. The headlights flashed and then went dark. Riley pressed on the gas, but the engine was dead. Blackness surrounded them.

"There is someone out there...?" Darius murmured. In the back seat, both dogs began whimpering in fear.

"Who?" Riley asked for clarification. He didn't need Darius to answer. He sensed the presence that surrounded them. The whole situation reminded Riley of an old movie about alien encounters. But this was not an alien. A soldier of the Dark One had come for them.

A deep roar crashed through the darkness with intensity. Darius grabbed the sides of his head, screaming. "Aaahhh!!! It hurts. Get out!!! Get out of my head!" He thrashed erratically in his seat before crouching into a fetal position, still screaming.

"Darius! Darius!" Riley yelled above his moaning. He placed his hand on Darius' head, willing the pain to go away. Darius responded, but only slightly. His screams slowly subsided to a whimper, but he could tell Darius was still in great discomfort. One touch was all he needed to verify what was happening. Darius was under a paralyzing demonic attack in the one place every human was most vulnerable, the mind.

The car began to rattle violently from side to side, tossing Riley and Darius back and forth in their seats. Riley watched helplessly as the front end of the car rose dramatically into the air before slamming into the ground, causing both he and Darius to lunge forward wildly. The impact from the seatbelt restraining his motion took the wind out of him. He heard the dogs yelp in pain as Duke and Spencer smashed into the back of the front seat. Riley couldn't be sure, but the car seemed to levitate for a moment and slide several feet toward the edge of the road. Toward the embankment. Toward the water.

As odd as it was, he knew he needed to obey the prompting that was flooding over him. Riley undid his seat belt and began frantically removing his shirt, his watch, and his belt. Anything that contained metal needed to be removed. Next to him, Darius continued to shake in torment, fighting his own battle, oblivious to what was happening around them.

Riley tried to unbuckle Darius' seatbelt, but the fastener was locked solid. The car lurched forward again toward the water, throwing Riley into the steering wheel. Riley felt one of his ribs snap as he smashed squarely into the center of the steering column. Fighting against the pain, he reached over and began to undo the Velcro straps of the harness that held his prosthetic arm in place. After a period of struggle, the arm fell to his side, now an inanimate hunk of plastic, metal, and rubber.

Riley took a moment to catch his breath, wincing against the pain in his side with each exhale. Unsure of his next move, he raised his head, a barely audible prayer leaving his lips. "Father, help us." Immediately, a wave of insight came to him and with it, a plan to save them. Slowly, Riley opened his car door and bravely stepped into the storm.

CHAPTER 31

The air was bone chilling cold. The kind of cold that clings to the body, sucking away any and all warmth. He could feel the air pulsating menacingly around him. The darkness seemed to be charged with energy, an extension of the spirit that was seeking to destroy them.

Riley could sense the spirit was angered he left the car. Good, he thought. That was part of Riley's plan to divide and conquer. He only hoped Darius was alert enough to read his mind. Otherwise, all could be lost.

A whirlwind of rocks and debris collided into him, thrown by the darkness. He crouched instinctively, doing his best to protect himself. He knew he would not last long as the target of the spirit's wrath. Riley needed to get to the other side of the bridge for his plan was to work. Another gust of debris smashed into his leg, this one containing exposed bits of metal shavings. The shavings sliced through his slacks and into

THE OTHER SIDE

his flesh. He fell onto his side, reeling in severe pain.

Out of the corner of his eye, Riley watched the car lurch several feet closer towards the brackish water. It was teetering on the edge of the embankment, inches away from plunging into the pond. Both the car and its contents could disappear into the water in seconds. There was only one thing to do.

Forcing himself to relax and to focus, he surrendered to the Holy Spirit he carried within, praying for the Spirit to arise and take control of his body. He felt power surge into him, providing him purpose in his movement.

Slowly, like a boxer rising from a knockout punch, Riley stood. There was strength in his stance. As if in retaliation for his resistance, the darkness intensified its attack. Riley ducked instinctively as a speed limit sign flew inches above his head, the thin sheet of metal a razor blade of fury. An instant later, he vaulted into the air, as a cannon ball of rusted screws, nails, and soda cans hurled below him. Riley marveled at the agility he was displaying, normally attributed to someone of extreme athletic dexterity. The power of God never ceased to amaze him.

Upon landing, he rolled to the left, avoiding the return arc of the street sign. However, he was now disoriented. He couldn't tell which way to run to get across the bridge and it was critical that he continued moving away from Darius.

Out of the fog, a soft mass collided with his legs. It was Duke. He must have followed him out of the car. "Go!!!" Riley shouted immediately, rising to his feet to follow. Within seconds Riley was pursuing his dog at a full sprint. Together they cut through the edge of the fog, searching for an exit from the madness.

Riley was just feet behind Duke when a metal cable, striking like a whip, collided with Duke's hind section. The impact sent the dog tumbling several yards. Riley stopped, his initial instinct to go him, but Duke lay motionless. Riley couldn't assess the damage, but he knew his companion was very hurt. Instantly the peace in his heart turned to fury, but he was still being prompted to flee, not fight. Reluctantly, Riley turned and began running again, only to stop. Darkness still surrounded him. If only he knew the way out.

As if in response to his plea, another furry body appeared from the mist, Spencer! The yellow lab seemed to understand exactly what to do, breaking into a sprint and penetrating the cloud. Riley followed, plunging into the darkness.

Within seconds, Riley broke free of the cloud, into the waning light of the early evening. The final rays of the sun were making a last ditch effort to resist the darkness. Yet it was just enough light for Riley to see the road before him. Beside him, Spencer was keeping pace as they

THE OTHER SIDE

ran down the road. He turned, stealing a glance at the cloud of darkness behind him. The cloud was rolling towards him at a fast rate. It was coming after him, exactly as he hoped.

'Riley?' The thought permeated his mind. He knew it was Darius. 'The fog is gone and, thankfully, that thing is out of my head. What do you need me to do?'

'Find Duke,' Riley thought. He prayed Duke was not injured too badly. And if he were, he just hoped Duke would survive. Riley slowed his pace, while still drawing the cloud further away from the bridge.

'I will find him,' Darius thought. 'But watch yourself. When I was under attack, I was able to pick up some information. It calls itself the King of the Nephilim, whatever that means. And it is wicked strong.'

One of the punished ones, Riley thought to himself. A spirit that serves Satan. It struck him as odd that the spirit hadn't just tossed their vehicle into the lake from the beginning. It obviously possessed the strength. It was almost as if the spirit was reluctant... a revelation formed in Riley's mind. He stopped running and turned to face the onrushing spirit.

The cloud stopped, only yards from where he stood, a bellowing mass of torment. Riley felt like it was waiting for him to do something.

Riley held his arms up towards the cloud. "Ahijah, King of the Nephilim," Riley's voice echoed back at him as it ricocheted off of the thick fog. "You interfere with the work of the Holy God of Creation. Desist and repent of your deeds. There is still hope for how you will spend eternity." A tempest of movement stirred up at the edge of the cloud. It was hard to see in the remaining light, but it appeared to be more debris. A fist of wrath waiting to throw the final punch.

"Judgment has already been established for you, but the Creator is merciful," Riley emphasized his point. The cloud flashed in response, a momentary brief light from deep within that rippled to the surface. The turbulence appeared to lose some of its intensity.

"I sense the conflict within you," Riley pressed, letting the Holy Spirit guide his direction. "You have a choice. Let's end this now in peace then perhaps the Almighty will take your actions into consideration on Judgment Day." The stirring of the cloud slowed to almost a stand still. It was as if the spirit was contemplating Riley's request. Riley heard the sound of crashing metal collide with the asphalt of the road as the swirling debris disappeared. Riley felt the spirit's emotion emanating and knew it wanted to be released from its prison on Earth. It wanted forgiveness from the Creator.

Suddenly, a new formation appeared in the cloud. Another tempest, only this one devoid of light. The intensity of this new form made the surrounding darkness muted in contrast. Riley sensed the presence of the demon immediately. The fact that the demon did not require a human host told him he was dealing with an entity much more powerful than himself. It had to be one of the Ancients, a member of the original Fallen.

He sensed the spirit was agitated by the appearance of the demon. Riley assessed his options as he watched the storm develop all around them. The darkness and the fog seemed to struggle against each other, each seeking dominance over the other.

Riley decided not to watch the outcome. He turned and began to run with all his strength. He knew the spirit would not win the battle against such a powerful demon.

If a battle occurred between the two entities, it was over in seconds. Apparently beaten into submission by the demon, the spirit descended on Riley in a rush, enveloping him in its grasp. Something hard smacked into Riley's shins and wrapped around his legs. Riley fell to the ground, writhing in pain. He reached down and felt the cold steel chain coiled around his legs. A second later, a remnant of rusted wire wrapped itself around his neck, making it impossible for him to take a breath. Slowly the wire around his neck tightened.

He clawed helplessly, trying to pull the wire away from his neck, but he wasn't strong enough. His lungs were burning, gasping for air.

He rolled on his side, his body reflexively jerking in a frantic effort to take a breath. He was losing consciousness. His eyesight was failing as intense pressure exploded in his head. The last thing he saw before all went dark was a bright light and the blurred image of a black form standing over him. Seconds later, Riley O'Connor was dead.

CHAPTER 32

The body of Riley O'Connor lay motionless in the darkness, the man's hands still clutching the wire that encircled his neck. It was done. The Anointed was no more.

Baal watched with wild amusement as a young man approached the corpse, cradling the limp body of a dog in his arms. Baal did not sense any life force within its crumpled form. It had passed from life just like its owner. How poetically human, he thought. A man and his dog together to the end.

The young man laid the dog gently beside Riley's body and began to work frantically to untie the metal cord from the man's neck. A few seconds passed before he began administering CPR. But it would be futile. Baal knew that the Anointed's esophagus was crushed.

Ahijah vanished immediately after Riley lost consciousness, and with him, the fog had dissolved into nothingness. Overhead, the soft blue light of the moon now cast an ominous glow. Baal would deal with Ahijah later. Insubordination would not be tolerated, especially from the most powerful of the Nephilim spirits.

What had that ridiculous spirit been thinking? Could Ahijah have possibly believed that the Creator would forgive him after all the evil he orchestrated against Him? Baal pondered the thought for a moment, quickly realizing it was insane. Even the Creator had limits to His forgiveness. Ahijah would burn in the lake of fire for all eternity like the rest of them, if Satan was not victorious in ruling the world.

Baal took one last look at the young man who was pounding in a rhythmic motion on the Anointed's chest. For a brief moment, Baal wondered about this young man. He had never encountered him before among the Anointed's chosen. Why was he with the Anointed? Whatever the reason, it didn't matter now. The first phase of his plans to destroy the United States was a success. The terrorist attack Thereon executed was devastating and with the next attack eminent, it would only be a matter of time until the country descended into absolute chaos.

Baal casually phased back into the spiritual realm, and just as effortlessly phased to a new location. Slowly the room of his destination took shape around him. It was a large room, oddly shaped for an office. He visited this place countless times since its construction centuries ago.

The office was lavishly decorated, mostly

with historic portrait art contrasted by modern accessories. Two large couches enclosed a square mahogany table. Other furniture in the room was purposefully retained by the occupant as a matter of tradition, though it didn't match the decor.

It was funny how humans honored tradition, Baal thought, noting the antique grandfather clock against the far wall. It stood solemnly by itself, a testament to another era, capturing the passage of time in fluid mechanical motion.

The innate desire of human beings to honor tradition proved beneficial to the kingdom of darkness. Throughout the centuries, humans shaped their religious activities into an experience of man-made traditions. The reliance on religious traditions versus the truths of the Bible has enabled Satan to capture the eternal souls of billions of people, then and now.

Baal reflected a moment longer as his eyes fell on a Bible located on a shelf of the massive bookcase. The ignorance of the human race. It was something he couldn't help but relish. All their religions, all designed to help them achieve some level of spiritual significance and eternity in Heaven. To Satan's benefit, most humans completely ignored the true path to salvation based on the sacrifice of the One. They either didn't understand it or chose to ignore it. They placed their trust for salvation in a church, a tradition, or in their good deeds—instead of having a direct relationship with the Creator. Either way, they were fools!

The current occupant of the office was just as much a fool as the rest, though he was a unique case when it came to his beliefs. President Matthew Harrison didn't believe in God, intelligent design or any form of higher power. He was a professed atheist, believing that man's only purpose in life was to fulfill his own desires. But when he met Baal face-to-face, he abruptly changed his stance.

On the evening of his presidential inauguration, Baal appeared to him disguised as an angel basked in white light. Baal told the man that God raised him to his position for a divine purpose. Believing Baal to be a direct messenger of God, the man quickly yielded to Baal's influence. The man himself remained completely unaware of Baal's evil motives.

Baal chuckled at the irony of the current situation. The office that was a public symbol for truth, justice, and liberty was secretly shackled to the kingdom of lies and deception. Baal glanced above, taking in the large insignia that graced the ceiling. Soon, what it represented would no longer exist.

A door on the far wall of the room opened to reveal a tall man impeccably dressed in a deep blue suit. The man quickly scanned the area before motioning behind him. A few seconds later, President Harrison entered the room.

THE OTHER SIDE

He projected a commanding presence, one that filled the room, giving the impression the large office was not going to be sufficient to support his needs. He walked purposefully towards the desk, each step confident, almost boastful of his power.

The president dismissed the agent before pausing to study the large wooden desk, running his fingers slowly across it, as if he didn't trust it was real. Baal knew that behind the man's facade of power and overriding confidence, lay a deep chasm of insecurity. Baal was leveraging the president's fault to create doubt in his decisions and to create fear that he could fail. Now, Baal planned to utilize the president's insecurity in the next phase of his plan.

Baal assumed human physical form, appearing out of nothingness to stand before the president. Though it had been expressly forbidden by the Creator, the ability to take direct physical form still existed. Both the higher ranking and most powerful angels and demons possessed this power, but few risked the consequences of making the transition. It was dangerous. While in human form, a demon could be captured by an angel and locked away for all eternity. But it was a risk that he and others were willing to take to usher in the destruction they desperately needed.

The president's back was turned to him, his gaze locked on something outside in the perimeter gardens. Baal took the moment to run his own fingers across the desk. Unlike the man, Baal could not feel the smoothness of the lacquered wood. To him, the desk was merely solid, but that was all. Soon things would be different for both Baal and the man.

Baal picked up the small gold picture frame that was positioned prominently in the center of the desk. It was a picture of this man's family. In the background, the skyline of New York City could be seen. The family looked so perfect —the man, his beautiful wife, and his two young girls. Not seeming to have a care in the world except to be with each other. It was like many of the pictures that adorned the large bookcase and lamp stands around the office. Family was important to this man. Baal wondered just how important.

Baal cradled the frame in his hand as he stepped behind the man. When he spoke, his words were soft, "It's time to make your decision, Mr. President. Which one are you going to sacrifice?"

The president turned, startled by the interruption. Upon seeing Baal, he fell to one knee. "I'm not sure I understand? Why do I have to sacrifice either one?" The president stalled.

"The terrorist attack that occurred today is only the beginning of what will come. The Creator has deemed that your country must be destroyed," Baal lied.

THE OTHER SIDE

"But why?" the president pleaded.

"Don't you understand? Everything that is happening is a test from the Creator. He wants to know that your allegiance is to Him," Baal said as he moved forward holding the picture frame for the president to see. "The choice is yours. Save your country...," he held his hand out towards the American flag that hung limply on a pole next to the desk. "Or your family?" He handed the man the picture frame. The president starred at it intently. Baal noticed the man's upper lip was beginning to quiver.

The president remained silent, unsure of his decision.

"This is the moment you have to make your choice," Baal pushed, leveling his gaze on the president. "Or the anger of the Creator will be thrust upon you and you will lose everything, including your life."

"What..." the president stammered, trembling in fear. "What do I have to do to save them?"

"Pledge your oath of fidelity to me," Baal pressed, sensing victory. "Grant me access to your mind and body when I ask for it. Resist me at any point and you and your family will surely perish."

The next words Baal heard provided him a small measure of satisfaction. Baal guessed right about the president. He was not the man he pretended to be in public. He did not place the welfare of his country and its citizens above all else. As the president sobbed woefully before him, Baal knew his work here was done.

CHAPTER 33

The intensity of the spotlights from the Marine helicopter cast the perimeter around them ablaze in an unnatural blue-white light. It was evening by the time they arrived and without the lights, it would have been near impossible for her to see what she was doing. She knew it should have been too late to save him. What just happened shouldn't have been possible.

Jessica tossed the drained epinephrine pen beside the military med-pack and began to gently massage the skin where she injected Riley. She wasn't sure if she needed to use the injection, but she wasn't taking any chances. Riley's breathing was labored, but at least he was breathing.

The urgency in her voice pierced through the quiet night surrounding them. "Riley... Riley.... Can you hear me?" To her relief, Riley's eyelids fluttered and then shot wide open. His eyes were blank, unseeing of the world in front of him. Jessica noticed the sparkle they usually held wasn't there. Something was wrong.

Jessica gently shook his shoulder, this time her voice was soft and nurturing, "Riley. It's me, Jessica. Can you hear me? Please wake up." She exchanged nervous glances with those assembled around her.

After a few moments, Riley's eyes closed. When they reopened, the sparkle returned. "What happened?" Riley said, coming to. He placed his hand to his head. "I feel like I went three rounds with Mike Tyson and lost."

"Who?" Jessica responded, somewhat confused. "Never mind," she said relieved. "It doesn't matter. What matters is that you are alive." She scooted backward, allowing him to look and take in his surroundings.

Both Stephen and Maria were kneeling beside Riley. The tears on Stephen's face were still fresh, his hand locked in Riley's as if he could arm wrestle him into consciousness. Noah was talking to the three men dressed in camouflage gear that huddled near the helicopter. Each man was holding a machine gun and one man carried a sniper rifle strapped in a holster on his back. One of the soldiers kept pointing at the sky and then motioning to a small book he carried in his left hand that she presumed was a Bible. She couldn't imagine what was going through their minds after what they just witnessed.

A wave of relief crashed over her, breaking

THE OTHER SIDE

through her doubt as the realization of what she accomplished sunk in. Riley was alive. She was still struggling to believe it herself. Like the apostle Peter, she made the impossible happen. She brought a man back from the dead.

"You saved me," Riley said between deep breaths. He spoke slowly, as if just waking up from a deep sleep.

"It was a team effort Mr. O'Connor," Jessica said.

"Why are you here?" Riley asked, obviously still reeling from the experience.

"Last night, Noah dreamed that you were killed after an encounter with a demon," Jessica said. She quickly relayed the details of the events that transpired that morning, including how they ended up on a Marine helicopter transport with armed guards. Riley only nodded, still dazed.

"But how did you find me?" Riley asked.

Marie patted Stephen on the back, "You can thank your son for that," she said. "He just knew where to find you. We only wish we arrived sooner."

"You know you performed a miracle," Riley said affirmatively, looking at Jessica. His smile told her everything she needed to know. He was both amazed and grateful. She was proud of herself too.

"With Marie's help, of course," Jessica acknowledged, giving Marie a quick fist bump.

Riley rose slowly to his feet, aided by Stephen. "What about Duke? Is he ok?"

"He's fine," Stephen responded. "Jessica healed him as well." As if in answer to Riley's question, Duke crested the hill running towards him, followed by Spencer and Darius. Duke leaped into the air, colliding with Riley, doing his best to jump into Riley's arms and lick every inch of his face, neck and whatever else he could put his tongue on.

"I thought I might have lost you!" Riley cried, holding the shepherd in a one-arm bear hug.

Jessica smiled, noting the tears in Riley's eyes. She realized tears were also streaming down her cheeks. She knew she was happy for Riley, but the tears were for a different reason. It was the first time since her aunt's death that she felt purpose again. She now knew without a doubt, that healing was her true calling.

"I can't believe you're alive! It is a miracle," Darius exclaimed, running to Riley's side. "I tried, but you were gone. Your throat was crushed... CPR wasn't working... this is incredible!"

Riley nodded at Darius, "Thanks for the flashback," he said, casually massaging his throat. He looked around at the others. "Have you all met Darius?"

"Not exactly," Jessica said, rising to her feet. Shortly after they landed, she and Marie rushed to Riley's aid. She encountered Darius sitting next to Riley, holding Duke in his arms. She was so focused on administering aid to Riley that she quickly forgot Darius was there. She now approached the mysterious man, "Hello, Darius. I am Jessica."

"Hello," he responded, taking her hand and offering a formal bow. The gesture struck her as somewhat flamboyant, but at the same time there was an element of charm to his actions. He straightened up abruptly, releasing her hand. "Please excuse my theatrics," he shrugged. "It comes from my stage training. It is my pleasure to meet you."

Most considered Darius handsome due to his dark complexion and chiseled features, but that wasn't what captured Jessica's attention. It was his aura. She stared at him for moment, intrigued by what she saw. His aura was vibrant blue, like the color of the oceans only seen in pictures taken from space. Only, the sea of blue was interrupted by streaks of black. Black usually meant evil, but she had also viewed that color around those who demonstrated leadership or a high degree of self-confidence. After all, black was the power of control, but it seemed in contrast to the center of his aura which appeared as a band of pure white that glimmered before her eyes.

"You think I am intriguing," Darius said assuredly. "So are you. Not only are you beautiful, your talent is amazing." His comment took Jessica by surprise. How could he know what she was thinking? A devilish smile appeared on his face. He bent down and patted the yellow lab that nestled against his leg. "This is Spencer. He is a little shy around pretty women."

Jessica felt herself blushing. Darius was not only charming, his personality was captivating.

"Please spare us the compliments," Noah huffed, a disapproving look on his face. Jessica hadn't noticed Noah walk over. "I have seen you before. You were in a vision I experienced." Noah looked to Marie for confirmation, who nodded in return.

Darius peered intently at Noah for a moment in response, but then returned his attention to Riley. "This is quite an amazing team you have assembled," Darius acknowledged. "Even though I knew what to expect, I am still impressed."

"Yes, God has blessed each of us uniquely in His own way. It is moments like this when I am humbled at what He can do through us with the unique powers He granted us."

"Don't get me wrong Riley," Noah interrupted. "I am very glad you are alive, but if God is all powerful, why does He let bad things like this happen?" It was a valid question, one that Jessica often asked herself.

Riley placed his hand on Noah's shoulder. "What we perceive to be hardship is being used for God's eternal plan. There is a reason for everything." Riley's tone was reflective.

"But you know why this happened, don't you?" Maria nodded in understanding.

Riley nodded affirmatively. "I crossed over again and I was met by a messenger of God. He gave me a glimpse of the future. Only I am not sure I understand what I saw or why God gave it to me. But He gave it to me just the same."

"Can you tell us? Are we going to be ok?" Jessica asked. It was a question she wanted to ask since she first met Riley. A question driven by fear deep within that was eating at her, slowly digesting her confidence.

A hearty laugh escaped from Riley. "Where is your faith, daughter." It was a statement, not a question. Riley's eyes appeared to illuminate before her. Perhaps it was just the reflection from the helicopter lights behind her, she thought. Even so, Riley's face took on a magical appearance, much like his aura. "There are no guarantees for any of us. That is why we must redeem the time."

"Sir, can you walk? We need to get back to Langley ASAP!" A soldier interrupted. "All hell has broken loose and they are requesting you to be at headquarters immediately."

Instantly, Riley's expression changed to alarm as he remembered the attack. "Yes, we must get going." The soldier immediately took off towards the helicopter to join his team who were already on board preparing for their return trip. A few seconds later, a high pitched whirl filled the air as the helicopter's engine engaged. Riley faced the others, "Before we go, I must share a word of warning." The others huddled around Riley, concern evident on their faces.

"The path before us is dangerous, we are all going to be tried. We are going to be tested. There is only one question we should be asking ourselves." Riley let the statement hang in the air, begging for someone to respond.

Jessica answered, not even realizing she spoke. The words came out as a whisper, each syllable seeming to catch in her throat, barely audible above the noise of the helicopter blades. "Am I willing to die for what I believe in?"

Riley's expression told Jessica everything she needed to know. She asked the right question. As they piled into the helicopter, the question repeated itself in her mind. She wasn't sure how to answer. She didn't want to die, but so many lives were at stake. It was only after a few minutes of contemplating her feelings that she came to a realization that gave her comfort. Perhaps God was finally giving her what she had been asking for— He was giving her a true test of her faith.

CHAPTER 34

Washington, D.C.

D eep under the Pentagon, below the lower-level shopping mall and the abandoned Metro subway line, an emergency communication session was just getting underway. Outfitted with state-of-the-art communication technology and protected beneath fifty feet of reinforced concrete, the Situation Room was an impregnable bunker designed to withstand a nuclear blast. Everyone within the government's inner circle of power was in attendance, including the president's cabinet, the senate majority and minority whip, the speaker of the house and the top leaders from all federal intelligence agencies. Natasha was outranked by most everyone in the room. Even so, she watched the spectacle before her, relishing the moment. Despite the protection the room provided its current occupants from an external attack, fear and confusion was running rampant within.

From the Homeland Security briefing she attended earlier that morning, Natasha knew the terrorist attack was the first ever to target the production and delivery of oil and gas. The possibility of an attack had been an increasing concern for a decade, considering the United States boasted more than two million miles of domestic pipeline that crisscrossed the country. Unfortunately, the responsible federal agencies never properly protected the pipelines and terrorists finally exploited that mistake to inflict a massive disruption to the oil and gas industry.

The attack occurred precisely at four o'clock in the afternoon. Within seconds, multiple sections of the country's oil and gas distribution network exploded into nothingness. The resulting damage transformed areas of the country into a war zone. Flames rocketed into the air in massive columns from the pipes that carried natural gas, while seas of flowing flames spilt across the landscape from those that carried oil. Brownish, black smoke bellowed forth in all directions, covering everything below in an acrid haze. At the various detonation sites, the smoke was so thick, fire crews were fighting the fires blind. Not even the rays of the sun could penetrate the shroud of chaos.

The face of President Harrison filled the large video monitor along the main wall of the room, bringing everyone to attention. As far as Natasha could determine, no one in attendance knew the president's location. Hours earlier, in a frenzied escape from the White House, the Secret Service had moved the president to a protected and secure facility.

Still, a part of her wished he was present with them. Then he also would be able to experience the chaos around her. The chaos of incompetency spawned by a power structure of career politicians who had no clue how to effectively lead others in a time of crisis.

Natasha studied the face of the president, noting the lines of concern etched deep into the man's face. She always desired the power he possessed and that fed her attraction to him. But at the moment, the president appeared anything but powerful. He reminded her now of a man defeated.

The president's normally styled salt and pepper hair was unkempt and showed the reality of his thinning scalp. Deep brown, sorrowful eyes peered from under furled brows and pale skin. It was obvious to Natasha, the president had been shaken emotionally and politically. He was a man who believed in diplomacy. In his ability to pacify the enemies of state through political maneuvering. In the levels and levels of bureaucracy and regulation that were supposed to prevent attacks like this from ever happening. But in a heartbeat, all of his beliefs were proven wrong. He was now a man who feared for the future, for himself, and for his country.

"What do you have for me, Gus?" the president asked, the tension in his voice evident as it blasted from speakers flanking the monitor.

"Just the key points, Mr. President," said a man dressed in a white button-down shirt sitting next to a group of worried-looking leaders in military uniforms. Before today, Natasha had never met Gus Winkler, but heard a great deal about the secretary of defense. He possessed no direct military experience, but was considered an academic expert on military strategy. He was the type of person that people either really liked or could not stand to be around. Her opinion of the man was still to be determined.

She noticed Gus' bloodshot eyes, magnified through the coke bottle lenses of his glasses. He probably hadn't slept since the attack occurred. She guessed that most of the people in the room were in a similar condition.

"Every major artery of the U.S. oil pipeline has been hit," Gus explained. "Computer hackers targeted the pipeline controls, overriding the safety systems and causing the pipelines to over-pressurize. Both natural gas and oil supplies have been disrupted indefinitely across the country. In spite of this, we have been successful in isolating the damaged areas and fire containment actions are underway."

"What about our refineries?" the president

asked.

"Our three largest refineries suffered significant damage from secondary collateral caused by the original explosions. The total damage and timing to get the refineries operational is still being assessed."

"Casualties?"

"About five hundred," Gus said, the number rolling off his tongue emotionlessly. "Most of them refinery workers and first responders. Fortunately, the explosions occurred in less populated areas where the pipeline was above ground, minimizing the number of deaths."

"Has anyone claimed responsibility?"

The secretary of defense looked around the room, hesitating. "Thereon is claiming they did it. And minutes ago, we were able to confirm this through our intelligence sources." The deep scowl on the president's face told them everything they needed to know. He was furious.

Natasha was not surprised by this reaction. In the past month, most of the internal resources of the CIA, FBI, and NSA were now rerouted to address and mitigate the looming threat posed by Thereon. Countless tax dollars spent and still Thereon was able to strike.

"My last question..." the president said, his words measured, but his anger clearly present. "Was the intelligence from the CIA wrong? Was this the attack we should have been focused on instead of a nuclear threat?"

"Mr. President," Bill Rogers spoke up, not bothering to identify himself. Natasha knew that he and the president were old friends, sharing a friendship dating back to their years at the Naval Academy.

"Yes, Bill," the president responded, leveling an icy stare at the director. "I trust you have a response?" the president asked.

The president was not giving any hint of their longtime friendship, Natasha thought. This was strictly business.

Bill paused, "We had no indications an attack of this nature was coming."

"What about Operation Kick-off? You must have known something like this could occur?"

"Sir, I repeat we had no indications that this attack was imminent."

"For Pete's sake!" President Harrison's anger erupted to fill the room. "You call yourself an intelligence agency!?!?" There was a long pause. "Do any of you think you have done a good job? Our country has been attacked because we all have failed. Every single one of us!" The president's accusation was met by quiet blank stares.

The president's voice broke through the silence, igniting the room into action. "I want answers now!"

Instantly, the room erupted into a multitude of voices, each trying to rise to the top. An argument broke out among the Joint Chiefs seated to Natasha's left. A man in a dull green military uniform, brandishing a breastplate of metals rose from the table and headed towards the exit door, a stream of curse words left in his wake. The scene was much the same in the other areas of the room. Natasha experienced this same situation before during her own agency's shake up several months ago. People shifting blame to others to cover their own inadequacies. It was the standard practice for Washington's elite, deny everything and do anything you could to deflect responsibility from yourself.

Natasha felt a familiar feeling of peace settle around her as she watched the chaos. Soft whispers entered her mind, buoying her confidence with subtle strokes of approval. She concentrated on the whispers. They sustained her through her divorce and other difficult times. She learned to trust the whispers, and on occasion, the clear commands that they would issue forth. Now was one of those times. The whispers were telling her to speak.

Natasha rose from her seat and walked directly towards the center table. She ignored the surprised expression of all those seated at the table as she deftly grabbed the speakerphone.

In that instant, time seemed to come to a standstill for Natasha. Every detail of her environment seemed to shine, imprinting itself on her memory. The white stubble on the president's cheek. The coffee stain on the left corner of the blue shirt worn by Bill Rogers. The incredulous look on the face of Gus Winkler. She saw everything at once, but wasn't sure how that was possible. What amazed her even more was what she did next.

"Mr. President, I have an answer." Natasha's voice broke through the mayhem as it reverberated through the speakers. The loud murmur in the room quickly subsided as everyone turned their attention to this new development. As Natasha scanned the leaders in front of her, surprised stares echoed back in curious contempt.

"Please identify yourself," the president demanded.

Natasha took a deep breath. This was her chance. With a slight smile breaking her lips, she confidently responded, "Sir, my name is Natasha Ellington, Deputy Secretary of Homeland Security. I know the solution to our problem."

CHAPTER 35

Hesitantly, the president acknowledged her, "Ms. Ellington, you have the floor."

Natasha took another deep breath. She knew she was committing political suicide, but she felt compelled to speak from deep within, as if controlled by an unseen force. She softly cleared her throat before speaking.

"Sir, it makes no sense to have an agency focused on foreign intelligence gathering to be leading an operation dealing with a domestic threat of this magnitude. The CIA is not equipped nor does it possess the resources to execute domestic counterintelligence effectively. Given this current state of emergency, I propose you place all federal intelligence and protection agencies, including the domestic operations of our military, under the authority of the Department of Homeland Security."

She knew it was a bold accusation she delivered against the CIA and an even bolder grab for power. There was a brief period of silence before an explosion of voices drowned out the room in deafening noise. Bill Rogers was on his feet, his arms reaching towards the Secretary of Homeland Security as if he intended to choke the life from him. Gus Winkler grabbed the speakerphone from Natasha grasp, throwing it on to the table before giving her a look of pure disdain. All around her, voices rose up in protest. What Natasha just proposed was unthinkable.

The president's voice broke through the chaos. "Quiet! Quiet all of you! I want everybody to settle down."

President Harrison continued, eyeing Natasha wearily. "Ms. Ellington. Give me one reason why I should take your request seriously."

Natasha picked up the speakerphone, ignoring the hateful expressions of those around her. "I will give you three, Mr. President." She paused intentionally, not sure what she was going to say. She had the full undivided attention of everyone in the room. A feeling of control pulsed through her. It was one thing to be the center of attention at a party. To be the center of attention among the highest seat of power in the country created a feeling in her that she could only describe as lust.

She hadn't rehearsed this moment. She didn't even know what she was going to say. The words came to her lips as if put there by someone else. "Reason number one. The DHS has the most extensive intelligence network of any fed-

THE OTHER SIDE

eral agency covering every corporation, every organization, and every citizen." This was a true statement. The Patriot Act and other successive acts aimed at curbing domestic terrorism provided the DHS with unprecedented access into the communications of American citizens. DHS also managed the largest network of domestic operatives of any federal agency, most of them undercover.

Natasha confidence grew as she spoke. "Reason number two. By previous executive order, we are the only agency authorized to take over all forms of communication during a national emergency. That includes all land, cellular, and internet-based systems. We also possess the only technology capable of scanning all these systems for suspicious communications." She noticed several people nod in agreement, apparently warming to her suggestion.

She paused deliberately. It all hinged on her next words. "The final reason and the one that is most concerning to me as an American citizen and a servant of the United States government," she paused again, for maximum effect. "I believe Operation Kick-off has been compromised by the very agent we are depending on to execute it. I have evidence that Agent Riley O'Connor has violated federal law in the recruitment of operatives and falsified official documents associated with those operatives on his team. I have further evidence that O'Connor's team is purposefully withholding information from federal agencies, including the CIA, relating to the direct nature of the threat against the United States. For what purpose he is doing this, I do not know."

Murmurs arose all around her. "This accusation is insane!" Bill Roger's barked, his face turning a shade of crimson red normally reserved for a root vegetable. "Do not listen to this rubbish!" He turned his eyes in contempt at Natasha, scalding her with the intensity of his stare. She ignored him, he was of no consequence at this point.

An odd hush settled on the room as Natasha and those awaited the response of the president. She was beginning to have doubts she was doing the right thing. She didn't really have any evidence against O'Connor, only theories and conjectures. If she were challenged on her accusation, all would be lost.

After a long moment of reflection, the president spoke. His words carried a tone of certainty that resonated loudly through the silent chamber. "By the authority of the office of the President of the United States and by the powers granted to me by the United States Constitution during a state of emergency, I am temporarily transferring power of all federal agencies including the federal military deployed in the United States, under the power of the Department of Homeland Security."

There was a collective gasp from the room.

THE OTHER SIDE

The president continued, "Effective immediately, I am also creating a new cabinet position to oversee the Department of Homeland Security and all other federal protective and investigative agencies. All existing agency directors will now report to the new cabinet secretary."

After a stunned moment of silence blanketed the room, Gus Winkler took the speaker phone from Natasha's grasp. She let it go without a fight.

"Ah...ah...Mr. President...this is quite a lot to digest. I am a little at a loss for words," his voice cracked as he babbled. "You never said...ah... you never mentioned what the title of this new position is. Nor did you mention the person who will hold it." There was a hopeful ring in the secretary's last words.

"Gus, you idiot! I am appointing the only person that appears capable of handling the position and saving us from further attack." The next words from the president sent Natasha's mind reeling. She struggled to make sense of it. She couldn't. Nothing made sense. The words resonated in her mind, forcing their way through her conscience, transforming into realization what was once an inconceivable thought. "I would like you all to congratulate the new Secretary of Domestic Defense, Natasha Ellington."

CHAPTER 36

The rain continued its relentless attempt to penetrate the large window near their table, altering the view beyond into a maze of colors and blurs. Even so, Riley stared through the window, lost in deep thought. It was the third day in a row of rain with more rain expected through the weekend. The impending forecast only served to intensify his already downcast mood.

The air conditioning system wasn't working well in the small Italian café either, evidenced by the humidity that could not only be seen, but uncomfortably felt. Large patches of condensation formed on the inside of the window in random patterns, occasionally merging into large droplets that streaked down the glass like tears. It was fitting for how Riley felt at the moment. Depression had him in its clutches with no chance for escape.

Riley was particularly discouraged by recent developments involving Natasha. It amazed him how fast Natasha established her power base across the consolidated federal agencies. The powers of evil were definitely at work, supporting her efforts to turn the federal government upside down.

Immediately after assuming control, Natasha fired every senior leader of each federal agency and replaced them with complete unknown appointees. There was one exception, Natasha chose to retain Branson Schaeffer and promote him to the Director of the CIA. Riley's feelings were mixed about Branson's appointment. Branson lacked the experience for the position, but at least Riley knew who he would be dealing with. Still, what Natasha did to his friends and colleagues was inexcusable.

Bill Rogers was devastated by the news of his dismissal. His life focus to protect the country was wrenched from him in a measure of heartbeats. Riley knew Bill's frustration at the situation was deeper, spawned by the betrayal of a life-long friend whom he trusted. The president turned on him and the entire country. Aggravating the matter, complaints about Natasha's austere actions from members of Congress and the Supreme Court had fallen on the president's deaf ears. The president's actions made no sense to Riley. None at all.

"It would be nice to see the sun again," Frank grumbled, breaking the lull that settled on their conversation.

Riley agreed. The darkness appeared to be winning over the light on most fronts these days. He studied the weary face of the detective. "I see you have been sleeping as well as I have," Riley said, trying to add a little humor into his voice.

"Sleep?" Frank huffed, filling his cup from the carafe on the table. "Only on Sunday." He easily drained the cup of steaming coffee, his third in less than fifteen minutes.

"Well, I appreciate the offer of lunch," Riley said sincerely. "I needed a distraction today." He liked Frank. Riley was beginning to understand him at a deeper level. Like everyone else, Frank had his own demons, but Riley knew he was a good man at heart.

"I figured you might need a little company," Frank winked at Riley. "A good detective does his homework."

"So he does," Riley said, smiling for the first time in days. Frank's comment, though simple, was significant. Today, he and Charlotte would have celebrated their 25th anniversary. He missed her so much the thought brought tears to his eyes. *Why God did you take my life partner?* It was a question he often asked himself. He knew it came down to a simple truth. God worked in ways Riley couldn't even began to grasp.

"Oh, I almost forgot," Frank said, reaching into a brown satchel at his feet and removing an envelope. "I brought those autopsy files you re-

THE OTHER SIDE

quested."

"Good. It will give me something to do," Riley replied sourly, reaching out and taking the envelope from Frank.

"I can't believe Natasha cancelled Operation Kick-Off!" Frank exclaimed, catching Riley's mood. "I bet you were pissed."

"Pissed would be a mild description," Riley commented, biting his tongue. He was furious. "It doesn't help that she also launched a formal investigation into my activities under suspicion of treason."

"What are you going to do?" Frank asked.

"I may not be officially on the case, but that doesn't mean I don't have a mission," Riley stated defiantly. "Thereon must be stopped and I have only two weeks left before the season opening football games. We both know the country won't survive another attack like this last one, particularly if it is nuclear."

Frank nodded in agreement. In the aftermath of the attack, fear was running rampant through the general population. The damage to the oil and gas pipeline infrastructure was significant. Within days, the country's gasoline reserves were drained, bringing interstate trade to a complete halt. Without the ability to be replenished, grocery stores were now empty and crime was exploding in response. The National Guard was deployed in every major city and given full authorization to use deadly force to control civil unrest.

Thinking about their current situation brought to Riley's mind an even more troubling scenario. Under such circumstances, Natasha would have every justification to implement even more drastic measures of control in the interest of national safety. The notion of the United States of America being transformed into a police state was more than a conspiracy theory, it was a certifiable possibility. The power she was yielding was frightening.

"Well, I may have an opportunity for you and the unique skills of your team," Frank said, a slight grin on his face. "I asked an analyst to scour Pastor Jessup's recorded sermons for comments made about his personal life and other clues to who he really is. I listened to several of the sermons myself," Frank shrugged. "I have to admit, he is an engaging individual."

"Any developments?" Riley asked, expecting the worst.

"Turns out, Pastor Jessup made several references to his earlier life...growing up on a farm in Iowa...graduating from a small rural bible college in Texas...being a widower at the age of thirty to his wife whom he met in college. All random stuff that sounds legitimate, but none of his statements can be proven. I think it's a massive web of deception."

"Can you elaborate?"

"I have a folder this thick of examples back at

the office," Frank said, holding his fingers in the air with an inch of space between them. "How about this? The bible college he attended is now defunct. It closed down twenty years ago. The main administration building was destroyed in a fire shortly after that, destroying all records. Hence, no way to prove he attended or not."

"Ok. Give me another," Riley said, chalking the first example up to coincidence.

"The pastor stated that he used the proceeds of a family insurance policy to start Summit of Light. The first income tax filing of the church listed their assets north of five million." Frank shook his head and let a laugh escape. "Anyway, insurance providers are required to report all payments to the IRS. There is no record of a payment to Anthony Jessup or anyone with a similar name." Now Frank laughed heartily, "It's all a scam. I went back five years from the first IRS filing just to be safe. Zilch!"

Riley nodded slowly. "That is very interesting. What about their financial dealings? Did you discover anything that might tie them to Thereon?"

"Nothing as tight as the monetary transfers, but there are some interesting coincidences." Frank filled himself another cup of coffee and waived the empty carafe at a passing waitress. "For example, the internet service provider utilized by Summit of Light is also the same one used by Thereon."

"So what?" Riley remarked, not really impressed with the detective's revelation. "There are lots of terror organizations who have legitimate accounts with internet providers all over the world."

"Yes, I agree. But how many terrorist organizations and churches have accounts opened on the same day and immediately after each other. We have the records with time stamps to prove it."

Riley stared at the detective in deep thought. There was definitely a pattern developing between Thereon and Summit of Light, but he needed more information. "What else can you tell me?"

"Remember Cooper Williams? He was the vice president who went loco at his investment firm a few months back." Frank twirled his fingers in a circle next to his head for emphasis. "It turns out that he handled a financial transaction for Summit of Light the week before his death. He placed a large short position against his own company, which is highly unusual. When the stock price dropped after the news of the shooting, Summit of Light raked in millions."

"That can't be coincidental," Riley acknowledged. He shook his head partly from disbelief, but mostly from disgust.

"This last tidbit is perhaps the most intriguing," Frank said, his lips pursed. "The only reported description of Mohammad Shakim

THE OTHER SIDE

Abdul appears to match the description of a key leader of the church."

"Which one?"

"The only one that matters..."

"Pastor Jessup?!?" Riley responded with shock. The coincidences Frank relayed were painting an intriguing story. Still, there was no tangible proof that Summit of Light and Thereon were working together. Even a financial exchange between the two organizations did not constitute conspiratorial behavior.

"You and your team have done a great job, but we are still no closer to figuring this whole thing out," Riley sighed, his frustration entering back into his voice. He needed a solid lead on this case and time was running out.

He stared out the window for a moment before turning back to Frank. "What about this opportunity you mentioned?"

"We have learned there is a construction project underway at the corporate headquarters of the church," Frank said, leaning in toward Riley. "With a few phone calls to our local office and a little luck, I believe I can get a few members of your team inside."

"Really?" Riley jumped at the news. "That is exactly what we need!"

Frank's face was beaming. He knew he was providing Riley with the one thing Riley so sorely needed. Hope.

Riley turned his gaze toward the window

once again, his mind racing around the detective's proposition. His mood began to brighten the more he thought about it. A burst of heavy rain battered the window in protest, perhaps an omen to what was to come. Even so, Riley perceived there would be a clearing ahead and the sun would return. The light of the world would rise again.

CHAPTER 37

Noah flew upward, propelling himself away from the explosion. He knew he was dreaming again. It was the same dream as before and he knew the outcome. The fire would consume him as it always did. There must be another way to escape, he thought frantically.

Moments before he was engulfed by the inferno, he willed himself away from the fire. He didn't have a specific destination, only that he would end up someplace far away from this nightmare.

Since his first lucid dream experience, his ability to control his dreams was developing quickly. He was now quite adept at creating dream realities and bending those realities to his will. When in a dream state, Noah was much like an artist with a blank canvas. If he could imagine it, he could create it.

Instantly, Noah found himself floating in darkness. There was no sound, no color. There was nothing. The world around him was empty. *Where was he?* He quickly reviewed the dream triggers he memorized to validate his lucid state. He was still lucid dreaming, but this was unlike any dream he experienced. He never dreamt of nothingness.

He willed the darkness to turn to light, but nothing happened. He willed himself to be on a tropical beach, with bright sunlight bathing him in warmth, yet nothing changed around him. The darkness remained.

This is odd, Noah thought. He mulled over the possibilities in his head. Though he was relieved he hadn't been destroyed in the fireball of a nuclear explosion, he was becoming very concerned with his current predicament. His dream was not responding and that was making him nervous.

He concentrated on waking up, willing the dream around him to dissolve, but still nothing happened. Doubt began to enter his mind. What if he couldn't wake himself up from this dream? Worse, what if this wasn't a dream and he was awake? *Where am I?*

His thought became a scream. "Where am I?!?" he yelled, beginning to glide through the darkness looking for an escape.

"Hello Noah." A voice permeated the darkness, feminine and sultry, beckoning to him.

"Who's there?" Noah shouted, coming to a halt. The darkness around him seemed to inten-

THE OTHER SIDE

sify, smothering him in silence.

Noah suddenly felt fingertips run gently down his back. His body pulsed with energy in response. He swatted at the space around him wildly, hoping to scare away whatever was there.

"What a surprise to see you here," the voice said, sounding at once far away and in his head at the same time. "You are indeed powerful to cross on your own."

"What are you talking about?" Noah replied. He began swimming through the darkness away from the voice. Instinctively he knew he needed to get away.

"Few have been able to do what you do," the voice replied curiously. "Enoch...Isaiah...Ezekiel. They were chosen by the Almighty to come here, but you are a surprise. You are not even a believer...*so* how are you able to do it?" The voice was strangely subdued, as if the question was more of a test.

Noah ignored the question, continuing to swim through the nothingness, seeking a way to escape. The thought occurred to him that if he remained silent, whatever it was wouldn't be able to find him in the darkness.

"You can't hide from me, young dreamer. Not in this place...this is my realm...the spiritual world," the voice drifted off.

Noah froze. *That couldn't be possible.* "Who are you?" Noah demanded of the darkness realizing this impossibility. He must be dreaming.

"I am your fantasy," the voice teased. "I am the one who can make all your dreams come true." Fingertips caressed his groin, causing him to flinch in response. "I know what you want. I know what you desire." Light erupted in front of Noah. Jessica stood before him. She was wearing a tight fitting white dress. Her hair and makeup was styled in a manner that Noah had never seen. She looked amazing. Instantly, she was gone and the darkness returned.

"I don't understand. Where am I?" Noah demanded.

"Wherever you want to be," the voice laughed. "Whoever you want to be, with whoever you want." There was another flash of light. Only this time, Marie appeared before him, wearing the same white dress. Then she disappeared just as quickly as Jessica.

"I can make you feel anything and control your every emotion..." the voice trailed only to return with a deafening roar. "DESPAIR!!!!" Noah recoiled into a ball, the pain, the hurt, the rejection was crushing.

"ANGER!!!!" Instantly, the pain was replaced with seething rage. Noah didn't know why he was angry, only that he was furious. He wanted blood. He wanted vengeance. He wanted destruction.

"LUST!!!!" The anger disappeared, replaced by the most intense feeling of desire he ever ex-

THE OTHER SIDE

perienced. It was like a fire burning within him, threatening to consume him if it did not have an outlet.

Noah felt the unmistakable sensation of lips kissing his. He jerked his head forward, searching for more. His desire was so strong. Then it was gone, as quickly as it had come.

Suddenly, the familiar feelings that plagued him through life took on an unbearable intensity. Weakness. Powerlessness. Despair. *What was happening to him?*

"Come with me, young oracle," the voice tempted. "Give into your pain. Give into your rage. Give into your desire. I can give you everything."

"Leave me alone!" Noah screamed at the darkness. This was a bad dream. That was all it was, he told himself. Nothing but a bad dream.

Noah felt the soft caress of a hand across his cheek, only this time, it lingered and moved down his chest toward his midsection. He tried to push it away but there was nothing there. He squirmed in the air, trying to flee from whatever it was.

"Give into me Noah. I can save you from all your fears."

"Get away from me!!!" Noah cried, smashing at the darkness with his fists, hoping desperately to beat his tormenter away.

The bolt of pain that rippled through his body stopped him instantly. Claws, like daggers, began to pierce him, cutting into his flesh. Noah screamed into the darkness.

The claws were all over him; tiny razors striking his body, inflicting pain everywhere.

"I can take the pain away," the voice bellowed above his screams. "I can replace it with pleasure." Instantly, an overwhelming sensation of pure ecstasy pulsated through Noah's body. It was indescribable. He wanted to relish the feeling. He never wanted it to end.

Within a heartbeat, the pain returned, rolling down his torso and legs. His body exploded into a raging inferno of burning agony. Noah screamed again before falling silent. His mind lapsing into a state of shock. There was no thought. There was only pain.

"Give into me Noah..." the voice demanded. "Give me your soul!"

"Stop! Please!!!" Noah pleaded into the darkness. He didn't even hear his next scream as he felt his flesh being torn off his body, one strip at a time. He wanted to die. Anything to stop the torturous pain. It was then Noah did something he never, ever did. He began to pray.

It was a simple prayer, a simple request from the heart, but he prayed with all the intensity he could muster. "Jesus, please save me! I know I don't deserve it. I know I have done wrong against you. But, I believe in you and I need you. Please save me!!!"

In the distance, a bright light appeared, but

THE OTHER SIDE

it was only a spec on a canvas of total blackness. Seconds later, the light expanded and deepened in intensity. Noah felt the light calling to him, but he couldn't focus on it. The pain was too great. He felt the claws dig deep into his flesh. Where they touched, fire spread through his veins. He felt his energy dissipating as if the claws were draining him of life. The fear of death began to grow within Noah.

Suddenly, the pain subsided, not completely, but enough to allow Noah a measure of relief. Noah opened his eyes and shut them just as quickly. The light around him was blinding. Warmth suddenly enveloped him, encompassing him in comfort. Noah opened his eyes again, only this time slowly, allowing his eyes to adjust. Noah's heart leaped. Floating before him was the most captivating being he had ever seen.

The being held in his hands a flaming sword, battling back the darkness with each slash, beating it away. Noah felt the claws release their grip on him and slowly slide from his body. The pain finally disappeared as the darkness receded completely. Only the searing bright light remained.

A voice booming with authority filled the space, "I was delayed in getting to you, my young dreamer. The forces are strong that seek to harm you."

Noah was too weak to respond, being so close to giving up, so close to death.

"I am the angel Michael, commander of the Almighty's army. Your prayer has been heard." A burning coal appeared in the angel's hand. It was deep crimson, the color of blood on fire. "If you truly wish to be saved, you must be exposed to the truth of who you are." The angel extended the coal towards Noah.

Hesitantly, Noah reached forward and took the coal in his hand. Instantly, a shockwave exploded within Noah, expanding through every inch of his body. It was like a bolt of electricity blazing a path through his veins. His entire body quivered in the intensity of the experience.

Immediately, Noah realized total clarity about himself. He traversed the currents of his own sorrow, swollen over the years into a raging river that he could not control. He stood at the base of the massive dam he built to harbor the pain of his past. And he came face to face with the molten anger that coursed within him. Anger at himself, so deep and so raw, driven by his failure and his fear.

For the first time, he understood his true nature, his sinful condition. So vile, so deep, and far reaching. He felt there was no hope as he thrashed against the wrenching inside his chest, an intense pain searing from his stomach to his heart. In its wake, there was only emptiness. Like someone bored a hole straight through him.

At almost the same moment, he experienced all the times when God was beside him. Helping him. Supporting him. Comforting him from his troubles, even though Noah never acknowledged His existence. God had always been there and Noah had been blind to it all. The enormity of God's love for him was overwhelming.

A voice filled his head, booming with authority. "For this is how God loves you. He gave His Son, Jesus Christ, to die for your sins so that you may have forgiveness. If you believe in him, and accept his gift of salvation, you will not perish but have eternal life." Michael placed his arm firmly on Noah's shoulder. "Do you accept God's gift?"

Suddenly, it all made sense to Noah. He understood who Jesus is and the purpose of His sacrifice for humanity. Noah no longer held doubt. There was no reason to resist what he knew was the truth. In that instant, Noah surrendered. "Yes!!! I accept Jesus Christ as my savior and his sacrifice for my sins."

Immediately, Noah felt an onrush of the most intense feelings of love and joy the he ever experienced. Every fiber of his body felt alive with energy and warmth. More than anything he ever wanted before, Noah wanted more of God.

Seconds later, Noah awoke to darkness. *Oh no,* he thought. *I'm still trapped!* It took a moment for his disorientation to clear and for him to realize he was back in his bedroom. He turned to look at his alarm clock, a sense of peace cascaded over him as he did. The soft red glow of the numbers told him everything he needed to know. It was 3:16 in the morning.

CHAPTER 38

"You have to believe me!" Noah pleaded, his voice straining with emotion. "I thought I was going to die. That thing...what it did...it was horrible!" Noah removed his book on lucid dreaming from his back pocket. The cover was worn and the spine was lined with deep white creases, evidence of the frequency it was read. "I'm done with this dreaming stuff." He tossed the book onto the coffee table. "Totally done! It was terrifying." Noah crossed his arms and shivered visibly, recalling a memory of his encounter.

Riley peered intently at Noah. The heartbeat, the breathing, and the alertness of Noah's eyes told Riley that Noah was telling the truth. He studied Noah a few moments longer. There was an unmistakable energy within Noah that didn't exist before. It was the energy of the Holy Spirit. Riley smiled inwardly. The Lord answered yet another prayer.

"Hey, what's going on?" Stephen asked,

chomping on a powdered donut as he wandered into the room from the kitchen. He stopped mid-bite as a stream of knowledge hit him. "No way! Really? I want to hear about this."

Over the course of the next thirty minutes, Noah relayed his experience in vivid detail. Both Riley and Stephen listened attentively, mesmerized by Noah's account. Riley didn't need his powers to know Noah was traumatized and emotionally exhausted from his experience.

"That is really some story," Stephen finally responded, picking up the book from the table where Noah left it.

"Stay away from that, Solly," Noah instructed, shivering again. "Trust me."

"Ok, Noah. I know you had a rough evening," Riley comforted. "But, I believe I can help us understand why this happened."

Noah nodded, but remained silent while Stephen began thumbing through the book.

"The Apostle Paul references an experience where he visited the spirit realm," Riley continued. "By his own account, Paul could not be sure if he glimpsed Heaven in his physical body or during a dream. We can't be sure what happened to Noah either. But in either case, I believe Noah crossed into the spiritual realm while dreaming, just like Paul."

"That makes sense, Riley!" Noah said, getting excited. "That demoness told me very few had been able to do what I did."

"But how is that possible?" Stephen asked.

"Have you ever asked yourself why we dream?" Riley's question lingered in the air.

Noah started laughing. "I ask myself that every day."

"Granted, you are a unique case, Noah," Riley acknowledged, trying not to chuckle. "I ask the question more from a perspective of general human understanding. Why do you think God gave us the ability to dream?"

"Scientific theory states it is so our brains can process and sort through all the information and experiences we encounter," Stephen offered before pausing reflectively. A moment later adding, "Dreaming was my escape before I was healed. During that time, my world made more sense in my dreams than it did in reality. And dreams were where I found my freedom to live."

"It is an interesting paradox," Riley offered. "How could something be one man's curse and another's man's blessing?"

Both Noah and Stephen stared at each other, neither one knowing the answer.

"Have either of you ever experienced a dream that was so intense that when you wake up, you still feel the emotions of your dream?" Riley asked his question, already knowing the answer.

Both Noah and Stephen nodded in agreement.

"How do you explain that? Why are we emotionally connected to our dreams?"

Stephen focused on Riley's question and answered, "We have body, mind, and spirit: the three elements of humanity. Emotions occur in response to a specific stimuli from one of those elements. For example, a physical stimuli such as a noise can generate the emotion of fear. A mental stimuli like doubt can create the emotion of worry. When I dream, I have physical and mental experiences that my brain processes, just like it does when I am awake. That means my emotions can still be stimulated."

Riley considered Stephen's explanation. "You are correct, you have explained why emotions linger from a dream, but you have not explained the role of the third element, the spirit."

"I think I know," Noah offered. "You once told me our spirit is the exact likeness of our body and mind, only without the physical form. When I dream, I have a sense of my body, I can think and react, but I don't have a physical body. That means my dream self must be like a spirit."

Riley smiled. "That is correct, Noah," he confirmed, pleased with Noah's explanation.

"But this still doesn't explain what happened to Noah," Stephen stated.

"I think it does," Riley asserted. "I believe our consciousness assumes the closest possible form to a spirit when we are dreaming. In rare instances, while in this state, one's consciousness is able to cross into the spiritual plane."

"Is that really possible?" Noah challenged. "Can this happen to anyone?"

"No, I believe God enables this to happen for His purpose only. For example, God gave the prophet Isaiah a vision of Heaven through a dream, so Isaiah could share God's message of redemption. Some fifteen hundred years later, Joseph, the husband of Mary, was visited by an angel in a dream and was told that his wife, a virgin, would give birth to the son of God."

"Isn't the Book of Revelations based on a dream?" Noah interjected.

Riley nodded affirmatively. "Yes, it was written by the Apostle John after he dreamt of visiting Heaven and witnessed the end of the world."

After a few moments of consideration, Noah visibly relaxed. "Thanks Riley. That really helps me understand. Just the same, I hope it never happens again."

Riley was about to respond, when he felt an onrush of information flood his mind.

"Are you all right, Dad?" Stephen said, noticing Riley's momentary disorientation.

Riley nodded. "I am fine son. Just a memory that I didn't know I had."

Stephen frowned. "I am not following. What do you mean?"

"During my last crossing to the spiritual world, the Lord told me He provided me with knowledge I would need to thwart evil. Only the information would be locked away in my psyche, waiting for the right moments to be revealed."

"What is it?" Noah said. "Does it have something to do with what happened to me?

Riley nodded affirmatively. Noah flashed a nervous glance at Stephen, who returned it with an equally nervous glance. They both locked eyes on Riley.

"Noah, I am going to need you to do something that is very dangerous."

Noah swallowed hard. "What?" he asked cautiously.

Riley took a deep breath, choosing his next words wisely. Noah was not going to like what he was about to ask of him. "As crazy as this sounds, I need you to go back into the spiritual realm."

"Back to the edge of hell itself?" Noah exclaimed, a stark look of horror appearing on his face. "Riley, it's not only crazy, it is more like impossible," he argued. "How can you be so sure?"

Riley understood Noah's fear, but knew that there was no other way. "Because Noah, nothing is impossible," Riley replied. "I know this with all my heart, because I also have the gift of faith."

CHAPTER 39

Dallas, Texas

Only one word described the spectacle before him. Majestic. As nervous as he was, Darius was eager to get inside and explore the massive structure. He had been thinking about this moment since Riley informed him he would be infiltrating the headquarters of Summit of Light. Now it was time for his first mission and he didn't want to make any mistakes.

Above him, twin towers rose multiple stories into the blue sky. Each tower reminded him of the Washington Monument, only the ostentatious towers were a collage of brilliant white bricks, deep blue windows and speckled tiles of gold. The towers were connected by a ten story glass building that semi-encircled a lush green courtyard of flowering vegetation, fountains, and gold statues.

The campus was vast, spanning several acres of green fields. A decorative fence made of iron protected the facility on all sides. The fence looked impossible to scale due to the sharp arrowhead protrusions that jutted at odd angles along each section of the twelve-foot barrier.

Darius adjusted the bright yellow badge that hung snugly from his front lapel, winking at Stephen as he did. Stephen wore a similar badge that identified him as a building inspector from the Dallas Department of Public Works. In tandem, he and Stephen fell into line behind a crew of uniformed construction workers dressed in work boots, blue overalls, and bright orange hard hats. A trio of security guards wearily eyed them as they walked through the main gate, but let them pass without any challenge.

Once inside the campus grounds, they followed the crew into the lobby of the nearest tower and quickly separated themselves by ducking into a nearby alcove.

"Ok, where to now?" Darius asked, peeking around the corner to make sure they were not being pursued.

"Just follow me," Stephen directed.

With Stephen in the lead, they navigated the main corridors of the complex as if Stephen had worked in the building for years. Eventually, they stopped outside an elevator that ran along the exterior of one of the towers. The walls of the elevator were made of glass, exposing the

THE OTHER SIDE

countryside around the building.

"You ready for this? Stephen asked, his face expressing genuine concern. Darius ignored him and tried to stare at the floor. He hated elevators. He never told a soul he was afraid of heights, yet Stephen knew.

"Let's get this over," Darius replied, stepping into the elevator.

Stephen entered a code into the keypad on the side of the elevator and pressed the button for the twentieth floor. Darius wasn't sure if it was the rapid ascension or the view of the ground disappearing below his feet, but he felt his stomach clench in fear. He shuffled backward against the elevator door and closed his eyes. It would be over soon.

The elevator doors opened to reveal a large, richly-decorated lobby. Elaborate white drapes framed large glass windows on either side. In the center of the room, on a large pedestal, rotated a six-foot replica of the church emblem. Darius studied the emblem, admiring the craftsmanship of the jade sculpture. A crucifix of white jade partially covered the face of a larger crucifix made of green jade. A third larger crucifix made of black jade was behind the other two, giving the impression of a three dimensional cross. The only thing that didn't make sense to Darius was that the white and green crucifixes were truncated at the top, so only the black crucifix was complete.

"Three arms face east, three arms face west and the center is facing forward, for a total of seven," Stephen said, noting Darius's frown of confusion. "Seven is God's number of completion."

"May I help you?" a voice asked from across the room. Darius and Stephen looked toward the far wall to find a woman sitting behind an immaculate glass desk, eyeing the two of them cautiously. Behind her, glass doors lay closed, barring entry to the rest of the floor. She quickly rose from her chair, apparently surprised by their unannounced visit.

"Is that nuisance fire alarm still giving you trouble in the conference room?" Stephen said, casually advancing toward the woman. Darius followed, not sure what Stephen was doing.

The woman looked surprised by the question, but quickly regained her composure. She smiled, but sternly inquired, "I'm sorry, what are you doing here?"

"Barry Waters from Public Works," Stephen stated with authority. "We are performing an inspection of the construction in the South Tower. My boss asked if I would check on the fire alarm while I was here. Is it still giving you trouble?"

"As a matter of fact, it is. It goes off at the most random times. Even the contractor who installed it, can't determine why." The woman stepped back, giving Stephen an appraising eye. "You look a lot younger than the guy who was

THE OTHER SIDE

here before."

"I am. That is why Marcus sent me. I'm his apprentice," Stephen said, pointing his thumb at his chest and doing his best to sound prideful. "Marcus threw his back out and can't use a ladder."

The women stared at Stephen skeptically. "Well Marcus knows I have strict protocols with visitors, regardless of the situation. You will have to schedule an appointment and come back later."

"But I have good news for you." Stephen said, feigning disappointment.

"You do?" the woman said wearily.

"Marcus gave me instructions on how to fix the alarm. I just need to get to the conference room." The women's expression became pensive. "It won't take long, I promise," Stephen assured, flipping through his clipboard, pretending to look at his notes. "We need to inspect the cabling from the alarm panel to the conference room. That will mean we may need to access the ceiling in a couple offices to trace the wiring. Do we have your permission?"

After a long pause, the woman smiled. "If you can help us fix this issue, I guess it is ok to let you do it now." She began typing on a keyboard. "I just informed everyone about the situation."

Stephen nodded appreciably.

"One more thing, you can't be in the conference room from ten to eleven this morning. The leadership team has a meeting at that time."

"Understood," Stephen replied. "Thank you."

A moment later, the woman pressed a button on the desk and the glass doors behind her opened. They were in.

That was easy enough, Darius thought as they walked into the corridor of the executive offices. *Is Marcus a real person? Did he really injure his back?* Stephen smiled as if reading his mind, but did not respond. He didn't have to. Darius shook his head in amazement. What Stephen could do was beyond his ability. Together, they really were a force to reckon with.

The executive floor was outlandishly decorated, reminding Darius of the fanciest casino penthouse suites he enjoyed as a gambler. Crimson colored carpet, an inch thick and soft as silk covered the floors. Each step felt like he was walking on a down blanket. Each wall was ordained with the most unique artwork he had ever seen, some of the paintings spanning the length of the room. This place felt more like a throne room for royalty than a corporate headquarters. He could get used to working in a place like this.

Stephen led them to a door on the left and entered into a room. He turned towards Darius. "Are you coming?"

Reluctantly, Darius pulled his eyes away from a spectacular painting that captured his

THE OTHER SIDE

interest. The painting displayed an angelic being, hands held behind its back as it was escorted by several other angels away from a bright light. The painting was familiar. It took him a moment to remember that, last year, he read a story that this painting had sold for ten million dollars to an undisclosed buyer. He thought it strange someone would spend so much on a painting depicting Satan being cast out of Heaven. It was even stranger that the buyer was the Summit of Light.

He entered the room to find Stephen with his ear pressed against the far wall. "Where are we?" Darius asked, looking around. The room was small and devoid of any furniture except for a small cabinet in the corner.

"This is the supply room for the executive floor," Stephen answered. "The conference room where the leadership team is meeting is on the other side of this wall. Don't worry, it will be safe to hang out here."

"Hang out?" Darius responded skeptically, not liking the implications. "Are you sure? We are as good as dead if someone comes in here?"

"Trust me," Stephen nodded.

"How do you know for sure?" Darius challenged. He hated feeling trapped.

Stephen smiled slightly and shrugged, as if he were embarrassed by the question. "It is hard to describe what happens with my gift. When I focus on a subject. I suddenly know about it. It is not a feeling. It is not intellectual. It is not a guess. It is deeper than that. There are experiences. There are memories. There are impressions. My Dad says it is the same for him, only he doesn't have the ability to use this power on demand. It just comes to him randomly."

Darius decided to back off. He didn't need to read Stephen's mind to know that Stephen believed what he was telling him. "Ok, if you say so."

With a slight groan, Darius settled back against the wall next to Stephen and slid down to a sitting position. If Stephen said they needed to wait. He would wait. And that was just what they did.

CHAPTER 40

FedExField - Landover, Maryland

Perched on a narrow platform situated between two massive banks of halogen lights, Baal and Asherah had a perfect view of the activities occurring below them. A maintenance crew busily prepared the football field, positioning several large rolls of bright green turf into small tracks that crossed the field from left to right.

On the far side of the field, a larger crew of workers was hastily assembling a massive metal stage behind the end-zone. This stage would serve as the primary broadcast studio for the game announcers, commentators, and sports media. With the most anticipated game of the college season only four days away, it was obvious there was still much to do.

"What do you mean the dreamer has been lost?!?" Baal exclaimed, struggling to control his anger at Asherah. Her failure created complications to his plan. Under his influence, the dreamer was supposed to become a servant of the darkness. A tool that they could use to guide them in overthrowing the Almighty.

"It was him, your brother," Asherah hissed. "He broke my bond. He destroyed the stronghold!" Her frustration getting the better of her, she conjured a ball of hellfire and sent it hurling into an adjacent light tower. The fire ball collided with one of the massive floodlights, causing it to shatter in an explosion of smoke and glass. "The Oracle was almost mine!"

"He is not my brother anymore," Baal replied, disdain dripping from his lips. The thought of Michael propelled his anger into hyper-drive. The archangel had foiled his plan yet again. Baal was tempted to follow her lead and throw a fireball of his own.

It wasn't a surprise, Michael was a worthy adversary, Baal's equal in all respects. Through the course of their eons-old battle, Baal thwarted the angel as many times as he himself had been defeated by Michael.

At their creation, Michael truly had been his brother. Formed from the same essence of the Creator to be kindred spirits linked through the ages. The Fall changed everything. Now they were eternally separated because Michael refused to believe Satan's claim that they were captives to the Creator. Baal shook his head in frustration at the memory of that day. He truly longed to be at peace with Michael, to enjoy his company once again. But that was impossible.

"I am sorry I failed you," Asherah finally said, breaking the silence. She sounded remorseful and he believed she was. They both knew what was at stake. They could not afford further setbacks.

"Well at least we don't have the Anointed to deal with anymore," Baal said, his eyes narrowing on the small van that pulled into the far end zone. Even at this distance, the letters imprinted on the side of the van were easy to see, ESPN.

Good, Baal thought. Thereon's henchmen were right on time. He returned his attention back to Asherah. "His team is inexperienced and lacks the fortitude to fight the type of battle we are waging. Losing the dreamer will be of little consequence."

"Sire, you are mistaken," Asherah corrected. "Are you not aware of what has transpired? The Anointed lives."

Baal stepped back in surprise. That was impossible. "What do you mean, he still lives? I witnessed his death with my own eyes."

"I learned it from the mind of the dreamer." Asherah said, obviously surprised Baal was not aware of this development. "He was resurrected by the healer and the truth-seer."

"Hellfire!!!" Baal shouted in rage. This time,

a fireball exploded from his fingertips, greater in intensity than the one Asherah had thrown. Baal watched as the fireball arched high over the far stadium wall and disappeared. He didn't care where the fireball landed or with what it collided. It just felt good to release some of his rage.

Why hadn't he known about the Anointed's resurrection? He forced himself to relax and returned his gaze back to the scene below. A large box was being removed from the van by two of the workers. They moved the box jerkily, as if they had no mind nor care for its contents. "Morons!" Baal spat. "Don't they know what they are handling?"

The men placed the box on the newly-constructed stage, quickly removing its contents and concealing them into the base of a small broadcast tower on the corner of the stage. Their work completed, the men returned to the van. Baal watched the van leave the stadium, following it until it disappeared into a service tunnel.

Perfect, he thought, everything was almost prepared. Almost. Now he just needed to make sure the Anointed would not disrupt his plans. "If the Anointed is still a threat, we must take extra precautions."

"Understood. What are your orders?"

"We cannot afford any further medaling from the Anointed. I will command all those under my control to engage in the hunt for those in the custody of the Anointed. There will be one objective... DEATH."

"What about me?" Asherah pouted. "I want in on the fun."

"I have a very special mission for you," Baal said, taking her hand. "One that you must not fail."

The demoness lowered her head in subjection and curtsied, "Yes, sire. What would you have me do?"

"I need you to spend some time in the human realm in human form."

Asherah perked up instantly, a broad smile on her face. He knew her desire for the physical world was as strong as his. "How delightful! I love breaking the Creator's rules. And why might I be doing this?"

"I need you to become someone," Baal said, walking off the platform into the air. He turned to look at Asherah one more time, studying her. "Someone who is very special." he reflected. A sinister smile expanded across his face. "Someone who has the power to destroy the Anointed." A moment later he was gone.

CHAPTER 41

Washington, D.C.

The grin on the young girl's face was infectious. A combination of surprise, wonder, and pure delight that forced Riley to smile, despite the seriousness of his mood. There were thousands of smiles in the enthusiastic crowd of onlookers. Children and parents alike were lined several yards deep along the gravel path that encircled the National Mall.

The young girl waved ecstatically at the group of Native Americans in full ceremonial dress dancing in rhythmic motion to the beat of drums. Several yards behind them, a trio of cowboys riding black stallions pretended to lasso imaginary cattle between displays of skillful rope tricks.

It was a beautiful morning for the unique parade, authorized by Congress for the purpose of boosting the moral of the public after the recent attack. The sunshine beamed across a cloudless blue sky, balanced by a cool breeze from the west. Riley could feel the small eddies of fall in the wind, miniature whirlwinds made from the essence of what was to come. Another summer was coming to an end in the capital city.

Riley continued to watch the procession pass, scanning the crowd as he lost himself for a moment in the proceedings. The ten museums of the Smithsonian that encircled the National Mall orchestrated the event, each showcasing elements of their exhibits and holdings. At the moment, a robotic triceratops from the Museum of Natural History was trotting down the path, chased by a larger robotic Tyrannosaurus Rex. The crowd responded with louder applause and shouts of surprise and excitement. The audience was getting quite the show. Riley was enjoying the distraction as well.

He noticed Frank, dressed in a dark suit and a bright blue tie, making his way towards him. The detective looked uncomfortable in his attire as he navigated through the maze of onlookers seated on the hill. Some men were built to wear a suit. Frank was not one of them.

"I didn't expect there to be a parade today, otherwise I would have recommended we meet across the river," Frank said, casually eyeing the Tyrannosaurus Rex. "Someone might get eaten around here," he added in a serious tone.

"It is all good," Riley replied casually. "I have been enjoying the entertainment." He squinted at Frank, "Nice suit. Did you just come from a job interview or a funeral?"

Frank huffed, "Neither, though either option is preferable to my reality. The Empress has implemented a dress code requirement for all active agents. She is over the top."

"The Empress!" Riley chuckled. "That name fits Natasha very well." Since assuming her new position, Natasha bullied, ordered, threatened, and even punished any who opposed her. She had become one of the most hated people in the federal government virtually overnight. "What's happened at the bureau since we spoke last week?"

"Things have settled down a little, but there is still a great deal of confusion in the rank and file. My new director is trying to make an immediate mark by implementing many new policies and a lot of people are getting caught up in the process. Too many good agents have recently resigned as a result."

"Why?"

Frank shrugged, "Natasha and her minions want people they can control. And anybody worth their salt in the agency won't be there for long. Either they are going to be fired or they are going to quit."

"What does that mean for you?" Riley probed, not liking the implications of what heard.

"Early retirement is looking better each day..." Frank paused, loosening the knot of his tie. "That is, if we have a country left. At least the public panic is beginning to subside. Look around us. Two weeks ago, no one would have come to an event like this for fear of another attack."

Riley nodded but was troubled by Frank's comment about retirement. He didn't need his perceptive powers to know that Frank was under extreme pressure. He paused to watch a group of astronauts in a lunar vehicle meander slowly behind a man driving a Model T. So much progress, he thought. So much that could be destroyed. The stakes before them where just too high. He turned to Frank, "What have you heard about the stadium attacks?"

"I wish there was better news to report. The chatter has increased significantly across the foreign intelligence networks in the last few days. Something big is going to happen. The agency is nervous. Really nervous."

"Is Natasha directing the agency to do anything in response?"

Frank furrowed his brow before wiping it again with his handkerchief. "That's what I don't get. The country is still at a state of red alert, yet we have less resources applied to domestic terrorism activity than we did before the pipeline explosions. If anything, Natasha has turned a blind eye to the eminent threat. It's almost as if she wants an attack to happen."

Riley sighed, his suspicions confirmed by Frank's comment. Another wave of applause arose from the crowd as three elephants from the National Zoo passed holding each other's tails with their trunks. For a moment, Riley wished he was in that crowd. A naive citizen, completely unaware of the reality that was crashing down around them. "I think she does want the attack. Either that or she is being controlled by someone who wants the attack to happen."

"If it is any consolation, we still have a team of agents scouring FedExField for a bomb," Frank offered. "But so far they have come up empty."

"Why doesn't the FBI cancel the game?" Riley asked. "It would be a logical thing to do. Isn't governmental action always driven by logic?"

Frank smiled at Riley's vain attempt at humor. "Cute. You know better than I do this is not a clear-cut situation."

"Don't get me wrong," Frank added after loosening the knot of his tie even further. "I believe you and so do many people in high places, but without more concrete evidence, this attack is just a theory. The government is not going to create nationwide panic by canceling the biggest college football game of the opening weekend. People would automatically think our nation was under attack."

THE OTHER SIDE

"We are under attack, Frank!" Riley stated abruptly, trying to contain his frustration. He knew Frank was doing all he could. He just wished he didn't feel so helpless. Time was running out. "So we do nothing and let thousands die?"

"Hey partner, I feel your pain too," Frank said, in an obvious attempt to console Riley.

"I am sorry," Riley offered in apology. "I know you are doing everything you can. Is there anything else the agency can do?"

"Maybe. But it's our Hail Mary play," Frank said, his tone subdued.

"What is it?" Riley pressed.

"I have a plan before the assistant director to authorize a small squad of agents to conduct surveillance on game day. They will be dressed as fans, in school colors, so it will be easy for them to fit in. Hopefully, they can stop anything before it happens."

Riley suffered a mental flash of knowledge. Another of the secrets planted deep in the recesses of his mind sprang to the surface of his consciousness. He grabbed his notepad from his pocket and began to scribble furiously. *How had he missed it?* The situation was more catastrophic than he originally thought. It was such an important clue, but he completely ignored it. *The colors of the uniforms were different in each of Noah's dreams!*

"What's up?' Frank asked, curious about

Riley's abrupt activity.

"Frank, you need to expand your search."

"Expand our search, what do you mean?" Frank replied, obviously confused.

"There is more than one bomb! There is more than one stadium that is going to be attacked."

Frank's mouth dropped at Riley's revelation.

Riley handed Frank the paper. "Those are the colors of the teams that will be playing each other. Match the colors, you match the teams, you find the stadiums that are to be attacked."

"How do you know the..." Frank stopped before finishing his question. Apparently answering his own question, he got up from the bench, preparing to leave. "I will get right on it."

"I'm not done, I have an important favor to ask you," Riley challenged. "Pastor Jessup has a meeting scheduled with the president in two days."

Frank pulled his tie off with a harsh tug and crumbled it in his hand with visible force. "Crap! Are you sure? Did your team uncover this in Dallas?"

Riley nodded, but didn't elaborate. "Frank, I need you to get me inside the White House for that meeting."

"Oh, you're full of demands today, Ace," Frank said as he stifled a laugh. He shoved his tie into his breast pocket and began to work on releasing the buttons of his cuffs. "You know that

THE OTHER SIDE

I have no authority to make something like that happen."

"Trust me Frank, you have to find a way. We are three days away from the season opener. I am convinced that I can stop this attack if I get access to..." Riley stood up, his gaze drawn to a commotion within the crowd below. An astronaut was throwing small colored envelopes into the eager hands of the spectators. For a moment, the crowd parted and that was when he saw her.

She was standing on the other side, slowly enjoying an ice cream cone. She was dressed casually in tight fitting jeans and a light blue T-shirt. Her red hair was held back by a navy blue ribbon, revealing an elegant face accented by high cheekbones. Slowly her gaze shifted to him. Her pale blue eyes locked on his. Then she smiled. There was no mistake, it was her.

"Char..." Riley's voice trailed off. He bounded from the park bench and raced down the hill, leaving Frank fumbling with the buttons of his cuffs.

By the time Riley reached the crowd, it had swollen to a mass of hundreds of people. Everyone vying to get the free exposition tickets being given by the astronaut. He lost his view of the woman as he entered the crowd, though now she was scarcely twenty yards away. Frantically he forced himself through the crowd, not caring who he pushed out of his way. He ignored the shouts of protest and profanity that he left in his wake. As he emerged at the far end, a wave of panic crashed over him. The woman was gone!

"Riley! Riley!" Frank yelled, trailing behind him. His hand gripped the revolver that was housed in his vest holster. "Riley, what did you see?"

Riley frantically scanned the area around them, looking for any sign of her. There was nothing. Did he imagined her? His gaze fell onto the ground, to the half-eaten ice cream cone that lay melting in the sun. He was sure of it. She was just here.

"Riley! Talk to me, man!" Frank grabbed Riley by the arm. "Are you ok, you look like you have seen a ghost?"

"It can't be," Riley replied softly. Riley closed his eyes and raised his head towards the sky. His face now displaying a mix of pain, confusion, and missed opportunities. "I know she was here!" He swore, not realizing he was shouting.

"Riley, calm down!" Frank grabbed Riley's good hand and pulled him close to him, holding on tightly. "It's ok. Tell me, what did you see?

Riley couldn't answer. Tears began to stream down his cheeks. "I saw her Frank. I don't know how it's possible, but it was Charlotte, my wife."

CHAPTER 42

Riley stared at the picture of Charlotte, struggling against a new wave of tears. It was an older picture from the early days of their marriage, and it was one of his favorites. She was holding a newborn puppy, smiling from ear to ear as she cuddled it closely against the nape of her neck. He wasn't sure what he liked the most about the picture, the look in Charlotte's eyes, the smile on her face, or the sense of delight the photograph conveyed. Today, he decided it was the smile. Oh, how he missed that smile.

Other photos lay sprawled across his bed, creating a colorful kaleidoscope of memories. Riley tossed the picture on the pile and settled back onto his pillow, closing his eyes in hopes he would finally succumb to his exhaustion. He had been looking at the pictures for hours in between long bouts of prayer and stretches of tears. He asked the others not to disturb him unless it was an emergency. He couldn't let them see him like this, not when he was so broken.

He now realized how much emotional carnage from her death he suppressed, how much he locked away deep within him, sealed from his conscious thought. Seeing Charlotte earlier unleashed those emotions with a vengeance, screaming to be heard, demanding to be acknowledged. The worst was the regret he felt. It flowed through him like venom, poisoning him with doubt and condemnation that he may have given up on rescuing her too soon.

Riley rolled over, a small whelp escaping from his lips. The wound in his heart was torn open, as it never fully healed. *Who truly heals from having their soulmate taken away?* Life without her was not the same, it was only a shadow of what it was before. Oh, how he missed her. Her healing touch. Her soft skin. The warmth of her embrace.

The love he held for Charlotte was unchanged in its fullness or passion. It had only intensified because the object of that love was no longer there to receive it. Like a candle flame fighting against a tempest of rain, he always held a glimmer of hope she could be alive. Now that glimmer was bursting into a real possibility.

He entertained the thought that Charlotte survived the accident. Maybe she was washed away in the storm and saved by a passing fisherman, only she was suffering from amnesia. That was a possibility, but a slim one. He resisted

THE OTHER SIDE

against the thought it was a figment of his imagination brought about by stress. He had seen her today, of that he was sure.

Riley sat up, resigning to the fact that he was not going to fall asleep. He picked up another stack of pictures and began browsing through them. One particular picture caught his interest. It was of him and Charlotte dancing at their wedding. She looked so beautiful that day. But she looked beautiful every day, he thought, a smile cracking his lips.

A drop of liquid appeared on the picture. He stared at the tiny bead for a moment, thinking it was another tear. He wiped it away and placed the photo onto the mattress. Unaware of what was really happening, he wiped his hand across his forehead, only to find he was sweating profusely.

An urgent knock at his door jarred him to his feet. "Riley! Riley! I need to speak with you, it's an emergency!"

Riley opened the door, revealing a panicked Marie. Like him, she was drenched in perspiration. "We are under attack!" she urgently proclaimed.

As Riley focused his senses, a vibration of evil rippled across his skin. The demonic presence seemed to envelop the house, saturating each room with the stench of its existence. He should have felt it earlier, but he was so self-absorbed in his meditation on Charlotte that he completely closed himself off to everything around him. "Get the others and meet me downstairs," Riley ordered. "Now!"

Within minutes, the entire inside of the house was transformed into a sauna, the temperature easily exceeding one hundred and twenty degrees. Riley knocked on Noah's door on his way to the first floor. "Noah, get up! I need you!" He continued downstairs after he heard the shuffle of feet and a groggy unintelligible response.

In the kitchen, Riley found Duke and Spencer, pacing uncontrollably around the room. Periodically, one of the dogs would stand on its hind legs near a window, peering into the darkness outside, only to fall back to the floor whimpering.

Marie and Noah burst into the kitchen to find Riley analyzing one of the windows.

"Are the others coming?" Riley demanded.

"I think. What's going on?" Noah nervously asked "Why is it so hot in here?" Noah further pressed, looking around the room.

"We are being attacked by a hostile spirit," Marie said, shifting her gaze to the ceiling. "And it has enveloped the house."

"Well if the spirit's here, there is only one thing to do," Noah remarked to no one in particular. "Let's get out of the house." Not waiting for a response, Noah moved past Marie and unlocked the back door.

THE OTHER SIDE

"Noah! Don't..." Marie screamed, but it was too late. Noah opened the door.

Instantly, a wave of pulsating blackness spilled over him and into the room. Flies. Hundreds, if not thousands, of the black insects cascaded through the door, blanketing everything in their path.

Riley closed his eyes against the onslaught and tried to back out of the room, swatting the air around his head. Tiny welts of pain peppered his body as the flies bit into his skin. He heard the others scream as the flies continued to attack. There was a crash of furniture as someone fell to the floor.

Riley persisted to smack the air around him, feeling his way to the door, eventually closing it against the onrush of blackness. He opened his eyes for a moment, only to close them a half second later because of the flies scrambling across his face. What he did glimpse, horrified him. The entire room was encased in moving blackness.

Riley fell into a protective crouch as the flies sustained their attack. The flies were everywhere. In his mouth, in his nose, in his ears. He couldn't even inhale without sucking in a mouthful of the putrid insects. That was when he heard Jessica's voice booming through the buzz of insanity around him. She was praying a forceful prayer, challenging the hostile spirit in the name of God. There were other voices who joined in the prayer. Riley felt a shift in the air,

307

a weakening of the spirit that was around them. Even though his eyes were closed, Riley detected a bright flash of light. In an instant, as quickly as they appeared, the flies vanished.

Noah slowly rose to his feet. There were tiny dots of crimson along his chest, arms and face where the flies had bitten him. Marie looked equally beaten up, in addition to the bites she sported a bright red lump on her forehead.

Jessica, Stephen and Darius, rushed into the kitchen. Jessica immediately attended to Marie and began to administer first aid, while Stephen locked the back door. Darius embraced Spencer and began checking him for wounds.

"Are you two ok?" Riley asked. Both Noah and Marie nodded.

"I am really sorry," Noah said, wiping a trickle of blood away from his cheek. "I didn't know that would happen."

"It's ok Noah," Riley responded. "I am the one who needs to apologize. I let my guard down." He walked over to Marie and inspected her forehead. Marie met his gaze, a look of fierce determination in her eyes.

"I expect the attacks by our enemy will only get worse," Riley added. "We need to be vigilant at all times and watch each other's back."

"What do we do now?" Jessica asked, turning her attention to Duke and Spencer. The dogs were in obvious discomfort and Spencer was whimpering slightly.

THE OTHER SIDE

"We stay inside for now and try to get some rest." We need to be prepared for anything."

Hours later, exhausted by the past day's experience, Riley settled into bed. It was then he felt a prompting unlike any he had before. Vibrations of extreme danger and sinister intentions pulsed from deep within him. He sprang from bed, his exhaustion replaced with alarm.

It could mean only one thing. More attacks were coming. In response, Riley fell to his knees and began to pray. It was the only thing he knew to do.

CHAPTER 43

Jessica's stomach felt like it was going to burst. She couldn't stop laughing at Stephen's hilarious antics.

Stephen began another impression, this time pretending to be the overzealous army sergeant from Camp Perry who had been their training instructor.

"The target is on the right about a half mile from here," Stephen described, his face clenching in furious concentration. "Keep an eye out for it, soldier. Don't miss it! We have one chance and one chance only!"

"Roger that, sir," Jessica replied, saluting. Again, they broke into laughter. It felt so good to laugh, a welcomed change to the recent craziness.

She knew Stephen was enjoying their time together just as much as she was. Stephen made her feel good. Maybe it was his carefree attitude. Or maybe it was the way he approached every activity with the enthusiasm of a child. Whatever it was, they just meshed.

Jessica cautiously pulled the SUV into the parking lot, scanning the area for any signs of danger. Despite Riley's attempts to calm her fears about future attacks, she couldn't help but feel vulnerable. The veterinarian clinic was located on the corner of a busy intersection in the trendy suburb of Reston, several miles from the manor. They hadn't planned to drive that far, but after several calls that morning, it was the only clinic that carried the medicine she needed for the dogs.

The attack last night could have been worse, but the dogs suffered most of the damage. Despite their thick coats, the flies inflicted hundreds of bites and managed to burrow deep into their skin. Jessica's main concern was to stave off infection, but the dogs also needed relief from irritation.

Riley didn't like the idea of the two of them leaving the manor, but agreed it was necessary. They were under strict order to return immediately after this errand.

"Are you ready?" Stephen asked, exiting the SUV. "Let's make this quick."

"Yeah, Solly. I think so," Jessica nodded hesitantly, still thinking about the possibility they could be attacked. Despite her response, she wasn't ready for what happened next.

Noah turned off his tablet. The movie he was watching finished long ago and he was staring at the screen, lost in his thoughts. He was feeling so good about himself the past few days, but his screw up last night placed him into a glum mood. Noah tried to push the thoughts of failure from his mind, but it was futile. If only he had dreamt about the attacks.

He watched the armed guard peer through the living room window to check on anyone who may be inside. There were four guards in total, one posted to patrol each side of the house. It was easy to feel like he was a prisoner without a cage, sentenced to live in isolation from the rest of the world.

Riley said it was a protective measure and it would be temporary, but Noah didn't think so. The last thing he wanted was another encounter with a demon. Not after what happened to Jessica and Stephen.

Noah's mind flashed back to the discussion with Riley, hours earlier. Riley recently returned from his meeting at Langley and was in obvious distress. Noah immediately detected something was very wrong. The recollection of Riley's words still made Noah's heart stop.

"I just spoke with Stephen. There has been an accident," Riley said, fighting back tears. "Stephen and Jessica are in the hospital. Stephen is fine, but Jessica is seriously injured. She is in the intensive care unit and her prognosis is unknown."

"What happened?" Maria asked, struggling to stifle her own tears at hearing this news.

Riley simply frowned, but the rage he was feeling radiated from his eyes. "A woman drove her car directly into them while they were walking in a parking lot. Witnesses report the woman stopped her car and then ran into the street, throwing herself into the path of an oncoming school bus. She was killed instantly."

It was a chilling statement. One full of implications that gave Noah pause. If the powers of evil were willing to kill others in order to stop Riley and his team, how did they have any hope of staying safe?

Noah's mind drifted to his own demonic encounter earlier that morning. What started as a peaceful walk with the dogs quickly escalated into a nightmare. Fortunately, Marie and Darius were there with him.

Appearing out of nowhere, a disheveled man approached them. Marie screamed, while the dogs began growling and snarling uncontrollably.

The man was skinny, of haggard appearance, with mud and debris coating his forehead, face and neck. Even more frightening was the man's face. Hollow eyes with tiny black marble irises were locked on them, conveying pure wickedness. The man suddenly produced a long hunting knife from his jacket pocket and lunged toward them.

Duke began pulling heavily on his leash, trying to position himself between the imminent danger and the group. Noah pulled back, wanting Duke to move with him in retreat, but the others didn't look like they were planning to run. Instead, Darius protectively moved in front of Marie with Spencer.

Surprisingly, Marie then stepped in front of Darius, raising her arms toward the man.

"What are you doing?" Darius shouted, grabbing her shoulder and pulling her back towards him.

"Trust me," Marie instructed. She immediately took another step toward the man. "I command you to leave!" Marie demanded, pointing at the man.

The man seemed to hesitate for a moment, but then pressed forward as if driven by some unseen force. He raised the knife toward Marie, now only an arm's length away.

"I command you to leave this man and return to hell!!!" Marie demanded a second time, with even more intensity. To everyone's surprise, the man dropped the knife and crumbled before them. Unexpectedly, the man rose dazed, only to run off into the park.

"What just happened?" Darius asked.

"I don't really know," Marie shrugged. "My instincts told me I could expel the demon. I was able to do it once before in the hospital with Noah. So I tried."

What Marie was able to do was a surprise to all of them, but it proved Riley was correct when he told them their abilities would continue to expand and manifest in new ways. It gave Noah hope that his ability might change for the better.

A tap on the window jarred Noah out of his reflection. Noah waved at the guard and gave him a thumbs up. The guard motioned back and then disappeared, seemingly to leave Noah alone.

Noah glanced at his watch, he really needed to get some sleep. Darius and Marie retired for the evening hours ago. Tomorrow was going to be a big day for all of them. They were going to the White House, though Riley didn't explain why. The only thing Riley told them was to be up early as they needed to prepare. Something told Noah that it was their turn to attack.

CHAPTER 44

Shocked, Riley surveyed the damage. It appeared as if someone spilled a box of massive Lincoln Logs over the White House grounds. Entire trees that towered for decades over the White House lay completely uprooted across the lush green lawn. The rest of the city wasn't faring any better through the chaos caused by the hundred mile per hour winds. Meteorologists called this weather event a "derecho." Riley called it a miracle.

The four of them waited patiently in a sedan outside the north gate for Frank to return from a nearby guardhouse. Riley prayed he was prepared for what lay ahead. He was physically exhausted, having spent most of the evening at the hospital. He was also emotionally drained, as Jessica's condition was not improving. She was in critical condition and was expected to be in intensive care for several days. She absorbed the full impact of the vehicle, purposely pushing Stephen out of its path. Stephen was beside him-

THE OTHER SIDE

self with grief and refused to leave her side.

"Here he comes, Riley," Noah noted, pointing towards the guard house. Noah adjusted his red bow tie nervously and ran his hand through his now close-cropped hair. Riley asked Noah to cut his hair as part of their disguise. Surprisingly, Noah did not resist. As it turned out, it was a good look for the young man.

Riley glanced behind him. Marie was grasping the hand of both Darius and Noah, as if she were trying to give them strength or draw it from them. She was dressed in a dark blue satin dress and her hair was pulled back into a ponytail. Next to her, Darius looked perfectly comfortable in his black suit. Somehow, Frank managed to have them added to a list of performers at the First Lady's luncheon, with Riley acting as their stage manager.

"Did the big guy upstairs make this happen?" Frank said, pointing to the sky as he crawled into the driver side seat.

"Maybe," Riley smiled. "It certainly is the distraction we need."

"I am not so sure of that," Frank said, whistling softly as he stared at the guard house. "This changes everything I planned. With the White House operating on generator power, all non-critical systems, including the guardhouse computers are offline. The Director of White House Security has closed access to the White House to anyone not on official business and who does not have government credentials."

Riley frowned. That was not good news. "Yet, something tells me you have an idea?" Riley pressed.

"I called in a favor," Frank replied coolly. "My connection told me to wait ten minutes and don't ask any questions."

"Be prepared and ready to do exactly what Frank tells you," Riley instructed his team. They all nodded in response.

As if on cue, several agents surrounded the vehicle, weapons drawn. "Hands up, no sudden movements," a tall agent with a blond crew cut barked. He waved his gun menacingly at Frank. "Slowly get out of the car. Keep your hands where I can see them."

Riley was surprised that Frank didn't protest. He didn't even show his badge. Instead he turned to Riley and winked.

Minutes later, after being handcuffed and frisked, they found themselves confined in a basement office of the White House. The overhead lighting was dim, as only two of the eight lights were on. They could hear the humming vibration of the generators coming from deep below them. One of the agents remained in the room, eyeing them warily.

Riley looked at Frank, who only nodded in acknowledgement. Hopefully, they would be able to explain themselves to the person in charge.

The door opened and a man with white hair and speckled rim glasses entered. He was a lean man, sharply dressed in a grey suit. The man's face was familiar to Riley, but he couldn't recall ever meeting him. The man nodded at the agent, who promptly left the room, closing the door behind him.

"Hi Frank," the man said as a broad smile expanded across his face. "Sorry about the theatrics, but it was the only way that I could get you in."

Frank held his hands up, "How about doing your brother a favor and getting these things off of me and the others." One at a time, the man removed the cuffs from each of them and deposited them in a pile on the table.

"Riley O'Connor, this is my brother, Jimmy Gillian, Director of White House Security."

"Your brother?" Riley questioned, surprised by the revelation. Divine coincidence had struck again. He shook the man's hand in appreciation. "Thank you."

"I should be the one thanking you, Riley," Jimmy said. "Ever since Frank met you, something is different about him. He's taken an interest in spiritual things. It is a blessing to my heart."

"Then you know why we are here?"

"Not exactly, but Frank told me a great deal about you and the battle you fight. I didn't believe him at first, not to mention that facilitating unauthorized access to the White House is an act of treason, but..." Jimmy paused as if he wasn't sure what to say. "Let's just say I experienced something last night that changed my mind."

"He says he was visited by an angel in a dream who told him to help you," Frank interjected, shaking his head in disbelief. "This is all too weird for me."

"We mean no harm to the president," Riley assured. "We believe he is in danger, and possibly compromised. I need to see him to know for sure." A look of concern crossed Jimmy's face at this news.

"I can get you to the Oval Office," Jimmy replied. "But if my involvement is to remain a secret, I cannot enter the public areas where we have surveillance cameras. The president's security detail will be outside the Oval Office and they will not give anyone access without permission from the president."

Riley glanced at his watch. The meeting was already in process. "Please take us as far as you can."

Riley and his team followed Frank and Jimmy to a set of marble steps leading to the first floor. At the top, they stopped in front of a large oak door. Jimmy turned and said, "The Cabinet room is immediately on the right as you exit the stairwell. Head to the south exit from the Cabinet room. This will bring you into a waiting

THE OTHER SIDE

area outside the Oval Office."

Riley and the others nodded as Jimmy slid a card through the door lock. Instantly, the stairwell door sprang open with an audible click.

"This is as far as I go. Good luck and God bless," Jimmy offered, giving Frank a quick hug. Riley and the others immediately hurried into the Cabinet room as Jimmy closed the door behind them.

Frank looked at Riley, "What now, Ace?"

"This is where I go to work," Darius said confidently, walking toward the door on the south end of the room. He paused and concentrated, placing his hand to his head. "There are two agents. One of them was just inside the office with the president. The agent seems confused. He is trying to figure out why there are three people with the president when only two people were on the official register. He is telling the other agent that another man appeared in the room, as if out of thin air."

"How do we get past them?" Frank asked.

Darius turned his attention back to the men on the other side of the door, concentrating. "That should do it." He turned to the detective. "Frank, I want you to flash your badge and introduce yourself to Agent Harris and Agent Tweed. I will do the rest." Darius adjusted his tie as if preparing to go on stage. "All of you wait here until I signal you it is clear." A moment later, he opened the door and both he and Frank disappeared.

321

Noah was fidgeting again and looked a shade paler than normal. "Have faith, Noah." Riley assured.

"But what do we do when we get into the office?" Noah asked, thinking about what Riley had shared with them that morning. Through divine revelation, Riley was informed the president was deceived by a demon and was being influenced to act against his will. It was their task to rescue the president from his bondage.

"As I explained earlier, you and Marie need to get to the president," Riley replied. "After that, trust yourself and use your powers."

'Mission accomplished' Darius projected to the three of them. Noah shook his head and tried to chuckle, though the nervousness in his voice made it more of a cackle. "I will never get used to that. It's freaky hearing someone else's voice in your head."

"Let's go!" Riley said, leading them through the door. Inside, Riley found Darius and Frank standing next to the agents, big smiles on both of their faces. The agents were oblivious to their presence, their gaze focused on something far in the distance.

Darius placed his arm around one of the hypnotized agents affectionately. "Agent Harris and Agent Tweed are enjoying themselves on a beach in the Caribbean. They will have no memory of this event," he said smugly.

"Craziest thing I ever did see," Frank said,

looking at Darius. "Don't you ever do that to me."

"Well done, Darius." Riley said, patting him on the shoulder. Riley motioned to Frank to come near him. The detective leaned in as Riley whispered under his breath. "I need you to get Darius and yourself out of here if things go bad."

Frank nodded gravely, stepped back and gave Riley a salute. "Good luck, Ace. It has been my honor to work with you."

"Save that salute for a real hero," Riley said. "I appreciate the sentiment but just take care of things out here. We need all the time we can get."

Riley stepped between the two agents and placed his hand on the door to the Oval Office. Immediately he felt bone chilling cold radiate through his hand. An extremely powerful demonic force was just on the other side.

Riley gripped Marie's hand. She looked at him, a fearful expression on her face. She felt it too. "Seeing a demon in physical form will send you into shock. Hold onto me and don't let go until you and Noah are near the president. I will be able to shield you from the full effect of what you about to see. But as soon as we lose contact, keep your eyes to the floor and follow Noah." In response, Marie reached behind her, pulling Noah close, clasping his hand tightly.

It was time. They were ready. Slowly, Riley opened the door and the three of them stepped through the doorway into the Oval Office.

CHAPTER 45

"If this attack by Thereon turns out to be true, we will need first responders and relief workers stationed within a ten-mile radius of each of these locations," President Harrison stated, his finger resting on one of the red circles drawn on the map unrolled across his desk. The president seemed unusually nervous today, Natasha thought.

She studied the map. Thick red circles surrounded the cities of Los Angeles, Houston, Boston, and Washington, D.C. These cities were identified in an urgent threat report from the FBI released hours ago.

"If a nuclear blast occurs, we will need to evacuate people within a five mile radius of ground zero," Natasha added. "Due to the risks involved, there will be no way to provide emergency services to those that remain in the blast zone, assuming they survive."

"We are talking about an evacuation of mil-

THE OTHER SIDE

lions. Can we handle that?" The president's question was directed to the man in a finely tailored blue suit. The man simply nodded in response, but remained silent.

Natasha eyed the man wearily. The man must have sensed her apprehension as he looked directly at her, a dismissive look on his face. She stifled the urge to interrupt the president and confront this unknown advisor. The man didn't even introduce himself when she arrived. To add to her frustration, Natasha expected to see the members of the President's cabinet at this meeting, only to find this unidentified man and oddly, Pastor Anthony Jessup. It didn't make any sense.

"That is when your people will be needed, Anthony," the mysterious man instructed. "Your organization has the capability and resources to manage the relief efforts. In addition to distributing food, supplies, and medicine, thousands will need spiritual guidance during this time. Are you ready?"

Natasha recalled a vague memory from an earlier cabinet briefing in which the president announced a pending partnership with Summit of Light Ministries. It would be spun as a nondenominational outreach effort to improve the lives of citizens through service and charity. It was going to be everything people liked about religious institutions with one caveat. Since it would be government sponsored, there would be no religion or any mention of God.

"All relief efforts will be coordinated through our headquarters," the pastor responded. "Since we have major church institutions in each of these cities, members have been given a directive to avoid the area around ground zero during the time period of the attacks."

"Are you sure they will listen to you?" the stranger asked. There was a skeptical look on his face.

"These people are civilians," the president added. "We can't order them to do anything."

"My parishioners will do whatever I tell them," Pastor Jessup responded smugly.

"You are talking as if the attacks are definitely going to occur?" Natasha interrupted. "We have no substantiated evidence that these attacks will actually happen. To have already informed civilians without my approval is completely out of protocol."

The strange man and Pastor Jessup exchanged a quick look, but otherwise ignored her. "You were saying pastor?" the man continued. This obvious dismissal sent Natasha's frustration over the edge. *Who do these people think they are?!?*

The door opening on the far side of the office drew their attention. Natasha's eyes widened in surprise as Riley O'Connor appeared in the room, trailed by a young man and woman, whom she recognized as members of Riley's special unit.

THE OTHER SIDE

Both Pastor Jessup and the nameless man appeared startled by the appearance of the intruders. They quickly moved toward Riley and his team, like wolves encroaching on their most prized pray. The stranger spoke first. "So you have finally decided to join our party. We could not be happier. It is not often we get the opportunity to destroy an Anointed."

President Harrison charged between the two men and approached Riley. "Who are you and how did you get access to this office?"

As the president neared, Noah and Marie stepped forward, hand in hand. With his free hand, Noah reached and grabbed the president's forearm. Instantly, the three of them fell to the ground, unconscious.

The stranger screamed at Riley, "You arrogant fool! You have just guaranteed their death!" He turned towards Pastor Jessup and directed, "You know what to do."

In a flash of light, Pastor Jessup vanished. Almost instantaneously, a light enveloped Riley surrounding him in a field of electric blue.

"It is time we end this, Baal," Riley challenged. His words boomed through the room as if spoken through a megaphone.

The stranger chuckled in response. "So you know who I am." He stepped toward Riley confidently. "Then you also know that you are no match for me. You are a mere mortal."

Riley stood his ground, blue energy radiat-

327

ing around him. "I may be mortal, but like Elijah, I also have the power to call down fire from Heaven against evil." Instantly a blue bolt of fire bolt smashed into Baal, hurling him backward into the far wall near Natasha. His physical body slammed hard against the cement wall with a loud thud, cracking the plaster. Natasha was sure he must be dead.

Amazingly, the man rose from the floor, apparently uninjured by the blast. He passed by Natasha without a glance as she crouched protectively on the floor. The stranger's form shimmered before her, transforming into something else. A vaguely human form, masked in obscurity, but with substance. Fear began to pulse through Natasha. She knew she needed to get away from this situation.

A glowing red dagger appeared in the abstract outline of an arm as another bolt of blue fire came forth from Riley. The arm moved with lighting speed, deflecting the bolt and sending it crashing through the bullet proof window behind Natasha in a fiery explosion.

Natasha darted from her protective position beside the desk and slid along the wall towards the nearest door. Out of the corner of her eye, she noticed Riley lower his upraised hands as she approached. A moment later, a crimson fireball slammed into Riley, blanketing the blue light in a layer of red. Riley stumbled under the impact of the blow, falling to one knee. The blue and the

THE OTHER SIDE

red forces violently struggled, seeking to snuff the other out of existence.

She was almost to the doorway. The only obstacle was the limp body of the president and the others that lay sprawled before her. There was no time to be concerned for him. She needed to get to safety and away from this insane battle. She scrambled to the door, only to trip on the fringe of the Persian rug that graced the sitting area. She tumbled forward, trying to retain her balance and collided with the body of the president. In that instant, everything around her changed.

CHAPTER 46

"We lost the president." Noah nervously said, scanning the horizon. The sky above was pitch black, yet light from some unknown source illuminated their surroundings. A desert landscape of red dirt was visible for miles in every direction.

"Where do you think we are?" Marie asked, trying to brush a blotch of red dust from her dress. The dust only streaked further, clinging to the fabric.

"We could be anywhere," Noah replied. "At least Riley's theory was right. Your power made it possible for us to crossover. I just wish I knew what to do next."

"This is so weird. I feel like I am in my body, but I know I can't be," Marie said, examining her hands. "Is this like it is in your dreams?"

Noah grabbed a handful of the red dirt, letting it sift through his fingers. It felt like sand, but was hot to the touch and a little sticky.

THE OTHER SIDE

"Pretty much," he shrugged. Noah took a few steps in one direction, looking at the horizon with a pensive scour. "Let's find the president. I don't want to stay in this place any longer than we have too."

Marie suddenly grabbed his arm. "Not that way. We need to go the other direction."

"Are you sure?" Noah questioned.

She headed away from Noah, leaving a trail of crimson mushroom clouds with every step. Noah hesitated, thinking through their options.

"You should follow her, young one," a voice beckoned from behind him. Noah spun around, finding himself face to face with a man dressed in a flowing silver gown and odd sandals that attached to his lower legs with thin leather straps. The man was bald with a pure white beard that extended below his chest. With a deftness that surprised Noah, the man easily bowed in greeting.

"Who are you?" Noah challenged, surprised by the man's sudden appearance. The terrors of his last spiritual encounter still lingered in his mind. He wasn't taking chances.

"I am like you, dreamer," the man responded, a slight smile on his face. Noah noticed the man did not have any wrinkles, yet somehow Noah sensed he was ancient. "I am known as Isaiah," the man added, taking another deep bow.

"The prophet Isaiah?" Noah asked, his jaw dropping in shock. He had studied much about

Isaiah and knew Isaiah prophesied the birth of Jesus Christ. He also was one of the few prophets who experienced visions of the end of the world.

The man moved closer to Noah. "I have been sent to guide you on your journey."

"What is this place?" Marie asked, having returned to Noah's side.

"You are in the nether region," the prophet replied. "A place between Heaven and hell. In my time, this place was known as Paradise."

"Paradise?" Noah blurted, stifling a laugh. "Are you serious?"

Isaiah bowed his head for moment, as if in reverence for something unseen. "Paradise was reserved for those who worshipped and served Yahweh, who is the Creator, the one true God. After death in the physical realm, those souls would come here. Before the Christ came to release and take us with him to Heaven, this place was as beautiful as the garden of Eden."

"What about other people? Those who did not worship Yahweh," Noah asked. He heard Riley preach enough about this topic that he knew the answer, but he asked anyway.

"Those unfortunate souls were sent there." Isaiah said grievously, pointing toward the horizon where the darkness of the sky merged into the red landscape. The area was illuminated, a swirling mess of black, red, and orange colors that pulsated in rhythmic intensity.

"This place was no longer needed after the

THE OTHER SIDE

Resurrection so the Holy One removed his barrier of protection. The evil one, who shall not be named, consumed it instantly and destroyed everything." Isaiah looked towards the darkness momentarily. "Come, we must go now."

"Where?" Noah asked, grabbing hold of Marie's hand. There was no way he was going to let them become separated. Besides he just felt stronger and more confident with Marie next to him.

"To the entrance of hell," Isaiah said as he approached Noah and Marie. "I must show you something. Please give me your hand."

Noah looked to Marie for confirmation. He wasn't sure what would happen. She nodded slowly in response, although her trembling lips told Noah she was as nervous as he was. Questions bombarded Noah as doubt crept into his mind. *Is this old man truly Isaiah or a demon in disguise? Where was he going to take them? Was it a trap?*

"Let's go with him, Noah," Marie said, giving his hand a reassuring squeeze. "I trust him."

Noah smiled. "That is all I needed to hear." Reaching out slowly, Noah grasped the hand of the prophet. The old man nodded approvingly. A moment later, they vanished.

CHAPTER 47

They appeared at the edge of a rocky outcropping, overlooking a large valley. Below them, bubbling liquid fire meandered for as far as the eye could see in two directions, a brilliant swath cutting through the darkness. Flames danced across the surface, periodically leaping high into the space above. It was the most incredible sight Noah had ever seen.

"This is the River of Atonement. It flows directly from the Creator and culminates in the Lake of Fire. On the far side of the river is the land of damnation...hell itself."

"Hell looks rather drab," Noah remarked casually. He envisioned something much more dramatic. He pictured hell as a place where people were in chains, surrounded by hideous demons with whips and lots and lots of fire. In contrast, the area directly across the river looked like the desert from which they had just come. "It is not like I imagined."

THE OTHER SIDE

Isaiah chuckled softly. "That is because we are on the outside, my naive friend. Hell is much more complex than humankind can conceive. It is a pit of darkness with layers as endless as the sins of humanity."

Isaiah ignored the exploding plume of fire that burst before them. The explosion caused Noah to jump back from the ledge in fear. The plume disintegrated just a few yards below from where they were standing.

"Each layer is progressively more severe in its punishments, its hopelessness, and its despair," Isaiah continued. "Unlike Heaven, where entrance is granted based on true relationship with the Creator, there is only one criteria for entrance to hell." Isaiah's face flicked brightly in the reflection of another exploding plume of fire. "Dying without acceptance of Christ's atonement for your sin."

Noah nodded in understanding, yet there was a part of him that still was not clear. "Why does hell have layers?"

"In the absence of one's acceptance of the Savior's gift of salvation to pay the penalty for your sins, the sins you commit sentence your soul to hell. The layer where your soul ends up in hell is based on the severity of the sins committed. Deep within hell, there are layers that are yet empty of human souls. Layers that wait for sins that have yet to be conceived by the human mind."

"Why are you showing us this?" Marie asked.

"You must return to this place to leave this realm. Through the fire, you will find what you seek. But I warn you both, do not cross this river, for you will be confined to hell, never to return."

Noah looked around them and then at the fiery river below. Crossing the river was definitely not an option. There was no way he would choose to go in that direction, but their other option was just as bleak. They were on a small plateau cut into a larger cliff. Vertical walls of red rock surrounded them on three sides.

"I don't understand," Noah said, "Assuming we could find our way to return here, how do we leave?"

"What appears as death to one, is truly life to another," Isaiah replied.

Noah frowned. The last thing he needed was a riddle to solve. "Can you be more specific? I don't know how to cross back to the physical realm."

"Join hands," Isaiah commanded, ignoring Noah's question. The prophet approached Noah and Marie. "It is time. I must leave you."

"What?!?" Noah shrieked, grabbing the robe of the sage tightly. "You can't leave us here."

"My young soothsayer, I will take you to the next step in your journey. But beware, the task ahead is marked with peril. Trust in yourself. Your faith will lead you home."

Noah shook his head in disagreement. This

THE OTHER SIDE

was not the advice he wanted. He was about to open his mouth to reply when Isaiah raised his hand in salute and then in a swift motion, brought it down onto Noah's shoulder. Again, the world around them shifted in a blur.

Noah found himself floating within a network of cables and threads stretching for as long as he could see in every direction. Some of the threads were the diameter of kite string, while others were as thick as a baseball bat. Noah could see a few in the distance that appeared the thickness of the trunk of a full grown Maple tree. Directly below them more threads and cables could be seen descending into the darkness.

"Floating like this reminds me of my lucid dreams," Noah stated, looking at Isaiah. The old man simply nodded, knowingly.

He raised a single finger at Noah, pointing at him. "The spirit world is malleable to the will of the soul. Remember that and use it to your advantage."

"We haven't much time. We have to get back to Riley," Noah urged. "How do we find the president?"

"Time in this realm is not the same as you know it," Isaiah said calmly. "Do not let that be a concern. You must focus on your mission."

"What are these cables and threads?" Marie interrupted, floating closer to a quarter size thread to inspect it.

"These are the threads of all those bound

to sin through a stronghold, demonic influence, or possession itself. The thicker the thread, the stronger the power of the Evil One to control that person."

"Of course," Noah realized. "When the angel saved me, I remember he swung his sword, appearing to cut something."

"Yes, the cord that held you in bondage," Isaiah agreed. "With the influence of evil removed, the guise of deception that kept you from belief in the Creator disappeared. Sadly, much of humanity lives under the Evil One's deception."

"Why does God allow this?" Maria asked. "Why doesn't he just do away with all of this and cut every cord?"

"Though it is in His power to do so, the Creator gave mankind the ability to choose his or her own destiny," Isaiah stated assuredly.

"You mean free will," Marie acknowledged.

Isaiah nodded. "Without free will, mankind is simply a slave. It is the choice one makes that leads to freedom or bondage."

"Mankind can choose to love God or reject him," Noah added.

"Well said my young dreamer," Isaiah said, releasing Noah's hand as he stepped backward. "Remember my young warriors, when you exit this realm, you must be connected by touch. Anyone not linked to you will be trapped in the nether region until the Day of Judgement." In re-

THE OTHER SIDE

sponse, Marie instantly grabbed Noah's hand and by the strength of her grip, she didn't intend to let go.

"I bid you farewell," Isaiah said. In an eye blink, they found themselves alone in darkness.

Marie clutched Noah tighter. "What do we do now?"

Noah thought for a moment, replaying their conversation with Isaiah. An idea began to form in his head. A crazy idea, but one that made perfect sense.

Now it was his turn to give Marie's hand a reassuring squeeze. For the first time, he felt confident in what he was to do. "We need to find the president's thread," Noah said, gazing into the distance. The threads stretched for as far as he could see. "Once we find it, we cut it."

CHAPTER 48

The power pulsing through him possessed a life force, desiring to be unleashed and consume all that stood in its way. Riley lowered his hands, feeling the force within him flicker in protest as he struggled to constrain it. He should be throwing every ounce of power he controlled toward Baal, yet the sight of Natasha in the middle of the battle made him hesitate.

She slid along the wall towards the exit, a helpless shadow of desperation and fear. Riley did not want to risk hurting her by accident. He knew she was just a pawn in Satan's plan, despite the havoc she had wrought.

His momentary expression of compassion was rewarded with a burst of pain as a bright red ball of fire slammed into his midsection. The force of the impact brought him to his knees as the power within him seemed to waiver. Out of the corner of his eye, he saw Natasha stumble and collide into the body of the president. She did not get up and he knew why.

Riley concentrated on the intense power that pulsed through him, focusing the torrent of strength that wanted to explode from his body. Blue flame erupted, creating a perimeter around him, consuming the remnants of hellfire left from the demon's attack. He never expected to possess such power, but he knew it was given to him by God for this exact moment and he intended to take full advantage of it.

Baal leaped into the air, somersaulting effortlessly towards Riley, his blade flashing in a wild arc. Baal unleashed another blast of hellfire before plunging his dagger towards Riley. Just in time, Riley rolled away from the descending Baal, avoiding both the fire blast and the dagger. As soon as Riley righted himself, he released a wave of blue fire at the demon. Baal took the full impact, the blast lifting the demon into the air and hurling him against the large mahogany bookcase. The bookcase instantly disintegrated from the impact.

Before Baal could recover, Riley sent forth another burst of fire, this one long and sustained. The fire engulfed Baal, lifting him and pinning him to the wall. Baal emitted a scream as he tried to fight, but the fire enveloped him.

Slowly, Baal's body begin to pulsate, fading for a moment then reappearing. Riley focused more of his power against Baal. He didn't know how, but the fire was somehow vanquishing the demon from the physical plane. Baal's dagger fell limply from his hand only to disappear before it hit the ground. The demon was now translucent. Like a ghost. Just a few more seconds and Baal would be gone.

"Riley..."

The voice stopped him dead. He desired to hear that voice speak his name every night for the last three years, but he knew it wasn't possible.

"Riley," the voice said again, "I am here baby. I'm really here. Look at me." He couldn't resist the temptation. Slowly, he turned towards the voice.

Charlotte stood before him, her arms outstretched, beckoning him to come to her. Her beauty was awesome to behold. She was radiant, dressed simply in a white cotton dress that accentuated her curves. Her pale skin emanated a soft glow and her ruby lips invited him. How could he have forgotten how beautiful she was?

There was only one thing he wanted now, to hold her again. He felt the power fading from his grasp as he lost focus on the battle. A moment later, the blue aura that surrounded him vanished along with the power to protect himself.

Riley stepped forward, "Charlotte..." Her name was barely a whisper on his lips. It was all he could manage. The madness of emotion welling inside of him left him speechless. He wanted to cry in relief. He wanted to curse himself for giving up on finding her. Now he wanted to take her in his arms and hold her, to make love to her, to feel the closeness that only they knew.

Yet, there was a part of him that resisted. A part of him that told him to flee. This couldn't be his wife. This woman could not be who she appeared to be. But his desire to be with Charlotte was too strong. He quickly dismissed the voice of reason that was sounding an alarm. He knew that it would all be worth everything if he could hold her just once more.

"Come to me, my love," Charlotte beckoned. "Please, I need you." Riley took another step toward her, his head shaking in bewilderment. He could almost touch her. Almost smell the pleasant aroma of her skin. One more step.

Charlotte stared directly at him, her mouth pursed in a slight smile. It was his favorite expression of hers. Given only when they embraced or when she was particularly proud of him. Oh, how he missed that look. Slowly, Riley reached his hand to touch her cheek.

Charlotte moved her hand toward his face, mimicking his gesture. At last, after so long, Riley fingers felt her flesh again. Any reserve of resistance he still held crumbled. He could feel her again. She was real. His Charlotte was alive.

"My love," Charlotte whispered as she clasped Riley's neck. "How I missed you. It is time you get what you deserve." An electric shock of white fire exploded through his body from where his fingers touched Charlotte's face. Where her hand touched his face, he felt his flesh burning. Charlotte looked unfazed. She continued to stare straight into his eyes as she slowly embraced him. Everywhere she touched, searing pain erupted. Riley screamed, his insides were on fire. He felt as if he was being burned alive. Still Charlotte continued to hold him, squeezing tighter.

"What's the matter, my love?" Charlotte taunted. "I thought you would be happy to see me after all this time." She grabbed his head in her hands, driving her fingers deep into his scalp. Her voice became shrill and screeching. "Surrender to me, Anointed. Only I can give you what you have lost."

Riley wanted to die, to finally be done. Of course Charlotte was dead. How could he have been so gullible? This woman was a demon...a destroyer...a lie.

'Give in to me, Anointed!' a new voice demanded. It wasn't Charlotte's voice, but a voice that dripped of rage. Riley could feel the presence of something trying to take over his mind and he felt powerless to defend against it. His pain was too intense and he couldn't focus.

Would it be so bad to give up? To let evil win? Riley resisted against the foreign thoughts in his mind. The demon's influence was growing within him. A vile presence that wanted to destroy him.

A flicker of red movement to his side caught

Riley's attention. Baal was leaping toward him. There was no time do anything other than lift his arm in a protective gesture.

Baal's dagger sliced through Riley's prosthetic arm as if it were made of papier-mâché, severing it in two. Riley would have fallen backward under the impact of the blow, but Charlotte held him rigidly against her, as if she could physically force her way into his body.

He couldn't feel the burning of his skin anymore. His body was beyond the pain and had gone numb. Riley managed to look at Charlotte once more. His knew his angel of light never existed. She was just a dream. A shadow of what was once and could never be. Now he understood who stood before him. It was his angel of death.

CHAPTER 49

Marie looked into the darkness that lay beyond. "I can feel the presence of the president," she said, pointing to an area directly in front of them. A web of threads blocked their path, merging into a tangled mess of blackness on the horizon. "He is still far away, but I can tell he is in that direction."

Noah touched one of the black threads in front of him. This one was about the diameter of a dime. "Ouch!" He recoiled his hand instinctively. The thread was so cold it burned.

He took a moment to assess their situation. In a fit of inspiration, Noah ducked under a thread and weaved himself between two others, trying to move forward, only to find his path blocked by impassable intersecting threads. He reversed his steps, accidentally brushing a razor thin thread with his arm in the process.

"Ouch!!!" He yelled as searing pain shot through his arm. Blast! This was not going to work. "How are we going to get through this?"

Noah asked dismayed. "The threads are everywhere."

Marie grabbed Noah's hand, looking at him intently. "You told me you could transport yourself anywhere you wanted in your dreams. Do you think you could do it here?"

Noah shrugged, considering Marie's suggestion. It was easy for him to do in his dreams. Could it be the same in this realm? It's worth a try, he decided.

"Hold on," Noah said as he grabbed Marie tightly in a hug. Noah concentrated, willing them forward into an area of the maze, just like he would will a dream to change scenery. The threads around them blurred for a moment, only to come back into focus.

"You did it!" Marie proudly exclaimed, giving him a tight squeeze. "I knew you could!" Marie's excitement sent a wave of pride through Noah. To be able to something right for a change made him feel good. The fact that Marie was complimenting him was even better.

"The president's presence is stronger. We're getting closer." Marie pointed into the darkness. "That way," she instructed.

With Marie providing direction, they worked their way through the maze until they came to a section of threads that were different. These threads were braided, like the cords of a rope. Some threads had interlocking black and white cords. In other threads, the cords were grey. Fortunately, these threads were widely-spaced, giving them ample room to move.

Marie floated adeptly between the threads, carefully inspecting each one. "I found the president's thread," she announced presenting a black and white thread the diameter of a softball.

"Awesome," Noah replied, retracing her route until he was beside her. He inspected the thread briefly. "Now we just follow it to the end." He wrapped his arm around Marie, pulling her close to him.

A moment later, to their surprise, they found themselves back in the center of the Oval Office. Noah looked down and stared at the odd sight below him. They were standing in the middle of a large wooden coffee table, the bottom part of their legs no longer visible through the table-top. Noah bent down to touch the surface of the table. His fingers passed through it as if it were a hologram.

"Uh, Noah..." Marie said, pulling on his arm. She was looking behind him, her eyes wide with fear. Noah spun around. He found himself looking at a scene that was frozen in time, as if he stepped into a picture. On the floor lay four bodies draped across each other. In front of them, Riley knelt under the embrace of an unknown woman, his face contorted in pain. Blood dripped from his eyes and the forearm of his artificial arm was missing. Behind them, a human-like form was wielding a glowing red dagger,

THE OTHER SIDE

preparing to strike Riley in his back.

"This doesn't makes sense," Noah said, confused.

"Yes, it does," Marie disagreed. "I think this is the intersection of the spiritual realm with the physical world. We are experiencing our world from the spiritual side."

Noah looked at his physical body and then back to Riley. Noah knew they needed to get back immediately, Riley was in danger. It was then he noticed the black and white cord terminating in the physical body of the president.

Noah instantly knew it was the cord they were searching for and quickly moved toward it. As he did, a steel axe with an oversized blade appeared in his hand. The fact that it appeared on his command, just like objects in his dreams, was not lost on him. A burst of confidence expanded from within him. He possessed power in this realm.

"I wouldn't do that, prophet," a voice commanded. "Not if you want to save yourselves."

Both Noah and Marie turned towards the voice. Pastor Jessup stood next to the president's desk, a menacing scowl on his face. Behind him, cowering in fear was the president. Noah hesitated, not sure what to do.

"Don't listen to him, Noah," Marie shouted. "He is lying!"

"Am I?" the demon dared. "Silly girl. This is my world and it is time I taught you both a lesson." A burst of red exploded from Pastor Jessup's fingertips and slammed into Marie, encasing her in flames. Her body began to thrash in pain as she fell to the floor. Her face contorted in agony as the flames around her slowly faded away.

"Marie!!!" Noah screamed, dropping the axe and rushing to her side. She was whimpering, her eyes tightly closed. Oddly, her body was slightly translucent and he could see through her. *What was happening?*

Noah looked up to see Pastor Jessup standing over him. Crimson red flames spilled from the man's eyes. "Don't you know whom you face?" The pastor gloated. "It is ill-advised to resist me. I am Belial! Destroyer of truth! You are no match for me."

He grabbed Noah by the throat and hefted him easily off the ground. Noah struggled in vain against the demon's grip. The demon's strength was incredible.

"It is time to extinguish your soul from this realm forever," Belial taunted. "Then I will do the same to the truth-seer."

It took less than an instant. Less time than it takes for a thought to be birthed into existence. Noah made a decision that he was done letting evil be a victor over him. Done with believing the lies of self-doubt that Satan had always whispered into his head. Lies that told him he was a failure and he always would be one. He would

THE OTHER SIDE

never surrender to evil again. From this point, his life purpose would be to fight evil with all his power. From deep within him, Noah felt a righteous rage building into a tempest.

Noah took a deep breath—and then unleashed his fury.

Immediately, Noah disappeared from the demon's grasp only to reappear behind the demon. Once again he conjured the axe to appear in his hand. In a single motion, he swung the axe with all his might, toward the neck of the demon.

The axe connected squarely, but Belial managed to vanish just as the axe made contact, reappearing a moment later on the other side of the room.

"Ridiculous mortal!" the demon hissed. The facade of Pastor Jessup melted away, leaving a hideous creature with a bulbous head, pointed teeth, and scales. There was dark smoke billowing from the side of the demon's neck where Noah's axe had found its mark. A bright ball of fire appeared in the hand of the demon. He hurled it at Noah.

Noah had just enough time to react. He instinctively willed a shield of energy in front of him. The fireball collided with the shield in a shuddering explosion, sending Noah flying backward. Expecting another attack, Noah disappeared, narrowly dodging another fireball. He reappeared directly above the demon, summoning the axe to appear in his hand and swung

351

downward with all of his might.

Belial fell backward, narrowly dodging the axe blade. Noah readied himself for another swing as the demon turned to face him, now brandishing a weapon made of flames.

"You are no match for me." Belial boasted, twirling the massive weapon in a dazzling display of skill.

"We'll see about that," Noah challenged, stepping back purposely, drawing the demon closer. As Belial raised his weapon for a killing blow, a second axe conjured by Noah appeared behind the demon. The second axe blade smashed deep into Belial, soliciting a howl of pain from the demon. Noah charged forward swinging his original axe at the demon's head. His axe passed through empty space. Belial had disappeared once again.

Noah scanned his surroundings, waiting for the next attack. After several moments, he let the axe disappear and rushed to Marie's side.

Marie was sitting up, her body having regained its solid color. That was a good sign, but Noah didn't like that her skin was deathly pale. "You're going to be ok," he assured her. "I am going to get us out of here." She nodded in response.

Noah approached the president's physical body. He summoned the axe to his hand and in a single swing, severed the cord just inches from the president's back. There was a momentous

THE OTHER SIDE

flash of light as the cord recoiled through the far wall where it entered the room. The remnant of the cord in the president's back burst into flames and disintegrated into ash.

Noah ventured one more glance at the statu-esque figure of Riley, stuck in a death struggle of his own just a few feet in front of him. He hoped Riley would survive. He hoped they all would survive.

Noah turned back to Marie, only to find her helping President Harrison to his feet. She was recovering quickly, the color having returned to her face. He smiled at her and said, "It's time to go home."

"Who are you?" the president asked, a bewil-dered look on his face.

"There is no time to explain," Noah replied. "I need you to come with me if you want to live." The president nodded, obviously not liking the alternative.

In a single motion, Noah wrapped his arm around Marie and pulled her tightly while he extended his other hand to the president, who grabbed it securely. Then Noah wished them to a safer place.

CHAPTER 50

Unsteadily, Baal rose to his feet, grasping the edge of the couch for support. The last blast of the Creator's light almost finished him. He was fortunate Asherah appeared when she did.

There was once a time when he bathed in that light, relishing in its completeness, in its purity. Then, he stood in a position of honor in the direct presence of the Almighty. Now that light was dangerous to him. Here in the physical realm, that light could destroy him.

Baal took a moment to collect himself, his strength returning with each passing second. The Anointed was locked in an embrace with Asherah, completely oblivious to his surroundings. *What a fool!* The Anointed possessed so much power yet was still a slave to human emotions. Baal positioned himself behind the Anointed preparing to deliver a death strike with his blade.

Baal swung the dagger fiercely in an attempt

THE OTHER SIDE

to drive the dagger deep into the spine of the Anointed. To his surprise, the Anointed turned at the last moment, raising his arm in defense against his thrust. Baal's blade cut through the Anointed's arm, sending the forearm hurling to the side of the room.

Baal had greatly underestimated the strength of this man. Despite Asherah's efforts, the Anointed was resisting her control. He prepared for a second thrust, this one aimed at the Anointed's heart.

"Don't kill him!" Asherah shrieked in protest. "I almost have him." Her voice was strained, belaying the effort she was exerting to gain control of the Anointed. The intensity of the struggle was evident on the Anointed's face. The turmoil within was causing him to shed tears of blood.

Baal hesitated. Possessing the Anointed was dangerous. A true believer could never be fully possessed because their spirit belonged to the Creator. However, the mind and body of a believer could be dominated by a demon, but only if the individual willingly surrendered to the demon's control. *Could Asherah control the Anointed?* The possibility was intriguing, but the risks were too high.

"He is stronger than you think," Baal warned, beginning to step forward. "Kill him now."

"No!!!" Asherah hissed selfishly. "I am so close."

"Then let me make it easier for you."

Baal took his blade and sliced a long swath across the Anointed's back. The torn cloth of the Anointed's shirt smoldered and burst into flame where the blade touched. The flesh around the wound turned black and then ashen white, poisoned by the blade that was forged with the sin of humanity. Riley O'Connor howled in pain, before falling silent. Asherah shivered momentarily. A slight smile forming on her face.

"Yes!!! I am…" Asherah's voice trailed away. The satisfaction on her face disappeared, instantly replaced with a look of shock. A sword of brilliant white suddenly protruded from her midsection as the air around her shimmered. The sword traveled upward, splitting her body into two halves that peeled away from each other. Each half burst into white light, burning into nothingness. In a flash, she no longer existed. Asherah was now banished from eternity.

Baal raised his dagger defensively as the room shimmered again and a blinding light filled his field of vision. When the flash receded, the archangel Michael stood before him, dressed in a white tunic overlaid with brilliant gold plate armor. So it has come to this, Baal thought. The Creator has sent his best soldier to the fight.

The angel's physique was massive. Perfectly formed in all ways, it was hard not to admire Michael's raw beauty. He was breathtaking. Baal once looked like that. He too had been a favored

THE OTHER SIDE

creation. The memory enraged Baal. He wanted to be that way again.

"It's been a long time since we battled in this realm, my brother," Michael said calmly as he looked directly into Baal's eyes. "I harbor a great sorrow that this will be our last time."

Michael kneeled next to the Anointed and placed his free hand on the Anointed's back. The Anointed's body tensed briefly as if jolted with electricity. The dead flesh peeled away as the deep wound of Baal's dagger disappeared, replaced by new flesh. Michael rose and continued towards Baal. "You have committed unpardonable sins. The pit of hell is no longer a just punishment for you. The Creator has demanded that you be expunged."

Baal stepped backward, making sure to stay out of the range of Michael's sword. He knew he was no match for Michael in this realm. Unlike demons, angels retained their full powers while in physical form.

Baal glanced at the Anointed who rested limp on the floor. *Was Asherah successful before she perished? Was the Anointed now a tool of the Master?*

"Goodbye brother," Baal said dismissively as the angel approached. "Another time maybe?" He willed himself into the spiritual realm.

To Baal's surprise, nothing happened. Michael continued toward him, sword poised to attack. There was a knowing smile on the angel's face. Baal willed himself into the spiritual realm a second time. And then a third and a fourth. Nothing. "What have you done to me?" Baal demanded.

The dagger in Baal's hand suddenly felt very heavy. He dropped it as he stumbled backwards, colliding into the president's desk and shattering a glass lamp into pieces.

Michael was almost on top of him now. There was no place for Baal to run. He scrambled over the desk, pushing himself to the other side. Pain erupted from his hands. He raised them to see shards of glass protruding from his palms dripping large drops of blood. *What?!? Blood?* The realization of what was happening almost drove him to his knees before Michael to ask for mercy. Almost.

"I regret it has come to this my dear brother," Michael said, tossing the desk to the side of the room with one hand. "There is no mercy for you, but at least the Almighty has granted you a measure of grace. He has transformed you into the creature you so desperately fought to destroy.

"But why?" Baal stalled, now backed against the window. He was trapped.

"You are now human so you can experience the beauty of God as they do." Michael paused, a distant look in his eye. "To feel His presence one more time."

A soft light enveloped Baal, emerging him in

warmth and peace. From inside him, he felt a force erupt.

It was a force he thought lost to him for eternity. Yet here it was once more, unchanged and even more intense than he remembered. It was the love of his Creator. God the Almighty. A love that was unmeasurable. He felt wetness streaming from his eyes as tears fell uncontrollably. Baal had never cried before. He never had a reason, until now.

"Our Creator is a loving God, and he is a just God," Michael proclaimed, raising his sword. "Our Creator has always promised to love, but he also promised to bring judgement on those who defy him. The wages of sin are always death. This penalty I cannot undo."

There was a sad look in Michael's eyes as he held out his hand to Baal. Baal couldn't be sure through his own tears, but he thought Michael was crying too.

"My brother, it is judgement time," the angel said slowly.

Baal fell to his knees, grabbing Michael's hand. "Please, spare me!" Baal pleaded. "Brother, I repent. I repent! I was wrong. El Olam ... El Shaddai...I repent of my ways. Please have mercy!!!"

As Michael's sword began a downward motion, Baal concentrated on the feelings flowing through his body. Feelings of unrestrained love, total acceptance, and complete understanding.

He squeezed Michael's hand, the angel an anchor to a memory of something Baal was eons ago. Baal's last thought before he transformed into eternal nothingness was directed at the Almighty. Not as a plea for last minute mercy, but more as a praise. It was a simple thought. *Thank you.*

CHAPTER 51

Blinked into existence, the landscape around them manifested from the blackness. Noah found himself staring at the same vast desert plain where they first arrived. Their appearance generated a series of small plumes of red glittering dust around their feet, which quickly settled.

"Why did we come here?" Marie asked. "This isn't where Isaiah told us we should go."

"I don't know," Noah said slowly. Something was wrong. He was sure he visualized the ledge on the cliff side overlooking the river of fire. Instead, they were back in the desert.

Marie looked to her left, toward the reddish glowing sky on the horizon. "The entrance to hell is over there. That is a long way to walk. I think you should try again."

Noah agreed. The last thing he wanted to do was extend their stay. He didn't relish the idea of having to walk anywhere, not when they might encounter more demons.

"You're taking us to hell?" The president exclaimed. "Are you crazy?"

"Not hell, Mr. President," Noah corrected. "The entrance to hell. Somehow, someway, our journey home starts there." The president didn't seem convinced. Noah decided not to tell him that he was in the biblical place of paradise. The president was already spooked as it was.

"Come on. Let's get out of here!" Noah reached for Marie's hand as he grabbed the president's arm. He closed his eyes, concentrating on the image of the cliff ledge. Suddenly, he felt the president pull away.

"Look, there is someone coming." The president pointed toward the horizon. Noah squinted, barely making out a figure in the distance that was running towards them. The axe appeared in Noah's hand almost instantaneously. He wasn't taking any chances.

As the figure approached, he began to make out details. It was a woman. Her hands were waving frantically as she ran towards them, leaving a trail of swirling red dust in her wake.

In a matter of moments, Natasha Ellington appeared. Her appearance was haggard and her eyes were full of desperation.

"Natasha!" the president bellowed, not believing his eyes. "Are you ok?"

"I have been wandering for hours," Natasha replied, wrapping her arms around the president in relief. "Where are we?"

THE OTHER SIDE

Noah noticed Marie scowling. "Is something wrong?" Noah whispered to her.

"Yes," Marie whispered back. "She bares the taint of evil and is not to be trusted."

Noah took this in stride. She may not be someone to trust, but he couldn't leave her here. That would be a fate worse than death.

"Everyone link hands," Noah demanded. "It's time to go." A moment later, they vanished from the desert.

They reappeared on the ledge of the cliff side, exactly where Noah wanted them to be. Below, the river raged fiercely. A tempest of seething destruction, looking more horrifying than before.

"This place is a dead end," the president said, venturing toward the cliff to peer over the edge. "What do we do now?"

"Now you die," a voice screeched behind them. Noah and the others turned to find themselves face to face with three demons. Each demon was twice the size of a normal man. The demon on the right stood on legs like a goat, but had the torso and head of a human. Two large horns protruded from the top of its head. The demon rocked back in forth on its hooves in anticipation. The demon on the left had human form, but with jet black vinyl skin. It carried a glowing yellow scythe as long as the demon was tall. The demon swung the archaic weapon easily in one hand in a flurry of movements, an eager smile on its face.

The demon in the center was the most terrifying of the three. Two reptilian heads, each brandishing a mouthful of razor sharp fangs that were longer than Noah's forearm, stared at him menacingly. The demon's body was long and rested on hundreds of insect-like legs and was covered in thick iridescent green scales that reflected the fire below. Two large wings extended from the demon's back. At the end of each wing was a series of sword length talons.

Instinctively, the group stepped backwards, towards the ledge. There was no place for them to run and the river of fire below bubbled menacingly. Noah's mind raced back to the words of the prophet Isaiah. *'What appears as death to one, is truly life to another.'* Noah glanced at the raging inferno below. *Could that be the answer?*

"Pastor Jessup sends his regards," the center demon hissed menacingly as it raised one of its wings, preparing to strike.

"Hold on and whatever you do, don't let go!" Noah commanded.

Everything was happening so fast, yet time seemed to slow for Noah. In front of him, the center demon was lunging forward, one of the beast's talons arching downward towards them. He felt Marie's arm locked firmly around his waist and the grip of the president's hand around his bicep. He caught Marie staring at him expectantly, a look of admiration on her face.

As the demon's talon descended towards them, Noah stepped off the ledge, pulling Marie and the others with him. As he fell, he looked upward at the cliff, expecting a demon to be following them. His mouth opened in horror at what he saw. Natasha was still on the ledge. *Why did Natasha let go of the president?* He didn't have time to figure it out. Seconds later, the three of them were swallowed by the fire.

CHAPTER 52

Riley awakened under an olive green canvas just a yard above his head. Though disoriented, he slowly raised himself to a sitting position, scanning his surroundings.

From his vantage point inside the tent, his view was limited to the courtyard beyond. Men and women in military fatigues raced back and forth in a frenzy, darting between small huddles of dark suits and police officers in deep discussions.

"Easy," Noah cautioned, appearing at his side to assist him. "You need to rest."

"I feel fine," Riley lied. His head was throbbing intensely, causing him to squint with every painful pulse of his heart. He steadied himself, trying to focus his thoughts. The last thing he remembered was Charlotte's face. "How long have I been out?"

"I am not sure. Marie and I woke up next to you about an hour ago."

It was then Riley noticed the empty

THE OTHER SIDE

stretchers nearby, similar to the one on which he sat. Several yards away, a team of medics were hovering around another stretcher. Riley thought he caught a glimpse of Natasha's curly dark brown hair through the commotion.

"The medic says you are injury free," Noah offered, a hopeful expression on his face. "I am just glad that you're alive."

"Alive...barely," Riley remarked dryly, recalling a hazy memory of blue and red fire exploding around him. "What about the president? Is he safe?" Riley asked, suddenly concerned.

"Yes, we rescued him," Noah responded, a bright smile forming on his face. "Marie and I kicked some demon butt!"

Riley couldn't help but chuckle at Noah's enthusiasm. "I knew you would." He reached out his hand to Noah's and clasped it firmly. "I am very proud of you, Noah. I mean it."

Noah smiled in return. They both knew their success was only possible because of their God-given gifts and the fact that they worked together as a team. Even so, Riley's compliment made the intended impact as he detected a surge of confidence rise within Noah.

"Riley O'Connor," a booming voice sounded over Riley's shoulder. He turned to find President Harrison entering the tent escorted by a trio of secret service agents who eyed Riley and Noah suspiciously.

367

"Sir," Riley responded, pushing himself off the stretcher to his feet. "It is an honor to meet you."

"Let's dismiss the formalities. Truth is, it is an honor for me to meet you," the president responded enthusiastically, extending his hand in greeting. "You and your team freed me from whatever spell I was under. To be honest, I have little memory of much of what has transpired the past few weeks."

"You are aware that we are still in danger!" Riley stated in alarm.

"Very well aware." The president glanced around him before leaning close into Riley so as to not be overheard. "Your team has brought me up to speed on the situation and the reason for your intrusion into the White House. Agent Frank Gillian has been dispatched to FBI headquarters along with Bill Rogers to formulate a tactical response plan to find the bombs and disarm them."

"Bill Rogers?" Riley remarked in surprise.

"Yes," the president affirmed. "About an hour ago, I restored Bill to his position as Director of the CIA. I need my best people on this."

"What about Natasha?" Riley asked.

The president grimaced at the mention of her name, turning briefly to look at the commotion behind him. "She didn't come back with us. At least not all of her. She is comatose at the moment."

THE OTHER SIDE

"I will fill you in on that later," Noah interjected.

"As a precaution," the president continued, "I am ordering the evacuation of the cities under threat and cancelled all football games across the country. The logistics will be a nightmare, but it will save lives if we can't locate those bombs."

Riley remained silent, still trying to process these new developments amongst the swarm of thoughts in his mind. He experienced a momentary memory of fighting against an unseen foe. It wasn't a physical fight, but something different. The memory faded as quickly as it came.

"Rest up. That's an order," the president said, placing his hand gently on Riley's back. "You have been through quite a battle. The Oval Office is a wreck and I truly don't know how any of us survived." He smiled warmly. "Speaking of that, when you are ready, I would like to talk with you alone."

Riley nodded in agreement. He knew the president would have questions. He only hoped the president was ready to hear the answers.

"Where are the others?" Riley asked.

"Darius and Marie went with a team of agents to FedExField," Noah said. "They left a few minutes ago."

"The stadium?"

The president leveled a stare at Riley, as if

Riley were testing him. Finally, the president's pursed lips expanded into a large grin. "Fortunately, Darius has a hunch he knows where one of the bombs is located," he offered reassuringly. "I have ordered the FBI's most elite weapons demolition team to accompany them to the stadium. Rest assured, we are going to do everything within the power of the U.S. Government to make sure it doesn't hurt a soul."

CHAPTER 53

Darius trailed the maintenance foreman through the dimly lit corridor below the stadium. Marie followed closely behind him, flanked by two heavily armed federal agents. Shortly they emerged into bright sunshine on the sideline of the field. By the thoughts Darius had detected from the foreman, it was obvious the man was not happy with their intrusion into his daily activities.

"Where do you need to go?" The foreman quipped hastily, checking his watch.

Darius pointed toward the far end zone to a large television studio constructed beside the field. "We need access to that studio," Darius replied confidently, recalling the image he received from the demon's mind. It was a fleeting image, but the thoughts associated with it were crystal clear. Revenge.

The foreman gave him a funny look before shrugging his shoulders and motioning for them to follow. Darius hesitated briefly, his mind jumping back to the odd experience that occurred in the Oval Office. It was only recently that Darius realized that he was unable to read the minds of people who were demonically possessed. He couldn't even detect their presence. Somehow, right before Riley's battle ended, he was able to probe the demon's thoughts. Darius still wasn't sure how or why it happened. He was just fortunate it did.

"Is everything ok?" Marie asked, coming alongside Darius.

"I don't know," Darius pondered. "Just wondering what we are going to find in that studio." Marie nodded silently in agreement.

The studio was constructed on a large stage about twenty yards wide and ten yards deep. The top of the stage was cluttered with television cameras, a maze of electrical cables and a large podium with several chairs. As they approached the studio, the two agents took forward positions, brandishing their weapons and scanning their surroundings for any threats.

"This is it. Just a studio constructed on a stage," the foreman said hesitantly, nervously eyeing the drawn weapons. "What did you fellows say you were looking for?"

"We didn't," the agent who identified himself as Max responded. "How do we get inside the stage?"

"There is a small access door on the far side." The foreman said nonchalantly. "Go ahead and

THE OTHER SIDE

check it out. Take as much time as you need. It's not like I have other things to do today other than babysit you folks." He promptly seated himself in one of the plush studio chairs set aside for the television announcers.

On the far side of the stage, they found a small plywood door on the supporting stage wall. Slowly, Max opened the door as the other agent took a defensive position, his gun pointed at the doorway. Max removed a pen light from his jacket and shined the beam into the darkness.

"Stay here until we check this out," Max ordered. The two agents nodded at each other and moved in unison, disappearing under the stage.

After a few moments, Marie pulled Darius back from the doorway. "Something is not right." She yelled into the darkness after the agents, "Watch out!!!"

Before she finished her warning, there was a brief burst of shouts from the agents. Darius watched in horror as the beam of light zigzagged in a random pattern followed by screams and then silence.

Hastily, Darius closed the door and pressed his body firmly against it, hoping he contained the strength to keep whatever it was inside. He waited for the impact, but it never came. He looked at Marie, uncertain what to do.

"We need to get help," Marie said, a pensive frown on her face. "I am not exactly sure what it is, but it's demonic.

"I am worried there isn't time for help to arrive," Darius said, shaking his head. "Do you think you can expel it from here?"

"I don't think so, I can barely detect it's presence at this distance. I need to be closer."

"Give me your hand," Darius said, extending his to Marie. "Let's try something." Darius positioned himself in front of Marie and peered intently at her.

"I want you to concentrate on my eyes," he instructed. "Take a deep breath, relax and concentrate." Darius repeated the command, beginning to probe into Marie's mind.

After a few moments, Darius felt Marie's awareness in his mind. "Good," he said in a slow, relaxed tone. He probed further into Marie's consciousness, seeking to be one with her thoughts. "Now concentrate on sensing the demon."

Immediately, Darius could feel his perception change. It was different from how he used his power to sense people's minds, but similar in ways he could not explain. Slowly, he projected his mind searching for the demonic being.

He could barely detect it, just a blurry speck, but he knew it was there.

"Concentrate harder," Darius pressed. "Focus on the evil." In response to his request, the speck slowly transformed into a distinct form.

"I can sense it!" Darius said in relief. "Now,

THE OTHER SIDE

when I give the word, I want you to expel it." Summoning his strength, Darius reached into the mind of the demonic being, seeking to connect with it. He expected to encounter resistance to penetrate the being's mind, but instead his mental probe passed through easily. Instantly his mind was flooded with graphic images of violence and destruction. Thoughts of hatred, rage, and pain permeated through the mental connection. The vileness of the brain he probed made him sick. It was indescribable.

"Now!" Darius commanded. A moment later, he felt a surge of energy passing through him from Marie into his connection with the demonic presence. Marie's voice expanded in his mind, squashing the vile images and thoughts he was receiving from the demonic mind. With intense effort, Darius channeled Marie's voice into the center of the evil chaos.

Instantly, his connection with the demonic presence was broken. Frantically, he probed to reestablish the connection, but there was nothing. The demon was gone.

Slowly Darius released Marie's hand. "I need to go in," he said. "Wait here, I don't think it will be a pretty site inside." With a quick jerk, he pulled open the door.

Ducking slightly to avoid the support rafters, Darius made his way to the corner, where a narrow swath of light was cast on the wall. After a few seconds of searching the ground, he picked up the agent's pen light, pointing it around him in a large arc.

The beam of light landed briefly on the piled bodies of the two agents before Darius hastily pointed it away from the gruesome scene. From his brief glimpse of the carnage, he was positive the agents were dead. Hesitantly, he pointed the light toward the far end of the stage. Slowly, he scanned the area. At the center of the wall, there was a small crate and beside it, a crumpled form. Darius approached the crate cautiously, keeping the light squarely focused on the form. It was a woman!

Darius was immediately struck by the frailness of the woman. She was alive but breathing with shallow, raspy gasps. The outline of her ribs was clearly evident through the remnants of a torn t-shirt. Her thin arms were caked with mud and fresh blood covered her hands.

"Are you ok?" Marie's asked, peering into the room from the door.

"So far," Darius replied, moving the beam of his light onto the crate. "Stay where you are. I think I found something."

Darius studied the wooden crate before him for several seconds. It was unremarkable with no identifying markings that indicated its contents. Eagerly, he shined the light inside only to find a pile of electrical cables nicely stacked in several coils. He frowned at his discovery.

There had to be more. He set the light on

the crate and began removing the contents. It didn't take him long to encounter a wooden shelf about two thirds of the way from the bottom of the crate. He scanned the shelf with his light several times before he noticed two small finger holes on either side. With a strong tug, he lifted the shelf out of the crate and tossed it beside him.

A bright red glow pulsated out of the box, filling the room. Alarmed, Darius stepped back. It wasn't the fact that he found the bomb that shocked him. It was the reality the timer was active and in less than twenty-four hours, the bomb was going to explode.

CHAPTER 54

"Welcome, Agent O'Connor. Please take a seat," President Harrison said, motioning to one of the leather desk chairs situated around a large oval table. "I appreciate you meeting with me so early this morning, particularly after the events of yesterday."

Riley nodded as he took a seat near the president, facing a large checkerboard of video screens. With the Oval Office in shambles, the president was using his war room deep below the White House as his temporary command post. It was hard to believe his death struggle with the demons occurred less than twenty-four hours earlier.

"I wanted you to be the first to hear the news. The bomb Darius found has been neutralized!" The president said proudly.

"That is great news," Riley agreed. "What is the status on the other bombs?"

THE OTHER SIDE

"Agents located the bombs at the three other stadiums late last night and removed them for transport," the president responded, beginning to pace in front of the video screens. "The bombs are due to arrive in a remote location in Nevada shortly for disarmament and if need be, detonation." The president smiled broadly. "Our nation owes you and your team a sincere debt of gratitude."

Riley exhaled loudly as he relaxed back into his chair. The weight of his burden finally lifted, he could feel the tension in his shoulders beginning to evaporate. "Praise be to God," he whispered thankfully, still digesting the president's news.

"Even with this victory, our country is still under threat from Thereon and other terrorist organizations," the president continued pacing. "We still don't know how Thereon is organized, nor do we have any real knowledge of their leadership. I am hoping the upcoming FBI raid on Summit of Light will provide the information we need."

Riley was aware of the raid only because Frank contacted him earlier that morning. Like the president, Frank was also hopeful that they would uncover information that could be used to fight Thereon. Given what he knew now, Riley had no doubt the church and Thereon were working together. But what bothered him most about the situation was the forces of evil were able to manipulate so many people for so long with seemingly little effort. It was a masterful work of deception.

"Now that my eyes have been opened to the true nature of these threats, I am gravely concerned for our future," the president stopped mid-stride, turning to face Riley. "That is why I am in desperate need of your assistance."

Riley analyzed the president, sensing the gravity of his request. The president picked up a blue folder from the table and handed it to Riley.

"What's this?" Riley asked.

"An opportunity," the president replied. "I have commissioned the creation of an agency so secret that only a limited number of people in the federal government will know of its existence."

Riley stared at the folder intently but did not open it up. "What is the purpose of the agency?"

"To fight the spiritual battle against Satan and his demons."

"I assume you want my team involved in this agency," Riley said wearily. Though the prospect of the agency was intriguing, the effectiveness of the agency would only be as good as the leader. "To whom would this agency report?"

The president smiled confidently before answering. "Directly to me. No liaisons, no federal bureaucracy, no congressional committees. This agency will be completely off the radar."

"I will talk it over with the team," Riley

THE OTHER SIDE

said, evasively. "We function better as an autonomous entity. I have serious reservations of having to deal with an agency head, given the unique nature of our activities."

"I anticipated that might be your response," the president responded reflectively, circling the table towards Riley.

"That is why I have chosen you to lead this agency, Director O'Connor," the president stated enthusiastically, making sure to place added emphasis on Riley's title. "You are the only person I trust to do it successfully."

CHAPTER 55

It was three days later when Frank appeared at Riley's doorstep. Despite the tiredness of his eyes and the grey stubble that marked his face and neck, Frank appeared more relaxed than ever. Gone was the tight, dark suit and tie, replaced by a white Cuban shirt and tan khakis.

"You look like a new man," Riley said, embracing Frank in a hug.

"I feel like one," Frank chuckled. "After the experiences of these past months, I have a new perspective on life."

"Me too," Riley smiled. "Let's go out on the deck and enjoy this beautiful day. We have much to talk about."

Outside, the midday sun shone brightly overhead against a cloudless blue sky. Both Duke and Spencer were next to them, resting peacefully. If the fall season was to have a perfect day, it was today.

"I read the official report, but tell me what really happened," Riley said, surveying the for-

THE OTHER SIDE

ested woods behind the manor. Though Riley trusted the information he received, he knew that information was often only part of the story.

"The raid on the Summit of Light headquarters went as planned. On paper, it was a success," Frank said. "The FBI confiscated their servers, their files, and anything else we needed." He paused, settling back into his chair. "Everything but the members of their leadership team."

Riley raised his eyebrows in mild surprise. The report he read did not mentioned that arresting the leadership team was an objective of the mission.

"Only a few of us were involved in the planning of the raid," Frank continued. "There was no way they could have known we were coming, yet they did. Who knows what information they took with them or were able to destroy before we arrived."

"Even so, we have a general idea of their whereabouts," Frank acknowledged. "So, it won't be long before we have them in custody for questioning. Which reminds me, I would like Darius to assist us in the interrogation process."

"Consider it done. I think Darius would welcome the opportunity to be involved."

"His potential to aid law enforcement is limitless." Frank added.

"Yes it is quite amazing," Riley smiled in agreement. "All the members of my team are...a-

383

mazing."

"True," Frank agreed. "That they are...and so are you."

Riley pretended to ignore the compliment. "Has the FBI uncovered anything that would connect Summit of Light to Thereon?"

"Yes, we now have solid evidence of a conspiracy between these two organizations. E-mails, bank transactions, payments to known operatives inside of Thereon. In my opinion, it should be a slam dunk case."

"I expected as much, particularly after I reviewed the autopsy report on the library shooter. She carried the same mark as other terrorists associated with Thereon."

Frank leaned forward, intrigued by Riley's statement. "What mark?"

"The symbol of the beast."

"What does it mean?"

"Based on the evidence I have reviewed from multiple cases, it is a mark taken by someone who has pledged themselves to aid the forces of evil. My guess is that Thereon has adopted it as their trademark."

Frank scratched his stubble, considering this new information. "It scares me that Thereon is still out there. It can't get any worse than a terrorist organization that is directed by evil spirits!"

This time, Riley was genuinely surprised by Frank's comment. "That is the first time I

THE OTHER SIDE

have heard you attribute anything to spiritual forces," he said curiously.

Frank frowned. "Six months ago, I would have bet my life savings that God was a made-up being that existed to give people hope and that angels and demons were figments of our imagination."

"And now?" Riley coaxed.

"Honestly, my world has been turned upside down," Frank admitted. "To know that Heaven and hell are real places. Well, that just scares the crap out of me."

Riley reflected momentarily on the change in Frank since their first meeting. Frank eyes were slowly being opened to the truth of this world. He patted Frank on the arm affectionately. "I am just glad to see you wearing something without a tie." That comment solicited a momentary laugh from both of them.

"In all seriousness, I am concerned for our future," Frank stated, staring into the distance. "After reading your report and hearing the president's own words on what transpired, our world can no longer deny this spiritual battle exists. I guess the question going through my mind is how do we stop something like this from happening again?"

Duke growled softly even though he appeared to be sleeping. Riley slowly rubbed his hand through Duke's thick fur, contemplating Frank's question. It was a good question, but he knew the answer was not what Frank wanted to hear. "This is a war that will continue until good finally trumps evil. The only thing we can do is fight for good and protect ourselves from evil."

Frank nodded. "I figured you would say something chivalrous like that. Still, can we really make a difference?"

"We have already," Riley stated.

"True," Frank agreed. "But the stakes are so much higher now." He studied Riley for a moment. "I still can't get over what those demons did to you. Did you know it was a trap?"

"Deep down, I knew," Riley said, nodding slowly. "Only I didn't want to believe it and I surrendered to my desire." The memory of seeing Charlotte's image was still fresh in his mind along with the reminder of his failure. Satan knew just how to attack him and Riley had given in without a fight.

"I understand that completely. I am sure it was a tough experience," Frank acknowledged. "Does that impact your decision about the President's offer? I mean have you thought through the implications of what he is asking?"

"It doesn't and I have," Riley confirmed. "And you?"

Frank nodded. "I must be crazy, but I feel this is the right thing to do. I will serve as the internal liaison between your team and all other federal agencies, acting through a puppet agency that I will oversee. As I understand it, they are

THE OTHER SIDE

going to give me some fancy title and a level of authority that carries weight across all federal agencies." Frank shrugged, obviously not sure if he liked his future job prospects.

"You know there are others out there?" Riley offered flippantly, a slight smile on his face.

"Others?" Frank questioned, the shock evident in the tone of response.

"Other people who God has specially gifted and should help us further fight this war," Riley nodded affirmatively, watching the surprised expression on Frank's face. "There are not many, but they are out there."

While Frank pondered this new revelation, Riley studied the patchwork of color in the canopy of nearby trees. He could see each leaf was distinctive in its color, shape, and size. Each playing its part with the others to form a beautiful picture. Penetrating rays of sun filtered through the leaves, illuminating each one to create a vibrant fresco of orange, maroon, and yellow. The symbolism was not lost on him. He was like a leaf. So were the members of his team. Apart they could impress. Together they could dazzle.

CHAPTER 56

"I was so relieved when I heard you awoke from your coma," Marie exclaimed, reaching forward and embracing Jessica tightly. "I have been so worried about you."

"Me too!" Noah added from the end of the hospital bed. "I have been praying a lot for you." He nodded at Marie adding, "We all have."

"Well your prayers worked," Jessica responded. Though she appeared alert, a slight slur trailed each word. "They are still heavily medicating me, but my doctor said my body is healing at an accelerated rate. They can't explain it."

"Well we know the real truth behind that," Marie said confidently. "Now there is so much we need to tell you."

"Yeah, like what happened to Noah," Jessica joked, giving Noah a big smile. "Your new look is really becoming," she added, measuring him with an appraising eye. "I mean it!" Noah cheeks flushed deep red in response, obviously embar-

THE OTHER SIDE

rassed by the compliment.

A shimmer at the edge of her vision grabbed Marie's attention. She looked momentarily toward the window where a radiant angel hovered just outside. The angel was watching them intently, floating in a relaxed stance. Marie noted that the angel's was carrying a sword, but it was sheathed, hanging freely by the angel's side.

"Are you ok?" Jessica said, glancing nervously towards the window.

"Absolutely," Marie responded, giving Jessica a reassuring squeeze. "All is as it should be. We are safe and we are together." She released Jessica hand, glancing one more time at the window. The angel held her gaze for a moment before reaching for his sword. In an agile, fluid motion, the angel removed the sword from its sheath and raised it in salute. Then as sudden as it had appeared, the angel was gone.

"Hi guys!" Stephen exclaimed, entering the room carrying a large white bag. Immediately the aroma of food filled the air. "Lunch has arrived." A moment later Darius entered carrying a similar bag.

"This really means a lot to have you all here," Jessica said. "Too bad Riley couldn't make it."

"He wanted to be here," Stephen said, removing several cartons of Chinese food and setting them on the table. "But he and Frank were meeting today to discuss some government business. He said he would come by and see you this evening."

"Well I guess that just means more for us," Jessica joked. "I am starving for some decent food."

"Me too!" Noah and Marie said in unison. Giggling, the three exchanged fist bumps.

"Will someone run to the cafeteria while I finish setting this up?" Stephen interjected. "I forgot to get utensils."

"Sure," Noah said, heading out the door into the hallway.

"I will go with you," Marie offered. "Just to make sure you don't get into any trouble along the way."

As they walked down the corridor, Marie casually locked her arm around Noah's. "We are really lucky we all have each other," she declared with a bright smile. "I am glad you talked me into joining the team."

"Yes we are," Noah replied as they entered the elevator. "And I am glad you're here too," he added, somewhat shyly. He reached to press the button for the lobby, but Marie intercepted his hand.

As the doors to the elevator closed, Noah looked at her oddly. "What are you doing?"

"Something I have wanted to do since you saved my life at the White House." Marie reached over and pressed the emergency stop button. She moved toward Noah, bringing her face inches from his.

"I don't understand," Noah said, stalling.

"Aren't you going to kiss me?" She asked, her lips expressing the faintest hint of a smile.

Not waiting for a response, Marie gently brought her lips to his. It was not a long kiss, but it left Noah wanting more. Slowly, he pulled back and opened his eyes.

Marie was staring at him, her dark brown eyes searching his. He was too surprised to do anything but stare back. The last thing he expected was to be kissed by Marie. Suddenly, Marie's eyes fixed on something behind him and she gasped in shock.

Noah whirled around in confusion, finding himself staring at a large hillside of pale brown rock and sand that extended to the horizon. Above him, an intense sun stood in the middle of a cloudless blue sky. As surprised as he was, he couldn't think of anything to say. His thoughts were still focused on the kiss he and Marie had just shared.

"I don't like this," Marie said, gripping his arm tightly as she studied their surroundings.

Noah scanned the area, doing his best to squash the mounting fear that was welling inside of him. They were in the center of a basin straddled by two large hills which extended in either direction for as far as he could see. The steep, sloping hillsides were covered by scant vegetation and the occasional large outcropping of stone.

Noah placed his arm around Marie, pulling her tightly next to him as they walked toward the nearest hillside. "I don't like this either," Noah agreed. "Let's hike towards the top of one of these hills. Maybe then, we can get an idea of where we are."

"Noah!!!!" Marie exclaimed, pointing forward in the direction they were walking.

Noah followed Marie's gaze to the top of the hill. Cresting the ridgeline, thousands of grotesque gigantic beings of various shapes formed a massive line against the horizon. As if prompted by Noah and Marie's appearance, the creatures began descending from the ridge towards their position.

"Noah, did we cross over again?" Marie yelled above the deafening noise of screams that were filling the valley.

"I don't know." Noah responded, pulling Marie in the opposite direction. They had only taken a few steps when he noticed a similar formation of creatures emerge on the opposite hill. Frantically, he began searching for a method of escape. It took him only seconds to surmise there was nowhere for them to run and they were out of time. In less than a minute, the demons would overtake them.

"How can there be this many demons in one place?!?" he cried in frustration.

As the first swarm of creatures approached, Noah hugged Marie protectively. She was trem-

THE OTHER SIDE

bling in fear, pressing herself deeply into his embrace. He had the strange thought that Marie should be immobilized at the sight of so many demons appearing in the flesh. Instantly, like the flashes of wisdom that would strike Riley, Noah knew the truth.

He brought his mouth to Marie's ear. Even though he was so close to her, he had to shout due to the noise around them. "Don't be afraid! It will be over soon," he reassured her.

Marie raised her head from his chest, her brown eyes now searching his intently for the truth.

"None of this is real." Noah paused, his next words catching in his throat because he didn't want to believe them. "This is only a dream... a dream of our future."

THE END

△△△

Author Note:

Thank you for reading my novel. My sincere hope is you enjoyed your reading experience. I encourage you to provide your feedback to me by writing a brief review. It would be very much appreciated. Until we meet again...

J.T. Todd

To leave a review, please click here:

Made in the USA
Monee, IL
15 April 2020